LOVE FAST

LOUISE BAY

Published by Louise Bay 2025

ISBN – 978-1-80456-043-3

BOOKS BY LOUISE BAY

All Louise Bay Books are available for free in Kindle Unlimited or on Amazon to buy.

Each book is a stand alone

The Colorado Club Billionaires

Love Fast

Love Deep

Love More

The New York City Billionaires

The Boss + The Maid = Chemistry

The Play + The Pact = I Do

The Hero + Vegas = No Regrets

The Doctors Series

Dr. Off Limits

Dr. Perfect

Dr. CEO

Dr. Fake Fiancé

Dr. Single Dad

The Mister Series

Mr. Mayfair

Mr. Knightsbridge

Mr. Smithfield

Mr. Park Lane

Mr. Bloomsbury

Mr. Notting Hill

The Player Series

International Player

Private Player

The Gentleman Series

The Ruthless Gentleman

The Wrong Gentleman

The Royals Series

King of Wall Street

Park Avenue Prince

Duke of Manhattan

The British Knight

The Earl of London

The Nights Series

Indigo Nights

Promised Nights

Parisian Nights

Standalones

An American in London

14 Days of Christmas

Hollywood Scandal

Love Unexpected

Hopeful

The Empire State Series

Sign up to the Louise Bay mailing list at www.louisebay.com

ONE

Rosey

The mirror reveals my three younger sisters in bias-cut, peacock-green satin, sucking in their cheeks and taking selfies. It also reveals a snow-white veil draping over my bared shoulders down to perfectly manicured fingertips. I should be the one giggling with excitement, unable to sit still for anticipation.

After all, this is *my* wedding day.

Frank might be older, and I might not exactly love him, but I'm grateful to him, and that's *almost* love, isn't it?

I take in a breath, the bones in my corset pressing against my rib cage. *I'm so lucky*, I remind myself. I'm never going to have to worry about where my next meal is coming from. I'm not going to have to tell my children not to make a sound when Mr. McAlister bangs on the door of the trailer, looking for rent. I get to live in a house with a yard and a top-loading washer. Frank says we're traveling overseas for our honeymoon. He's keeping the destination a secret. I've never even made it across the border into California. Never been on an airplane. Before Frank, I'd never been to the grocery store and not had to do mental arithmetic as I added every item to my cart to ensure I had enough money to cover the necessities. Marriage to Frank promises so much.

I. Am. So. Lucky.

Except, no matter how many times I say it to myself, how much I *will* myself to feel it, I can't drown out the voices screaming at me, telling me I shouldn't be walking down the aisle in thirty minutes.

"Are you going to get pregnant right away?" Lydia asks out of nowhere. "Cement the deal?"

The room tilts a little and I close my eyes. *A child?* The boning in my corset is going to leave bruises. Everything's just so tight. I can't breathe.

My sisters are happy to accept the niceties that come with me dating the co-owner of the second-biggest car dealership in Eugene, Oregon. They know this isn't a love match. It doesn't occur to them that it should be. Frank's been generous with my family. When we started dating, he obviously felt he had to seduce the entire family. He gave Kitty a job and had a chat with the sheriff when she got caught up in an argument with her boyfriend. He took all five of us out for dinner after our fifth date, and bought everyone Christmas presents three months later, after he insisted everyone spend the holiday at his house.

And when he proposed, he also announced he'd bought the trailer we'd grown up in, and gave it to me as an early wedding present—his way of making sure my family was taken care of. Frank is kind. He's generous. I could do a lot worse.

So why aren't I looking forward to being married to him? Having a *child* with him?

My mother comes out of the bathroom. She's wearing

lipstick, which I've only witnessed two other times in my life. She's wearing a long, pastel-blue dress that looks like it was meant for someone else. It's just so formal. I don't think I've ever seen anyone look so unlike themselves. I look down at my gown. Maybe the congregation will feel the same way when they see me dressed up like this.

She meets my eyes in the mirror and pulls back her shoulders, like she does when someone accuses her of something. "You look beautiful, Rosey. You always do. A smile would complete the picture." It's an accusation in disguise: *Why aren't you excited that you've landed a man like Frank Goad? You're going to have a charmed life. It's good for your whole family.*

But she doesn't say it, because if she does, I might disagree with her. She won't risk it. She always told me my face would be my fortune. And in her eyes, this day confirms it. I'm marrying into money.

I nod and force a half smile. "I think I just need some air."

"Someone open a window," she calls, but my sisters ignore her. I don't want an open window. I want to look up at the gray Oregon sky and ask God whether I'm doing the right thing.

Before she can stop me, I gather up my skirt, toss it over my arm, and beeline toward the hotel room door. "I'll be five minutes," I call over my shoulder.

"Rosey Williams, come back here," my mother calls. Her voice closes in on me, and before I can make it out the door, she grabs me. "Get back here."

"My hair and makeup are done," I say. "I'm ready. There's thirty minutes before I need to be downstairs. I just want to talk to Frank about something." It's a lie. Frank is the last person I want to see. Despite the way he's always trying to help me—help us—he's not the person I'd run to in a crisis. Not that he doesn't care about me. I think he really does. But the only person I can count on is me. I learned that lesson a long time ago.

"About what?" she hisses. "You're going to be walking down the aisle to him soon enough."

There's a crash behind us and my sisters start assigning blame. In the split second my mother's distracted, I manage to slip out the door. My heart pounds in my chest like I've just escaped a kidnapping. Slamming my whole palm against the elevator call button, I glance back down the corridor. No one's chasing me. Yet.

The elevator doors spring open immediately, like they're a getaway car idling at the curb. I expect Frank to be waiting for me in the lobby, but when the doors open, there's an eerie quiet I wasn't expecting.

I'm wearing a wedding dress. It's not like I can fly under the radar, but I casually cross the lobby to the front door like I'm in sweatpants and my Oregon State t-shirt.

I just need some air. Some time to breathe. To think.

I step outside and it's like there's a roof on the world, it's so completely full of low clouds.

"Okay, God," I say out loud. "I don't think we've actually had this talk. But I need to know whether you think I should be marrying a man twenty years older than me who I don't love because he bought my mom's trailer and kept my sister out of jail?"

I wait for a sign. A frog or two falling from the sky. A bird shitting on my dress. Anything.

God doesn't respond.

I stamp my white pump into the gravel beneath my feet. "Fuck."

"Need a lift somewhere?" a woman's voice asks from my

left. A figure in a white shirt and black pants pushes off from where she's leaning against the wall.

Is she talking to me? A woman comes into view and I realize it's Polly Gifford. We went to high school together, but ran in different circles. From what I heard, she got married at nineteen and had three kids before she turned twenty-three. "Polly?"

She twirls a bunch of keys around her finger and rounds the hood of the cab parked in front of the hotel. "I've got an airport pickup." She shrugs. "I can drop you there."

My chest lifts as I consider her suggestion. The airport? "Where would I go?"

She chuckles. "The fuck outta here? I don't know. You just don't look like you want to be here. You can stay and ask God for guidance, or you can get a free lift to Eugene Airport. Choice is yours."

A thrill chases down my spine as I consider her offer. My phone is tucked into my bra—the only way to hang on to your phone with three sisters—so I wouldn't need my wallet. But I don't even have a jacket.

Or my freaking passport.

My heart sinks. No one's letting me on an airplane without ID. I chew on the inside of my lip. It's in the safe in the honeymoon suite—the room I just left. Frank made me apply for my passport when he told me we were going on an overseas trip. Why didn't I bring it down with me?

Because I wasn't planning on Polly Gifford offering me a ride out of my life.

Polly taps the roof of the cab. "Enjoy your wedding day, Rosey Williams." She opens the cab door.

"Wait!" I say. I don't have a plan. Or a place to go. I just know that I don't want to get married. Not today. Not to

Frank. "I need to grab my ID. It's upstairs. Can you wait five minutes?"

She looks at her watch. "That's all I can wait. If you're not back in five, I've gotta go."

"I'll be back." I turn and run across the lobby toward the elevators. "God, if you're listening, you better have me back down here in five minutes," I mutter.

The elevator's waiting and I jump in, suddenly filled with energy and purpose. On the way up to the suite, I don't second-guess myself. Not once. As much as I like Frank, the idea of me jilting him at the altar isn't as horrifying as actually marrying him. I can't go through with it. I just can't. Maybe I should stay and face the music—look Frank in the eye, listen to my mother's chastisement and blame. But I can't face it.

I just need to get away. Escape.

In no time at all, the elevator doors open. Full of determination and a steel I don't recognize in myself, I let myself back into the honeymoon suite, hoping no one notices.

"Oh, you're back, finally," Mom says, from the chair where Kitty did my hair. Armed with a can of hairspray and a teasing comb, Kitty stands over Mom. Anything could be about to happen.

"I gotta get Frank my passport," I say, heading for the safe. "He needs it to check us in apparently."

"You *saw* him?" she asks, horrified, only narrowly missing a squirt of hairspray to the eye.

I type in the code to the safe but it doesn't open. Shit. This is all I need. I can't have forgotten the code. That can't be God's plan for me. The idea of a trip to the airport fills me with such relief, getting stuck here can't be my destiny.

"No, I ran into Pete in the lobby. He's gonna get it to Frank."

"Well, why didn't he come up to get it? He can't expect you to be wandering around in..."

I tune Mom out and type in the code again. This time the click of the lock feels like I've reached the summit of a roller coaster. My hands start to shake. I'm excited and terrified at the same time.

I pull out my passport and hold it up toward Mom, careful not to let my driver's license slip out from the pages where I stuffed it last night. "It's fine, Mom. It gives me something to do so I don't get nervous." I eye my purse next to the window, but I can't risk taking it. Mom will know something's up.

She rolls her eyes, and Lydia takes her attention by asking her to referee an argument she's having with Kitty.

I take in the scene. My mom, snapping at Kitty and trying to cajole Marion into standing up so she doesn't wrinkle her dress. Kitty and Lydia trade insults like they're playing snap like we did when we were younger during endless rainy days stuck in the trailer. The suite is twice as big as the trailer I've called home for all twenty-eight years of my life, but it's still too small for all of us. We've spent our lives on top of each other, arguing, competing, surviving.

I'm done.

I curl my hand around my passport, grab Lydia's gray hoodie from where it's slung on the back of a chair, and slip out.

I race toward the elevator, stuffing my passport into my bra. If I run into anyone, I don't want to have to explain why I'm holding it.

As I get into the elevator, I press the down button a thousand times in the hopes it will get me to the lobby faster. After all this, I don't want Polly to have driven off, but as I get to the first floor, I see the amber plastic light of her cab over the flower arrangement in the lobby. I take in a breath. This is it. I made it.

I keep my head down, like anyone's going to miss the girl in the white dress sprinting toward the exit.

"Excuse me!" someone calls behind me, but I pretend I haven't heard them. I need to get to Polly. I need to get out of here.

Polly must see me coming, because she opens the passenger door. I'm just a couple of yards from the exit when I feel a hand on my arm and my heart sinks.

I stop and turn, accepting defeat.

I've been caught.

When I look up, I expect to see Frank staring back at me—but it's a small man with jet-black hair who I don't recognize. "You dropped this," he says, handing me Lydia's hoodie.

I laugh. I'm still free. "Thank you!" I say, beaming at him.

I forget any pretense of making a graceful exit. I run to the cab, to Polly, to freedom.

Nothing, not even God, is going to stop me.

TWO

Byron

When I left my hometown of Star Falls, Colorado, nearly fifteen years ago, I never thought I'd be back. Not even for the holidays. I knew I didn't belong here. Which is why it's so surprising that being back feels... not as strange as I expected it to. And the plaid shirt I'm wearing feels oddly comfortable. I don't know why I kept it all these years. I found it at the back of my closet in New York and stuffed it in my luggage, reasoning that I'd seen eighteen Januarys in Star Falls and none of them were warm.

I upend my suitcase on the floor and start to unpack. Every time I've been back here over the last two years, I've always lived out of my luggage. But this trip feels more permanent. Not that I'm back for good—hell no—but I'll be staying longer than I have on any of my previous trips. Eventually, I'll move from the cabin I've rented into one of the lodges at the Colorado Club—the billionaires' playground I'm constructing on the edge of town, a little way up the mountain. I want the construction workers to focus on the lodges that will be bought or rented by the centimillion-aires and billionaires who will attend the Club's grand opening at the end of next month.

My personal accommodations can wait.

I can't bring myself to put on the cowboy hat and boots that are almost mandatory in Star Falls, but I put on the steel-toe boots I had couriered from *Safety With Us* in Brooklyn to my apartment in Tribeca, and my Colorado Rockies baseball hat I've had since I was a kid. I make a mental note to scuff my shoes up a little before I go into Grizzly's tonight. The leather practically gleams, they're so new.

Going to the only bar in town, if you don't count the Snowdrop Inn—which I don't—isn't something I've done since I've been back in town. And apparently, it's *been noticed*. I should have known my every move in Star Falls would be carefully catalogued, but I've had other things on my mind—like the fact I'm sinking my entire fortune into the Colorado Club.

When I asked Hart McEvoy, the Club's general manager, why we weren't getting more local applicants for all the jobs we're advertising, he informed me that there's still *local hostility* toward the Club. We have hundreds of positions to fill, and although many of them have been taken by people from across the state who will live in staff hous-ing, I need local people to be part of the Club, too. They'll be more reliable and less likely to leave.

It irritates the shit out of me that people are being so short-sighted.

I'm here, bringing jobs, bringing *life* to the town, and people still find a reason to bitch and moan. I need to win them over. My worn jeans and new boots are part of my I'm-a-local-guy persona. I grew up here. I *am* local. It just doesn't feel like it, since I've been away almost half my life. New York feels like it's always been home. Star Falls is just the name of a place on my passport that reminds me where I was born.

I lace up my shoes, lock up. Not that there's any danger of a burglary in Star Falls. It's dark out and I can only just see the tops of the familiar mountains I know cut through the clear sky all around me.

The one thing New York City doesn't have is a sky like the one over Star Falls. The fucking stars always get to me. Every time. Even when I lived here and had never seen another sky, I knew the one I was born under was special. It never gets fully dark here because of all the goddamn stars. There's no doubt it's beautiful.

I slide into my truck and head the mile into town toward Grizzly's. I just want to show my face. And maybe accidently run into a few people. Star Falls understood what an influencer was long before social media was born. I figure if I can get certain big personalities in town on board with the Colorado Club, the "local resistance" will melt away and Hart will have people lining up for all the jobs we have to fill.

My first target is Jim Johnson. Or more specifically, his wife, Sue. She's the most influential person in Star Falls. But I need Jim on board first. I need him to soften up the ground for me before I try to get Sue to change her mind about the Colorado Club.

I pull up outside Grizzly's and realize I haven't scuffed up my shoes. People are going to clock my spotless boots as soon as I walk in the place and label me a city boy. Which I am. Except tonight, I'm trying to win people over. Or at least not alienate more of them.

The ground is frozen, and there's not much boot-dirtying mud around, but after kicking my tires and stepping on my own feet, the leather no longer gleams like a flashlight with new batteries. Hopefully no one saw me. I hate to think of the rumors this town could invent if anyone saw me trying to scuff my own boots.

I left town before I could legally drink, so I only ever went into Grizzly's to look for my father. I open the door and am instantly transported back twenty years. The scent of stale beer and the crack of pool balls brings me to fourteen again, desperate to find my father. My mom had collapsed and I'd gone to fetch Dad. But he hadn't been at Grizzly's. Or maybe he'd been in the back playing poker. Losing at poker, knowing him.

I head straight to the bar, slide onto one of the tan leather stools and order a beer. The bartender is young, skinny with a tattoo of what could be a Chinese dragon in red ink on his arm. He doesn't know me and I don't know him. Suits me just fine.

One of the reasons I haven't come into town over the last couple of years when I've been back overseeing things at the Colorado Club is because I don't have any connections in this place. My dad was found dead a couple of towns away after a bar fight. My mother remarried three years later while I was in New York and moved to Southern California with my sister, Mary. There's nothing here for me.

"One beer coming right up, Byron," the bartender says. Maybe I don't know him, but apparently he knows me.

I shouldn't be surprised. There won't be a person in Star Falls who doesn't know that Mack Miller's kid is building something on the side of the mountain. I just hadn't expected that my face would be so easy to put to my name. The way this town gossips is another reason I've avoided coming back. People are just so in each other's business. After my dad died, my mother cried for weeks, not because Dad was dead, but because she knew everyone would be talking about it, saying how she was better off as a widow.

"Well, well, well," a woman's voice says from behind me. "Look who just rode into town. Finally."

Part of me wants to ignore it. Whoever it is doesn't have malice in their tone, but by responding, I'll be opening a can of worms—and I'm not sure I'm ready. I'm not sure I'll ever be ready.

"Hey, you got a hug for an old friend?" the voice asks.

There's no getting out of this. I turn on my stool and come face-to-face with Eva Maples. I haven't seen her since the day I graduated high school.

"I haven't seen you since the day we graduated high school," she says. "Heard you were back in the area." She pauses and gives me a look full of meaning—what meaning, I'm not sure. "You never made it into town until now." She shakes her head disapprovingly, but holds out her arms. I bend and pull her into an awkward hug.

She laughs as she pulls away. "Never were a hugger, were you, Byron? Too much of the tortured poet in you." She fiddles with the back of her apron. "You just drinking or you wanna order some food?" She leans in and whispers, "Don't say I told you, but steer clear of the chicken meat-balls." She clears her throat and resumes her normal voice. I glance around to see who's listening. Everyone, it seems, though at least they're pretending not to. "The wings are the best."

"Sounds good," I say. "Do you have a side of broccoli?"

She laughs, pats me on the shoulder and walks off, like I just told her the funniest joke she's heard this year. Except I wasn't joking.

I'm still trying to figure out whether or not I'm going to get that side of broccoli when a heavy hand drops on my shoulder.

"So, Byron Miller. What you doing at Grizzly's? I hear you have a fancy bar up on that mountain." Jim Johnson— just the man I was looking for. Things might have changed over the last fifteen years, but apparently you can still always see Jim at Grizzly's at eight on a weeknight. When I was growing up, Sundays were the only days Jim stayed away from the local watering hole.

I hold out my hand. "Jim Johnson," I say. "Good to see you again."

He shakes my hand, nodding. "We've been waiting for you."

There's nothing I can say to that. I should have come before now. The town has taken my absence as a sign of disrespect.

"Can I buy you a beer?" I ask.

"That you can, son." I try to suppress the shiver that runs down my spine when he uses the term *son*. He slides into the seat next to mine and I order his drink. "Wanna tell me a little bit about what you're doing up on that mountain?" he asks.

"Yeah," I say. This is why I'm here, after all. I might have a permanent PR associate in place at the Colorado Club, but she's focused on getting the Club coverage in high-end international publications, courting celebrities, getting the zero point one percenters talking.

I should have been managing the residents of Star Falls from the beginning. Instead I've buried my head in the sand, hoping I could build a resort on the edge of town and maybe no one in Star Falls would notice.

"You've probably gathered it's a retreat. A place where

people from all over can come and appreciate the great state of Colorado."

He narrows his eyes and takes a slug of the beer that's been put in front of him. "Is that right? And you going to encourage these visitors down to our town?"

This strikes me as a trick question. On the one hand, he might see the benefits of having people with a pocketful of cash spending it in Star Falls. On the other hand, he might not want a bunch of strangers interrupting their peaceful way of life.

"That's something I've been thinking about," I say. "I'd like your thoughts on whether that's something you'd like to see."

He lets out a small chuckle.

"I'm creating a lot of jobs," I say. "Opportunities. If people want them."

"I hear you're shipping people in from out of town."

"There will be plenty of staff housing so people don't have to be local, but I'm advertising in the *Star Falls Gazette*. Got it online too. And there's flyers being handed out at Marty's Market and the post office. We're just not seeing the interest from the town."

A silence settles between us. Jim isn't a bad guy. He's not about to run me out of town for daring to change small-town life in Star Falls. At the same time, he's protective of this place and its residents. Perhaps more so than his wife.

"How's Mrs. Johnson?"

"You can call her Sue. She's good. We can see the lights of your place from our back porch."

I scan his face, looking for signs of anger or frustration, but I don't see any. I relax my shoulders. I've spent the last three years of my life getting the relevant permissions and permits from local and state officials, and there were never any complaints from anyone from Star Falls.

"How's it look?" I ask.

"Pretty," he replies.

There's a beat of silence before I say, "I'd love to have you come and look around if you'd like."

He sucks in a breath. "Listen, son. I'm not interested in fancy restaurants and spas and whatever the hell else you've got going on up there." He takes a sip of beer and I wait for the *but*. I know there's one coming. "I've been walking through those woods and across those mountains for a good five decades now." He glances around the bar. "Just like a lot of other people in this town."

I nod, keen to hear what it is he's trying to tell me.

"I do it less in the winter. Don't want to take any unnecessary risks. But I still like to wander with my dogs. You know?"

"Right," I reply.

"And we're hearing rumors about electric fencing and checkpoints and... I'm not sure that's going to go down so well. From what I hear, you've got your hands on fifteen thousand acres of land—that's pretty much everything of the mountains and the valley that you can see from this town. Much more than the five hundred acres your father had."

I take a swig of my beer. My father's farm had been small by Colorado standards. He grew apples mainly, and some other fruit. The farm had been in the family three generations, and I was supposed to be the fourth. At least, that's what Mom always told me.

When Dad died and we discovered the huge loans he'd taken out on the farm, I don't know if I was more relieved or horrified. I was no longer locked into a future I didn't want, but I also didn't know what the future would look like otherwise. My father's gambling meant I had to forge my own path, but it also meant the farm's lineage had been cut short.

Until I bought it back five years ago.

"You're right," I say to Jim. "Fifteen thousand two hundred forty-four acres."

"And as well as you buying up some of the neighboring farms, some of that land belonged to the state before you."

I nod. I'd bet Jim knows exactly the boundary line of the Colorado Club. I'm not quite sure what he's getting at, but no doubt I will soon.

The sound of chairs scraping against the floor catches my attention. Someone comes up from behind Jim and offers me his hand.

It takes me a minute before I realize it's Walt fucking Ripley. Our mothers had been best friends since school and got pregnant with us both at the same time. "Hey, man," I say. He's unmistakably Walt, but older and forty pounds heavier. Then again, it's been fifteen years since I laid eyes on him.

"Byron," he says with a nod.

"Can I get you a beer?" I ask.

"You bet your ass, you can. I figure you owe me for going off to New York without me."

Walt had been the guy who stood by my side at my father's funeral. The guy who'd told me it was going to be okay when I found out we were going to have to move because the family farm was being sold by my father's creditors to pay back all the loans he'd taken out to pay off his gambling debts. He was the boy who helped me formulate a plan to get out of Star Falls. Of course I hadn't forgotten him. I just hadn't let myself think about Star Falls after I left. It held too many painful memories.

"I've just been telling Byron that I still want to roam around with my dog," Jim says.

I understand Jim's frustration. The problem I have is that the promise the Colorado Club makes is exclusivity, privacy, and security. If celebrities want to escape LA, I want their first thought to be the Colorado Club.

"We can figure it out," I assure Jim. "There aren't going to be electric fences."

"There shouldn't be *any* fences—electric or not," Jim says. "This is wilderness. Wilderness isn't fenced off and claimed by an elite couple of thousand people in the world."

They're both staring at me, and I know they're right. It's just, for the Colorado Club to work, it needs to have a boundary. I nod. "I hear you."

"It's God's country," Jim says. "Not Byron Miller's."

I don't ask him whether he'd welcome people wandering across his land. It's not worth the fight—I'm not going to win, even if it is a double standard. But if the idea of having the land I own fenced off is a problem for the residents of Star Falls, I'm not sure what I can do about it.

I'm saved from having to think up a reasonable answer when Jim turns to see someone come through the door. I pick at the edge of the blue and white label on my beer bottle, wondering if there's a solution to the problem. There's got to be.

I turn to assure Jim that we'll figure something out, but his attention isn't on me anymore. He's looking over my shoulder. I turn to follow his gaze and see a woman in her mid-twenties with long dark hair, walking toward the bar. She looks a little bedraggled, although she's pretty. She's definitely not from around here. Nothing too unusual in that, aside from the fact this woman is wearing sneakers, a faded gray hoodie, and a wedding dress.

I glance at Jim and he shoots me a look that says, *What in the hell?*

I still don't have any answers for him. I glance at Walt to see if he understands what's going on, but he looks as confused as I feel. I turn to the woman again, just as she slides onto the barstool one down from mine.

"I'd like a drink," she says.

The bartender who knows me better than I know him says, "Well, you've come to the right place. You want to be more specific?"

Her eyelids flicker as she takes a breath and thinks about it, like she was expecting the bartender to decide for her. Now that he hasn't, she's having to make a decision she hadn't planned for. "Do you have tequila? On the rocks?"

She picks one of the three brand names she's given, and when the glass appears in front of her, she hesitates before she brings it to her lips. She takes the tiniest of sips and lets out a huge sigh. It seems she's been waiting for that drink all day.

"You just get into town?" Jim asks the woman.

The woman doesn't hear him at first. She's staring forward and thinking so hard, I can almost see her thoughts in front of her face. She's worried. And out of energy. Like she's reached the end of the road.

Then, as if Jim's words have taken a couple of seconds to register, she turns to him. She offers him a tight smile and nods—she's not interested in small talk.

Jim goes to follow up on his question, and both Walt and I interrupt him at the same time.

"I'm sure we'll come to some understanding," I say, just as Walt tells Jim I'm not about to stop him walking his dog wherever he wants.

"Let me have a think about it, Jim," I say. "And if you have any other questions—"

"I have a few things I want to talk to you about," he says. He's about to launch into his list, but he stops himself. "Why don't you settle back in. Catch up with your buddy here." He slaps Walt on the back. "But don't be a stranger, you hear me? I'm gonna run. Gotta get back home by the time *Love Island* finishes."

I want to laugh, but I stop myself. "Say hi to Sue from me."

"You sure you want me to? Your presence will be required at Sunday dinner if I do that."

I nod. "Say hi to Sue for me."

"See you Sunday," he says, as he drops some cash on the bar and heads out.

I wasn't expecting the warm hum that settles in me. I walked out on this town fifteen years ago and Jim's acting like I've only been gone a couple of months. It's almost like they always knew I'd come back, and they've just been waiting.

"So you're going to come to dinner on Sunday?" Walt says from beside me.

"You're going to be there too?"

"I'm there every Sunday. I married Patty."

My eyes nearly fall out of my head. "Patty Johnson? How'd you manage that?" Patty Johnson was one of the most formidable girls at our high school. She was two years older than us and ran the school more than the principal did. Just like her mother before her, she was an influencer before the time of social media. She decided what was cool and what wasn't. The sweater every girl should own, the boys the girls were allowed to ask to the spring formal. At fourteen, when she took up the flute out of nowhere, every kid in the school badgered their parents for lessons.

Walt laughs. "It took me a while to win her over, but perseverance paid off."

"He married Patty?" I say to Eva, as she delivers a bowl of chips.

"A thousand years ago," Eva says. "It's been a while, Byron Miller."

For a second, I wonder why it's been so long. Everything's so welcoming and warm and familiar. For almost a minute, I can forget all the pain that came with this place.

"I gotta go," Walt says. "Patty watches *Love Island* with Sue. I have to go pick her up." He pauses, and I want to make a time for us to catch up, but I stop myself, because what's the point? We'll catch up, and I'll probably never see him again. I'm here to do a job—get the Colorado Club up and running. I'm not here to take a walk down memory lane. However nice that walk might start off, it'll soon turn dark and muddy, and before I know it, I'll be waist-high in cow shit.

"I'll see you Sunday," he says.

For a second I'm confused, and then I remember Jim's invitation. It's not like I'm planning to go. But maybe I should. I do need to get Sue on board. We've got to fill the vacancies up at the Club.

I chuckle. "Maybe you will."

He gives me a two-fingered salute and heads out. I order another beer and surreptitiously scan the rest of the bar. Is there anyone else here I need to talk to? Any other old-school influencers?

The runaway bride next to me is on her phone. She has long fingers, and she's gripping the device like she's holding on to a life raft. I wonder if she really is a runaway bride or if she's an extra from a film or a model from a photo shoot. None of the potential explanations for the white dress explain why she's sitting on the stool next to me.

I wouldn't consider myself a nosey person. Not normally. But I've come back to Star Falls after fifteen years and nothing much seems to have changed. The woman next to me is the exception. I'm surprised Jim didn't ask her to fill out a questionnaire so he could report back to the rest of the town about who she is and why she's at Grizzly's. This town likes to know every single detail of each other's lives.

The bartender asks if she wants another drink. The woman pauses for a second before she asks for tap water. I want to offer to buy her a drink, but then it would get awkward, because she might think I'm making a pass at her. I wouldn't be. Not that she's not attractive—she is. Big blue eyes and flawless skin and dark hair that's curled at the ends and seems to go on forever.

I'm staring.

If we were back in New York right now, I would have had a drink thrown in my face at the very least.

But we're definitely not in New York, and I'm not sure she's even noticed my staring. She's too lost in her thoughts. Probably she's thinking about the groom she jilted or the town she just rolled into. I'd pay more than a penny to know what exactly is on her mind.

When the bartender delivers the water, the bride asks, "I checked at the little inn on the corner, the one with the snowdrops in pots on the stoop? To see if they had any rooms for the night—two nights maybe—but they were completely full. They suggested I try here. Do you have rooms?"

There's only one inn in town—snowdrops or no snowdrops.

"We don't have rooms," the bartender says. "Tanya probably meant for you to ask around in here." He briefly slides his gaze to me. "We have a few Airbnbs in town but I think most things are fully booked." She looks a little confused. And she should be. It's not like Star Falls is hosting an annual film festival or anything, but the Colorado Club has booked out the Snowdrop Inn for senior managers who are still looking for accommodations. And I booked out Beth and Mike's two cabins because they're the closest accommodations to the Club. I'm only living in one of them, but I didn't want a nosey neighbor keeping track of my comings and goings.

She turns, and her gaze hits me like a thunderbolt. She's gorgeous. A smattering of freckles across her nose and full bee-stung lips that I'd be intent on kissing if we were in New York. But we're not in New York. We're in Star Falls, Colorado, and the cabin next door to mine is the only avail-able accommodation in town.

THREE

Rosey

If I'd stayed in Oregon, I'd be halfway to my honeymoon right now. I'd be on my way to Mexico or Tahiti or maybe even Paris.

Instead, I'm freezing my ass off in a bar in god-knows-where. Okay, so I'm pretty sure I'm in Colorado—the state where I landed. Other than that, I'm clueless *and* also homeless. The bus stopped when it was already dark. From what I've seen of the town so far, it could be the backdrop to a cozy mystery or the home of a serial killer. Either one doesn't seem particularly appealing. But the bus driver told me about an inn in town, and stupidly, I assumed I'd get a room, so I got off two stops before the end of the line.

I figured no one would look for me here. Beyond that, I don't have a plan. When I got up this morning, I'd planned to be Frank's wife by now. Now I'm sitting in a bar halfway across the US, and I'm definitely *not* married.

My mother's going to kill me.

I need another tequila. But no, I need to be sober in case

I need to practice the self-defense moves I learned in high school. The town being home to a serial killer and all. Possibly. Maybe. I also need to be sober in case drunk-me is tempted to respond to Frank's text, telling me I'll come to my senses. That was after I texted him to apologize for dumping him not-quite-at-the-altar.

"Ask around?" I scan the bar. Who would I ask? Letting the world know I'm totally lost and alone doesn't seem like the wisest plan. Not to mention, the last thing I want is for someone to ask why I'm dressed like this.

By the time I got through security at the airport, the plane was already boarding. I didn't have time to look for a change of clothes. When I landed, I had a little more luck. After buying a bus ticket, I prioritized footwear. I picked up a pair of sneakers on sale, but then I had to run for my bus. By the time I reached Star Falls, all the stores were closed.

The bartender is barely twenty-one, but he looks at me like he's seen plenty of brides on the hunt for a bed while on the run. His eyes are full of pity and knowing. "I know Beth and Mike have a couple of cabins just outside of town."

My heart lifts in my chest at the real possibility of a bed to sleep in tonight.

"But I think they're rented at the moment." He looks at the guy sitting next to me. Is this Mike, of Beth and Mike? I turn to look at him. If it is, Beth is a very lucky woman. Mike is hot. I know I was engaged to be married up until ten thirty this morning, but I'm not dead. The guy next to me is tall and dark and swarthy. I don't know exactly what *swarthy* means, but I know this guy is it. His hair isn't long, but it's not short either. It's definitely long enough to get a fistful of when he's buried between my thighs.

Holy crap! I snap my head back to focus on my glass of tap water. I'm staring. More than that, I'm *fantasizing*. It's not something I've done in a while. My life has felt all too real recently. I make a silent apology to Beth and then turn my attention back to the bartender. "If Beth and Mike are lucky enough to have their cabins rented, is there anyone else in town who has a place? Or rents out a room?"

The bartender shoots another speaking glance at Mike before saying, "You could try Colbert's Farm, but I think it's booked."

Mike interrupts. "I'm renting Beth and Mike's cabins. I'm in one. You could take the other if you needed it for a couple of nights." He's wearing a blue plaid shirt that looks as soft as spun clouds.

So not only is the hot stranger not one half of "Beth and Mike," he also might have the solution to my accommodation problem.

"It's available?" I ask.

He nods. It's not an enthusiastic response, but at this point, as long as it has a bed and a flushing toilet, I'll take it.

"Is it far?" I ask.

"Just up the street, about half a mile out of town." He glances at the door and then back at me.

I don't bother to ask him the price—it's my only option and I'll just have to hope it doesn't drain all of my savings. I glance at my engagement ring. It's such a pretty ring. I picked it out myself. Frank wanted me to have the exact one I wanted, so we went ring shopping together after the engagement. I hadn't given any thought to engagement rings, and I picked it out because it reminded me of the kind of flower six-year-old me would have drawn. Small sapphire petals surround a large central diamond. It's pretty, but now it feels heavy on my finger. Like I shouldn't be wearing it.

I slip it off and slide it onto the bar. I'll have to give it back to Frank. I guess I could mail it. I push thoughts of tomorrow away. I will know what to do after a night's sleep.

"I'm Rosey, by the way," I say to the stranger. I really hope he isn't a serial killer.

He nods. "Byron."

"Good to meet you, Byron." I want to ask him if he's named after the poet. Whether his parents were romantic and whether he reads poetry. All of a sudden I have a thousand questions, but from the look on his face, questions are the last thing this man wants.

I don't ask him if I can have the key right away, even though that's exactly what I want to do. I want to go now. Get out of this dress. When I first put the hoodie on, I could pretend people weren't going to necessarily think that I was wearing a wedding dress—I tricked myself into believing that people would just think I was wearing a white skirt with a hoodie. But since the zipper broke when it caught on the arm of the airplane seat, there's no doubt I'm wearing a full-fledged wedding gown.

The problem is, I don't have anything else but this dress to put on. I don't know why, but somehow, the idea of taking it off tonight and having to put it back on in the morning feels worse than just sleeping in it.

"You want to go now?" he asks, staring ahead at the multicolored bottles behind the bar.

"Whenever you're ready," I reply. This guy has done me a huge favor. I don't want to rush him, but let's get the hell going already. He hasn't finished his beer, and he probably came to relax. Let off some steam. He looks stressed. Or maybe not stressed as much as irritated. That can't be just down to me. When I first walked in, he wore the same expression, way before he knew I was going to be bothering him for a room for the night.

He slides his beer across the bar, stands, and pulls out his wallet. "Let's go."

"Oh, you don't need to—I mean, I can walk. I just need a key." I hope this guy doesn't think he's getting lucky tonight. He's hot and everything, but like, I was supposed to marry someone today. One is enough.

"Key's in my cabin. I'll give you a ride." He holds out his jacket. "Put this on. It's freezing."

"I'm fine—"

"Put the jacket on. It's cold outside."

I tighten my jaw at his command. I didn't escape Oregon just to be ordered about in Star Falls. But once again, I can't say no. I need a bed for the night and this guy's cabin is my only option. I figure I'll put his jacket on and just be grateful he hasn't asked about what I'm wearing. If he's going to murder me, my DNA will be on his clothes. And enough people have seen us leave together that even if I'm dead, at least this guy will go to jail.

I slip on the navy jacket, cuffs falling past my fingers. It feels like a huge blanket. I didn't realize how cold I'd been until now. I look up at Byron, his hands thrust into the pockets of his dark blue jeans, his eyes narrowed like he's trying to figure something out. He glances around the bar, and I follow his eyeline. There's a ripple of heads lifting, checking out what's going on.

He sighs. "Fuck," he mutters under his breath. "This town never changes. It's addicted to gossip. Let's go."

He sounds pissed off. At the town? Me? His evening being interrupted? Probably all of the above.

Nothing I can do about his mood. Hopefully it means he won't quiz me about what I'm doing in town, how long I'll stay or where I've come from. I don't have any answers at the moment. I certainly don't want to think about Oregon.

Every minute that ticks by makes it more and more impossible to go back. I left wanting to escape a wedding, but the more I think about it, I've escaped more than just being Frank's wife. I escaped my entire life.

And I'm not sure I want to go back.

If I'm honest, I haven't liked my life in Oregon for a long time. I don't like the person I was there, either. I want to be someone else, with different circumstances and a different future. I just need to figure out whether that future can start in Star Falls, or whether I'm just as far as ever from a life I actually want.

FOUR

Byron

Rosey needs a place to stay and I'm probably the only person in town who can provide it. That's my fault, since I've rented out every available place in Star Falls. Giving her the cabin next to mine for a couple of nights is the least I can do. The only thing that makes letting Rosey stay palatable is that she's not from around here. If I take a shower at four in the morning, the patrons of Grizzly's won't be talking about it the next day because she doesn't know anyone.

By all accounts, Rosey's only going to be here for a couple of days. The wedding dress is a clue she's not looking to stay. She's looking for escape.

I know the feeling.

I put some cash on the bar to cover both our drinks.

Rosey stands in my jacket, which completely drowns her, and tries to get the attention of the bartender. She offers me a smile. "I only have my phone to pay, so I just need to—"

"I've got it covered," I say, nodding to the cash I've laid out on the bar.

Her eyes go wide. "No, you can't. I mean—"

"Come on." I head out. I don't want to argue about paying for a shot of tequila. "Consider it a welcome to Star Falls."

I hold the door open for her. She pauses before dipping under my arm. As she passes me, her arm grazes my chest, and at this brief touch, we both jump apart like we're two magnets with our poles pointing toward each other.

"Sorry," I mutter. I don't want her to think I'm flirting. I'm not. The last thing I want is a one-night stand in a town that probably has my inside leg measurement in a central repository somewhere. As well as being gossips, the residents of Star Falls have long memories. A single indiscretion will last a lifetime.

I lead her toward my truck. She seems thoughtful, or maybe disappointed.

I open the passenger door and she climbs in. "*Star Falls*..." she says. "The name seems a little... ominous. Don't you think?"

"Ominous? Because...?" I always thought Star Falls was a pretty name. Almost too pretty, given how ugly life got here for me.

"I'm just being silly. I've had a bad day and I'm not in the most positive mindset."

"A falling star is a meteor shower," I say. Maybe there's a little defensiveness to my tone. I wanted to escape Star Falls so badly when I was younger, but I can't see what a stranger passing through town would have to complain about. "Meteor showers are... cool."

She laughs, and I realize I sound a little unhinged. "I guess. I don't know why, but it makes me think of someone who has fallen out of favor. A Hollywood movie star no one likes anymore. She doesn't belong."

My eyes widen at her description. We couldn't be coming at this from any further apart. Star Falls says "interstellar wonder" to me and "washed-up misfit" to her. "Wow. That's... depressing. You *have* had a bad day." As soon as I say it. I wish I hadn't. If she walked out on her wedding ceremony, a bad day will be a massive understatement. "Sorry if I'm being insensitive."

"Why? Because of this old thing?" she says, pulling at her dress. "Gives me away a little, doesn't it? Yeah, well, however bad a day I'm having, a guy I know is having a worse time." She glances down at her lap.

I want to ask more, but I don't want to prove my heritage as a Star Falls native son. No nosey gossip-hunting from me. It helps that our journey is at an end.

I pull off the main road and park in front of the two cabins.

"Here we are," I say.

She ducks to look out the window. "A perfect place to be murdered," she mutters.

I push my palm over my jaw and blow out a breath. "We haven't had a murder in Star Falls for at least twelve months." My tone is deadpan.

She snaps her head around to look at me, her eyes wide and wondering.

"I'm kidding," I say.

"Oh yeah, I can tell you're a real joker," she replies sarcastically.

I *was* trying to make a joke, but I don't know why. It's not like I'm trying to get to know her. But something inside me wants her to feel okay. "You'll be safe here. I'm next door. There's nothing to worry about."

I bet at least half the town doesn't lock their houses at night. She doesn't need to be concerned about being murdered.

I pull my mouth into a contorted smile. "I'll get the key."

I grab the key to the empty cabin from the hook inside my front door. I'm about to hand it over, when I remember the lock being stiff when I checked the place out when I first arrived. "Let me make sure you can get in." I leap up the steps to the porch and put the key in the lock. It fits like a glove. "Yeah, it's fine. It didn't fit so great when I tried it the other day."

I turn to find her at the top of the steps. "Thanks," she says.

"Do you need anything?" I ask. I'm not by nature a hospitable person, but this woman is having a really bad day. Maybe it's something about the air in this town, or maybe I'm overcompensating with kindness to lessen her fear of being axe-murdered.

"A new life?" she suggests. She gives me a half smile, and my breath catches in my throat. Her eyes kind of sparkle in the moonlight.

"New lives aren't available until morning," I say.

She gives me another small smile and for some reason it feels like the promise of something more. I shake it off. I don't need to be reading meaning into a pretty stranger's smile.

"This is great. Thank you," she says.

"Heaters are electric. If you have any problems, need a cup of sugar, anything, I'm right next door."

"Thank you, Byron." She narrows her eyes.

I hold up the key, which is attached by a chain to an oak disk with Star Falls Cabins etched on it. "Welcome to Star

Falls, Rosey," I say, sounding like the head of tourism for this tiny town I've avoided for so long.

My insides twang at how warm and entirely genuine the smile she beams at me is. I love New York, but it's full of fake smiles. My gut tells me there's nothing fake about this woman.

I realize I'm staring at her, so I give her a two-fingered salute and head back to my cabin.

Inside, I busy myself, turn on the TV and grab a tub of leftover curry I have in the refrigerator. I can't get Rosey's smile out of my head. Nothing can stop the images of her flashing through my brain. Where did she come from? Who was she going to marry? Why did she run away? Her escape clearly wasn't planned, since she had nothing with her but the clothes on her back. Her *wedding* clothes.

Shit, she's got nothing to change into.

I slide the cold curry onto the counter and head into my bedroom, pulling out a couple of t-shirts and some joggers. They'll be comically large on her, but at least she'll have something other than her wedding dress to wear tomorrow.

I stride over to her cabin, but pause as I get to the porch steps. I don't often question myself, but I don't know if I'm doing the right thing by disturbing her. I'm no Good Samaritan. My reaction to Rosey isn't normal for me. First giving up my privacy to give her a place to stay and now making sure she has a change of clothes? Is this who I am in Star Falls, or has Rosey sweeping into town shifted things somehow?

I have no explanation, but she answers the door as soon as I knock, like she's been waiting.

"Just in case you needed a change of clothes. They'll be too big, but at least..."

Her face is full of confusion, and for a second I wish I'd

stayed the fuck in my cabin and finished the curry instead of trying to help.

"That's so kind of you," she says, like no one's done anything kind for her in her life. "You're a good man, Byron." Her tone hits me right in the center of my chest. I've been called a lot of things in my time, but I'm not sure *kind* or *good* have made it to the top of the list. Somehow, when she says it, that's how I feel. I get the urge to do more. To offer to cook her dinner, run her a bath, do something—anything—else.

Instead, I nod and turn away before I make an epic fool of myself. "Sleep well, Rosey."

I need to get to bed myself. Maybe a night of rest will help quiet all these strange... *urges* I'm having. By tomorrow morning, the runaway bride will probably have moved on and I'll never see her again. She'll learn soon enough that Star Falls is a place you run *from*—not *to*.

FIVE

Rosey

Thank god I didn't throw my cellphone away in the airport trash, like I considered doing. For some reason I thought Frank would chase after me, aided by the GPS embedded in my phone. Then I remembered I don't live in a spy thriller. Why would a man I humiliated come after me? He probably hopes I'm dead right about now.

The upside of having my phone is being able to figure out there's an outdoor supply store in town that opens at nine. I slept in my dress because I couldn't face putting it back on in the morning, even though Byron was kind enough to give me a change of clothes. And a wedding dress covers me slightly more than Byron's tee—any way I cut it, I'd look like an escapee from an asylum. But I can't go another moment wearing it, which is why I've been standing outside Snail Trail for the past fifteen minutes. Me and a gigantic moose. Not a real one, of course. It's as tall as me and painted glossy brown, with large cartoon eyes and antlers that obscure a chunk of the Snail Trail window.

A woman with a bright red sweater comes to the glass door, flips the Closed sign to Open, and unlocks the door. I can't get in there quick enough. I don't have a ton of savings, but over the years, I've managed to put a little away. Mom would always take the majority of our paychecks. For rent and food and other bills. She'd let us keep a small amount for clothes and a rare trip to the movies. Mom would kill me if she knew any of us had a savings account.

"Hi there," the woman says. Her smile is contagious, even first thing in the morning. "Please come in." She pokes her head out of the door. "Morning, Marv." I'm pretty sure she just spoke to the moose, but given my outfit, I'm not fit to judge anyone's mental health.

"Thank you," I say as I glance around, trying to figure out what I can wear. Anything is better than what I'm currently in. I don't even have a change of underwear. I need everything.

"Can I help you with anything?" the woman asks.

I exhale. It's not like I can cover up the fact I'm dressed in a wedding gown, half covered up with a t-shirt, zipless hoodie and a man's jacket. "I've had an unexpected detour, and I need a full change of clothes. Or two."

I figure I can start working out a plan once I don't feel so conspicuous. The wedding dress needs to go.

"Well, I'm sure we can get you set up," she says. "My name is Marge. Shall we start with..." She looks around the store. "Pants. Then we can decide on everything else."

I allow myself to unclench my stomach muscles and take a deep breath. Everything inside settles a little. It's baby steps but this feels like a way forward. I haven't decided whether I need to go back to Oregon today and face the music or give myself a few days. Or maybe even a few weeks. No matter what I decide, I'm going to feel better after a change of clothes and some time with Marge, whose friendliness is a balm to my spirit.

"So, have you come from the Colorado Club?" Marge asks as she starts shunting hangers from one side to the other on the rack. "We hear it's getting busier and busier."

"Erm, no. At least I don't think so." Is "Colorado Club" a colloquial term for the airport or something?

Marge pulls out a couple of pairs of pants and laughs. "You don't know what I'm talking about, do you? I take it you don't work up there on the mountain?"

I shake my head. "I got into town last night. Kind of a spur-of-the-moment decision to leave Oregon."

"Oregon." She gasps. "Oh, the dress! It was... you were in Grizzly's last night! Oh, you sweet girl. What a mess."

Marge doesn't know how right she is.

"What's the Colorado Club?" I ask.

She looks over her shoulder as if to check that no one's listening, despite us being the only ones in the store. "You didn't see it? Just north of here, not exactly halfway up the mountain, but not in our valley either."

Marge must not realize that she hasn't actually answered my question. I shake my head. "I came in last night and was just focused on getting here as early as I could."

"Well, I'm staying positive. I think we should see it as an opportunity for the town. I don't see a downside, really." We move to the next rack of clothes and she starts pulling out sweaters and jackets.

"An opportunity?"

"Yes, lots of people with lots of money will be close by. And wealthy people like to shop and drink coffee. Hopefully they'll do that in Star Falls. Look what's happened to Vail. My momma's ninety-three this August, and she says people didn't really come to Colorado to ski when she was a kid. A lot can happen in a short space of time in this world. The Colorado Club could put Star Falls on the map."

I'm still not getting what the Colorado Club is.

"And even if the wealthy people want Gucci, there are going to be a lot of people working at the Club who will need good outdoor clothes." She holds up the bundle she's been gathering.

"So the Colorado Club is... a hotel?"

She smiles. "Kinda. I think. A hotel with lots of land and activities rich people like."

"A resort, then."

"Exactly. Good for our little town. Don't you think?"

"Sure," I say as she ushers me into the changing room.

"Try these on, sweetie, and I'll be out here if you want some advice or a different size."

I strip off the wedding dress and dump it in the corner of the room. It's filthy now after a full day of traveling. Wedding dresses weren't designed for wear and tear, I guess. Durability certainly wasn't one of the attributes I was looking for when I tried on dresses. I'd left shopping to the very last moment—or so the bridal store told me. They said that normally brides come in as soon as they have a date fixed. They also told me most brides bring their moms. My mom had no interest in coming. Anyway, it was easier to go alone. And quicker. I picked the second dress I tried on and, luckily for me, it didn't need many alterations.

I pull on a sweater over a white, long-sleeved t-shirt and look in the mirror. The pants are navy blue and weirdly lightweight, and the sweater has pockets on the side. It's practical and warm, and best of all, it's not a wedding dress. I'll take it.

I hear more voices in the store and mentally high-five myself for getting here early enough to avoid prying eyes.

"I'm sick of it, Marge. He completely takes me for granted. And there's never any notice," a woman's voice says, her irritation obvious.

As I come out of the changing room, I see a redheaded woman perched on a stool by the cash register. "I might take myself up to the Colorado Club. Get a new job. I've got a ton of waitressing experience. They might even make me a manager."

"You want a jacket?" Marge asks me.

I really need to give Byron back his jacket. His truck was gone already by the time I woke up, so I didn't have a chance to return his clothes this morning. I hope he had another jacket to wear. "Yes, please," I call, though Marge is already halfway across the store, searching out the perfect coat.

I smile at the woman with a high ponytail, perched on the stool by the counter. She mouths a *hi* back.

"Did you say the Colorado Club is hiring waitresses?" I ask. It's not like I expected to stay in this town when the bus dropped me off last night. But unless I decide to head home, I don't have anywhere else to go. If there's a job here, that might be reason enough to stay.

"They're hiring more than just waitresses," the woman says. "They want housekeeping staff, restaurant staff, admins. There are a lot of openings from what I can tell. Are you job hunting?"

"I might be," I say. "I just got into town and I'm not quite sure what I'm doing, to be honest."

"Honey, I was *born* in this town and I'm not quite sure what I'm doing." Her smile is all warmth and understanding. I'm unexpectedly touched, and a lump forms at the back of my throat.

Marge appears with a couple of coat options. "I would recommend the long length. It's still winter here and it will be for a while." I nod and decide to go with the one she's suggesting, which is padded and looks like a giant duvet with arms.

"I don't know where you're staying, but the Colorado Club is offering staff accommodation for out-of-towners," the stranger chimes in. She shrugs and smooths down her black pants. "If you're interested."

"Thanks," I say. "I'm Rosey, by the way."

"Donna." She nods at Marge. "We're sisters-in-law."

I take the pants in two colors. The sweater too. I collect three t-shirts and a five-pack of socks. I'm able to pick up some panties and a bra, as well as a hat, gloves, and a new pair of boots. My sneakers are still wet from the puddle of water outside the cabin I stepped in this morning.

Marge rings everything up and puts it all in two large bags. "We're open until six, so just come on by if there's anything else we can help you with," she says, sliding the bags toward me.

"Let us know how it goes if you go up to the Colorado Club," Donna says. "I work at the vet's and the diner, so I'll see you around."

We say our goodbyes and I head out, patting Marv on the head as I exit.

I look like I'm about to hit the trails. But it's better than looking like you just jilted your fiancé at the altar and hopped a flight out of town without a plan.

I turn right to head up Main Street and find out what else this cute little town has to offer. I could do with a coffee and a chance to think. I've never seen a place so pretty. The mountains stretch up behind the town like dramatic scenery in a play. But it makes the place feel cozy. Protected.

As I'm staring up at the clear blue sky stretching into infinity behind the mountains, a young kid offers me a flyer and I take it. Across the street, there's a café with a gigantic black tea cup in the window. I head toward it while I glance at the flyer in my hand. It's a notice about job opportunities at the Colorado Club.

I'm pretty sure this is what they call fate.

SIX

Byron

I can't get Rosey out of my head. I don't even know her last name and I'm playing through all our interactions from last night—not that there's much to replay. Just the way she looked in my jacket. The way her hand felt when I gave her the key to the cabin next door. That goddamn smile.

The Colorado Club needs to recruit thirty members of staff by the end of the week or we won't be able to complete training before the grand opening. I'm sitting opposite the glass windows that look out onto the Colorado Rockies, but I barely see the looming mountains. All I can think about is the woman in the ripped wedding dress, who rolled into town without a bed for the night.

When I left this morning, all the lights were off in her cabin. She was either still asleep or she'd already left. Maybe she went back to wherever she came from, and decided to give her fiancé another chance.

Or maybe not.

"We've had a couple more applications today but I'm

hoping that's going to increase," Hart says. "We've got four people in town handing out flyers, and as of thirty minutes ago, the shuttle bus between the Club and the town will run every thirty minutes."

"People need to know that the place is easy to get to if their car breaks down or they don't have access to transportation," Janet, the head of my HR department, says. "And it's good for our sustainability charter too." I brought Janet in from New York, and it's clear that's where she'd rather be. She doesn't get the culture here in Star Falls. It's understandable. If last night at Grizzly's taught me anything, it's that I'd forgotten how much this town is a law unto itself. I've sunk a lot of money into the Colorado Club, but that doesn't make me the king around here.

"Thanks for the update. Janet, you and I need five minutes," I say, effectively dismissing Hart.

We're in one of the lounges, but because the Club isn't open yet, we're the only ones here. I could have these meetings in my office, but it's good to be visible to what staff we've managed to secure. Besides, it's good for me to see what's going on around here—things I might miss if I were stuck in my office.

"Are you sitting in on interviews?" I ask Janet, once Hart has left.

"Absolutely. For the more junior positions, I'm not leading the interviews, but I'm there."

"I think you need to take a step back," I say. Janet is a seasoned New Yorker. I can be blunt with her.

"Okay," she says. I hear the edge of a question in her tone.

"I went into town last night. There's clearly a local issue —wariness around the changes the Club will bring. I think we need to make things less formal."

"More *folksy*?" she says, raising a cynical eyebrow.

God, I miss New York sometimes. Not as much as I thought I would, but enough.

"People need to be interviewed by their direct managers. We have the first tier of management in place—that couldn't have happened without you. But a lot of the recruitment decisions we're making now are around more junior staff. They have a different perspective. Maybe it's folksy they need. Or maybe they don't trust New Yorkers."

Janet pulls her shoulders back. "You're right. And I guess you can take me out of NYC, but you can't take NYC out of me."

"Right," I say. "We both know this isn't a permanent position for you."

"For you either, right? You'll be back in New York as soon as this place is up and running?"

"Exactly," I say. I have no intention of leaving New York permanently. But for the next six months, I need my focus to be here. There's too much at stake for me to be on the other side of the country. I miss my friends and the anonymity of the city. I miss the energy, the constant hum of traffic and people. I'm not leaving for good. But in the meantime, the mountains aren't such a bad backdrop. Mountains that have been here seventy-five million years and will tower over this valley for millions more. No matter how long I stay in New York, I know this view will be back here, waiting for me.

"How long until the VP of HR arrives?"

"Thursday," she says. "But she's coming from Switzerland. And before that, Paris. She's not going to be *folksy*."

"No, but she's in the hotel business. She'll do okay."

"So I'm fired?" Janet looks hopeful.

I chuckle. "Not yet. But almost. I'll get you back to New York as soon as I can."

"And I'll be going back to Miller Investments, right? Or am I fired from that too? You're looking kinda comfortable here."

"I'm not going to be back in New York for at least six months. I need to be on the ground here. But you're not getting away that easily. I need you back here every month at least. Senior management coaching, one-on-ones..."

"I can cope with once a month. You never know, I might even start to look forward to a little mountain air."

We stand and something catches Janet's attention out the window. "The first shuttle from town just arrived."

I glance down and see Rosey step off the bus. She's no longer wearing a wedding gown. She looks like she could have been born in Star Falls, complete with hiking boots and a beanie.

"Looks like we have our first local candidate of the day. Don't worry. I'll get someone else to interview her so we don't scare her off."

"You think she's here for a job?" I ask. This morning I convinced myself she was just passing through. She definitely said she only needed the cabin for a night or two.

"She doesn't work here at the moment, and the bus isn't for day-trippers," Janet says, making a valiant effort at keeping the *duh* out of her voice.

If she's looking for a job, she'll need a place to stay.

"Is the staff housing finished?"

"Enough for staff starting this week. There's another block due to finish construction this week. Furnishing will be complete at the end of next week."

If she gets a job here, Rosey will need the cabin for a couple of more days. I can't shake off the feeling of conflict in me. I like the idea of Rosey being next door for a few more days. But if she works here? That will make me her boss.

"We're on track," Janet assures me, bringing me back to the moment. Right—staff housing, the grand opening, our readiness to receive guests. That's what I should be focusing on, rather than what it might mean to Rosey if I'm her boss.

Because it doesn't mean anything. She's just gotten out of a serious relationship, if her wedding dress is anything to go by. She's running from god-knows-what. And I'm focused on making the Colorado Club a success. Failure isn't an option. Everything I've worked for since I was seventeen years old is on the line. If this place doesn't work—

I can't even finish the thought. Failure isn't even a possibility I can contemplate. And not just because my fortune's at stake. There's something less tangible I could lose, too.

Despite the fact that I've been gone fifteen years, this town has a long memory. The Colorado Club is the key to Star Falls seeing me as a native son making good, not as the kid whose dad lost all the family money gambling and got killed in a bar fight.

The bus starts to maneuver around some crates that have been stacked in front of the main entrance of the Club. Presumably, now it's dropped Rosey, it's going back down the mountain to trawl for more candidates. I make a mental note to tell the project manager, Kathleen, to start clearing the entrance. We're having a photographer come up in a week or so for publicity shots, and we can't have it looking like a construction site.

As the bus pulls away, it reveals Rosey standing alone out front, looking up at the Club. She doesn't see me, though she's practically staring right through me. Maybe it's the reflection or where I'm standing. I have to stop myself from waving.

"Should someone go down and check what she needs?" I ask Janet.

"If she can't figure her way through the front door, I'm pretty sure I don't want her working here."

"Right." I nod, pulling my gaze away from Rosey. "Will you interview her right away?" I ask. Maybe I should join the interview. It might help Rosey feel at ease.

Jesus, what is my obsession with making her feel better? I need to get a grip and focus.

"She may have to wait a little. I have to get Sally to conduct the interview, as you don't want me doing it. But I'll get her situated." Janet eyes me suspiciously.

"It's just... I want to encourage local applicants," I say, trying to justify my interest. "Maybe I should go down." The moment the words leave my mouth, I wish I could take them back. What am I going to say to her? *Howdy, neighbor, looking for a job?* Rosey knows me as the guy next door. Not the boss. Not the rich guy from New York City. And that's exactly how I want it to stay.

Maybe that's why I feel drawn to her—because in this town where everyone knows who I am and who I was last time I lived here, Rosey only knows me as the nice guy from the bar who gave her a place to stay when she needed it most.

I check my watch. "I have a call, excuse me." I need to get out of here or Janet's going to accuse me of having a crush on the woman who just arrived for an interview. And she wouldn't be wrong.

SEVEN

Rosey

I'm wrestling with the key to my cabin, trying to pull it out of the lock, when my cell rings. I pull it out of the deep pocket in my extra-warm coat, which I might never take off it's so cozy. A chill shudders down my spine. I'm not exactly fielding calls left and right at the moment.

Since Frank and I traded messages when I arrived, I haven't heard a word from anyone in Oregon. Not from him, my mom, or any of my sisters.

It's like I'm on some kind of pre-booked vacation and they'll see me when I'm back. No big deal.

But the caller isn't a number I recognize, so I answer.

"Rosey, it's Sally. It was so good to meet you this afternoon. I'm excited to say we want to offer you a job."

I hold my breath, worried that if I let it out, I might squeal with excitement.

When I arrived at the Colorado Club, I wasn't sure what job I'd be applying for. Without a résumé or a personal recommendation, I didn't have much going for me.

But I explained that I was traveling through town and hadn't thought about staying until I heard about the Club. Sally was more than understanding and said I could be considered for a waitressing position. The pay is a little more than I earned at Frank's garage, and I can live onsite in staff housing at half the price of the rent Mom charged me. It feels like the perfect opportunity just landed in my lap.

Why wouldn't I say yes?

A car pulls up behind me. I spin on the porch and see Byron in his truck. He's been so kind—letting me stay in the cabin, lending me his clothes. I don't know if it's his kindness or something about the evening light, but he's even more attractive than he was when I first laid eyes on him. Which is saying something, because last night I was pretty sure he was the best-looking man in America. With his face framed by the car window, he looks like a movie star or a tortured poet. He pushes his hands through his hair, giving emphasis to his natural pout. I let out a small sigh.

"Rosey? Is everything okay?"

Sally's voice on the line brings me back to myself. "Oh, yes, thanks so much. When do I start?"

I can't help staring as Byron emerges from his car. He's tall and broad and perfectly proportioned. Whenever I looked at Frank, his shoulders seemed too narrow for the rest of his body, but there's nothing about Byron that doesn't fit. His legs are covered in dark denim, and his long fingers close around the keys to his truck in a tight grip I can almost feel around my wrists. My nipples tighten against the fabric of my bra.

Our eyes lock and my stomach tumbles like his gaze has caused some kind of internal earthquake. All of a sudden, any doubts I had about saying yes to the job I just got offered melt away. I want to stay in Star Falls awhile.

"Tomorrow at nine thirty? Staff housing won't be available for another week. Will that be a problem?"

I can't tear my eyes from Byron. He's come home just at the right time. I need to ask him if I can extend my stay.

"I'll figure something out, no problem. See you tomorrow at nine thirty. And thanks, Sally," I say hurriedly and hang up.

I take the four steps down from the porch as Byron heads back to his cabin. "Hey," I say, holding up a brown paper bag from Marty's Market. "I have celebratory hot chocolate. You want to join me?"

He turns, a look of uncertainty on his face. All of a sudden, I'm self-conscious that I've asked a perfect stranger over for hot chocolate. It's not just because he's so handsome and... magnetic or something, but I kind of don't know how to be outside of my old life in Oregon. Am I being too friendly? Too enthusiastic? He's the only person I know in Star Falls. And he's a good guy. He's been good to me and the least I can do is offer him a drink. Right?

Maybe that's not how things work. Mom never allowed anyone in our trailer, so I'm not exactly practiced when it comes to extending invitations. Then again, I'm not in Oregon anymore.

He shrugs. "Sure. What are you celebrating?"

We take the steps up to my cabin.

"I got a job today. At the Colorado Club," I say, excitement flooding back. I don't know if it's the job or Byron saying yes to the hot chocolate. There's a lot to be excited about.

"Huh," he says. "Well, congratulations." He doesn't sound impressed, but that doesn't dull my happiness.

We head inside and it's a little awkward, since I've essentially just invited Byron over to his own house.

"You never did tell me why you rented two cabins," I say. I take a saucepan from the cupboard and fill it with milk before putting it on the stove.

"Thought I might need both."

Is he being deliberately vague? What would he need two cabins for? But I shouldn't pry.

"So, are you like me? Just passing through?" I ask, trying to get the conversation started.

Byron's not a big talker. But based on the fact I survived last night without him taking an axe to my neck, I figure he's at least not a murderer.

"I'm back here for work," he says. "But I also grew up here."

I grab a wooden spoon from the drawer and lean back against the sink while the milk heats. I don't unzip my coat because I can almost see my breath in front of me, it's so cold in here. "That's cool. You can see family when you're not working, then."

He winces at my words. I've obviously said something wrong. I'm not good at this entertaining-friends-at-home thing, but I want to be. I start switching on the heaters to try and warm the place up. "I wish these things were on a timer. I hope it doesn't take long to heat up."

"We should take the hot chocolate on the porch," he says. "Then you'll feel the difference when you go back inside."

"Sounds like you've done that before. I guess you know all the tricks, growing up in a place like this."

He winces again. How many times can I put my foot in my mouth before the milk comes to a boil? I pull my beanie back on and resolve not to be so nosey. I grab mugs, heap a few spoonfuls of cocoa mix into each one.

"I have a favor to ask you, actually," I say. "Well, at least, I think it's you I need to ask."

"I see. The hot chocolate's a bribe, is it?"

I snap my head around, horrified. "No! Of course not," I say.

He smiles at me. "It would take more than a mug of hot chocolate to bribe me."

I narrow my eyes, thinking what I could add to sweeten the deal. "What if I told you I have marshmallows?"

"Damn," he says, fisting his hands. "I thought I could resist. Whatever you need, Rosey. It's yours."

I laugh, partly because the tension between us seems to have dissolved, and partly because he's funny. I wasn't expecting that. I pour out the milk into both waiting mugs. The way he said my name replays in my head, and my smile stays planted on my face as I sprinkle each mug with marsh-mallows. Our fingers touch as he accepts the mug from me, and our eyes meet. If this was a different place and I hadn't just ditched Frank at the altar yesterday, I'd think we were flirting. But that can't be what this is.

My cheeks heat and I turn away to collect my mug so he doesn't see.

He holds the cabin door open for me and we head outside.

A handmade wooden bench-swing hangs from the roof of the porch. Byron takes a seat, propping his crossed legs up on the porch railing, like he's lived in this cabin his entire life. He fits. The colors of his clothes melt into the surrounding trees and mountains. The scruff of his beard looks like it's been there ten years rather than the two days the length suggests. He looks solid and part of this place in a way that makes me feel safe—like I can stay for a while.

"Tell me what you need, Rosey." He's looking over the

tops of the pine trees on the other side of the road, out into the dark. The humor in his tone has gone, replaced with an intensity that feels more natural.

I realize I'm staring at him, at his chiseled jaw and the turtleneck sweater that ends just where his beard begins.

"Oh yes. The cabin. You... I'm not sure if it's your decision, but I'd like to stay for another week if that's possible. The Colorado Club has housing for staff members, but it won't be ready for a week. I don't know if you needed this place or—"

"You can stay," he says. "That's not a problem."

Everything just seems to be slotting into place. This cabin. The job. As soon as I need something, it drops in my lap—like Star Falls is magic or something.

"That's great. Thank you. And you never did tell me how much it costs per night. I can pay you in advance if that works better for you."

"You don't need to pay me. It was going to be empty anyway."

"What? I have to pay you. I'm going to be here a week."

"Seriously," he says, still facing forward, almost like he doesn't want to look at me. "It's not a big deal. I just thought I might need the place. But in the end, I didn't. You did."

"I have to pay you. This conversation isn't over."

He huffs out a laugh. "If you say so." He takes a sip of his hot chocolate and makes a humming noise that reverberates over my skin and echoes between my thighs. If I didn't know better, I'd say it almost sounds like a growl. A sexy, powerful growl, rather than a growl where I think a limb might be in danger of being gnawed off.

"You approve?" I ask.

"The marshmallows make all the difference," he says.

"Otherwise, I might have charged you rent." His tone is serious, but his humor is back. Maybe this is him—a mixture of stoicism and humor. He lays his head back like he hasn't a care in the world. It's the first time I've seen him relax. In the bar last night and even when he pulled up tonight, it seemed like he had the weight of the world on his shoulders. With a little hot chocolate and a porch swing, Atlas has set down the heavens and earth.

We sit in comfortable silence for a few minutes. Byron speaks first. "My dad died when I was a kid. My mom remarried, moved away and sorta reinvented herself. So coming back to Star Falls is... tricky. There's no family to visit."

While I've been trying to start inane chitchat, Byron has gone bone-deep straight off the bat. It's intense but not awkward. "I'm so sorry," I reply. "I just assumed you'd be visiting family. That was insensitive."

He glances across at me and shakes his head slightly. "It's different than I thought it would be." A couple of beats pass and I can tell he's thinking. "I hadn't been in town at all before last night at Grizzly's. I've been keeping myself to myself."

If he had stayed away last night, we wouldn't have met. Marv and I might have occupied the same stretch of Main Street for the night. "Too busy?" I ask.

"Maybe," he says, pulling in a breath it feels like he's needed all day.

"Or maybe you've been avoiding people?"

He turns to look at me. "Says the woman who rode into town in a wedding dress."

I can't help but laugh. "Yeah. I'm definitely avoiding a lot of people right now. Just not in this particular town."

"Did something happen?" he asks. The question's open-ended on purpose, I suspect, but I know he's asking about the reason I called off the wedding.

He went deep, so I'm going to dive right in.

"It took standing in the white dress with minutes to go until the ceremony for the reality of the situation to sink in. I thought I could marry a man I didn't love to make my family happy." I don't know why I'm telling him this. He wasn't prying. But he's sharing his secrets, so I don't mind so much telling him mine.

He doesn't say anything but I don't feel any judgement from him.

"He's a good, decent man, and I know I've hurt him," I say. "But he deserves someone who loves him back."

"We all deserve that," Byron says on a whisper.

"I should have realized sooner." I don't know if I'm talking to Byron or myself. Both of us, maybe. "I caused a lot of hurt feelings and wasted money. Hopefully, one day, he'll see it's for the best."

"No regrets?" he asks.

"None." I sound resolute, because I am. Calling off the wedding was the right thing to do. I'm just not sure whether running away was.

"So what now?" he asks. "You start fresh in Star Falls?"

"Maybe," I say. "I don't have a plan figured out right now."

"But you have a job," he reminds me.

"Yes. I have some breathing room to strategize."

"Ahh," he says sagely. "So you're pre-plan."

I grin. "Pre-plan. Yeah, I like that." I take a sip of hot chocolate. "What about you? Are you mid-plan?"

He nods slowly. "Yes, definitely mid-plan."

"That's vague," I reply, wanting more detail.

"I'm also pre-sharing my plan." A smile curls at the

corners of his mouth. It makes him look younger, more carefree.

When I laugh, there's a howl in the distance in response.

"You've got the wolves' attention," he says. Our gazes meet, and there's heat in his eyes I wasn't expecting. "As well as mine."

My stomach flips and I look away. There's no doubt now Byron's flirting with me, and the flutters in my stomach say I don't mind a bit. Why would I? The last two years with Frank have been... disheartening. There was no flirting. No flutters. No love between us.

"Is having your attention a good thing?" I ask.

He pushes out a breath. "God only knows. You just jilted a man at the altar and I... I have stuff going on." A grin slowly unfurls on his face. "But you make a great hot chocolate. That's for damn sure."

EIGHT

Rosey

The uniforms at the Colorado Club have less than nothing in common with the gray polyester coveralls I had to wear at Frank's garage. I used to itch just looking at them. Nothing I'm wearing right now could withstand a flamethrower the way a Eugene Auto Sales uniform could. My plain black pantsuit—black trousers, a fitted white shirt, and a black vest—might not be fireproof, but it feels anything but plain. I feel like I should be a patron of a fancy restaurant, not a server at one.

"You look great," the girl with the sleek black bob says from where she's changing beside me.

"Thanks. You too. The suits are nice, right?"

There are three of us starting today. I'm glad I'm not the only one.

Bob Girl lowers her voice. "I heard Hugo Boss designed them."

I couldn't tell you exactly who Hugo Boss is, but he sure does make nice clothes.

"They feel..." The fabric is soft against my skin and fits like it's been tailored specifically for me. The outfit is unadorned but makes me feel sexy. Pretty. Prettier than I felt on my wedding day. But I also feel so comfortable, because it's such a good fit. This uniform makes me feel like I'm meant to be here. Like *I* fit.

"Sophisticated," she says. "I guess billionaires want their waitresses to look expensive."

"Billionaires?" I ask.

"Yeah, you know—the guests who will be staying here."

I nod like I understand what she's getting at. It's a hotel. It's not like everyone's going to be a billionaire.

"I'm only here to find a husband," the woman on the other side of the locker room says. "I heard they take centimillionaires too. I'd be okay with that."

She and the other girl laugh. I feel like I'm missing something.

"What's a centimillionaire?" I ask. That seems the most obvious question of the five I have in my head right now.

"You know, someone with over a hundred million in the bank," Bob Girl says. "I'm Akira, by the way. This is Eden." She nods at the husband-shopper.

"I'm Rosey."

"Where are you from?" Eden asks. "Because I know it's not Star Falls."

I smile, not quite sure how she's so certain. "Oregon."

"Oh, so you just came for the job too?" Akira asks. "As soon as I saw 'exclusive private members resort,' I packed my bags."

"Private members resort? I thought this was a hotel?" I ask.

"You can't come here unless you're a member," Akira

says. "You have to apply, be accepted, pay a membership fee. It's a whole thing."

Wow, that sounds... weird. "So... not a hotel," I say, hoping for a confirmation.

"It is," Akira says. "And it has lodges and chalets too. Some are owned and some are rented. But you can only get into this place if you're a member."

Eden's eyes grow wide. "And guess what? Annual membership is a hundred and fifty thousand a year. You gotta be rich to afford that. I just hope some of them are single."

A hundred and fifty grand a year? Just to be able to come here? That's insane. "So it's like an all-inclusive?" I say. One of the girls back at the garage went to an all-inclusive in Jamaica for her honeymoon. Everything was free once you got there. She said she and her husband had the time of their lives.

"The exact opposite," Akira says, who seems to know everything I don't about the Colorado Club. "You pay the membership, then you have to pay for everything else on top. So drinks, food, your room—everything."

"I don't get it," I say. "Why would you do that? Why wouldn't you go to Aspen and not spend a hundred and fifty grand a year to come here?"

Akira just laughs. "Because the people who come here only want to mix with other people who are as rich as them. They want the slopes to themselves. They want caviar on every menu. They want waitresses dressed by Hugo Boss. Millionaires go to Aspen. Billionaires come to the Colorado Club."

"You should really get a job in the marketing department," Eden says. "You make it sound like heaven for VIPs."

"That's what it is. A roped-off section of heaven."

"And we're lucky enough to work here," I say on a laugh.

"Until we land rich husbands and become guests ourselves," Eden says on a wink.

"I heard the real big fish is the owner of the place. He's a multibillionaire apparently," Akira says.

"And about a hundred years old, no doubt," I say.

"Even better!" Eden says, and dissolves into laughter. "The only problem is, he might never be here. Someone that rich probably doesn't get involved in like, running the place."

"Apparently this guy is here," Akira says. "One of the reception agents thinks he's gay. Or hopes he is. Apparently he's in the gym a lot. He's got quite the bod, by all accounts."

"Does he wear a ring?" Eden asks. "How old is he? I need details. Is he definitely gay? Is there flexibility?"

"Flexibility?" I ask, unsure what she's talking about.

"Like is he bisexual?" Eden asks. "I could make that work."

"We need to go," I say, not wanting to tumble down that particular rabbit hole. "We're meeting Hazel in the lobby. Maybe we'll get to see the owner on our tour."

"If I see him, I might propose on the spot," Eden says.

"Sounds like an excellent way to lose your job," I reply.

Eden mutters something and we make our way out of the locker room. We head to the main lobby, where we've been told we're going to start our tour.

"I'm Hazel," a tall Black woman says. "I'm heading up your induction today. Any problems with your uniform, fill out the form you received over email."

Akira puts up her hand. "If we're not open yet and there are no guests around, why are we wearing uniforms?"

Hazel mostly covers up her irritation. I'm not sure if she's been asked the question a hundred times and is sick of it, or she just doesn't like questions. Either way, Akira doesn't seem to notice.

"If you're in member areas, you must always be in a uniform. No excuses. Yes, you're training, but it's best to start as we mean to go on. The uniform helps create a mindset of professionalism and service." She doesn't invite any further questions. "We're going to start with a tour and I'll give you some information about the resort and our expectations in terms of our approach to members and service." She pauses and winces slightly. "There will be pop quizzes along the way. I wanted to tell you up front so you don't get a shock."

"You're going to test us?" Eden asks.

"Yes. The service we provide to members needs to be consistently first class across the entire resort, so there's an expectation for all staff to share a baseline of operational knowledge. The tests help us ensure consistency and understanding. They also help us understand how well senior management are communicating."

I'm not sure what she said, but I'm starting to feel real pressure and we're only three minutes in.

Hazel takes a step closer to us. "Look, we're not trying to catch you out. That's not the aim. We just want you to know the resort well and be able to communicate with members properly. If they want to know what time the slopes open, we want you to be able to say, *The lifts are manned twenty-four hours a day and lighting is available on the green, blue, and red runs on request.*"

"Oh, so it's not like... questions about the menu?" Akira asks.

"It will be that too, but the members here will have huge expectations of you, so you'll need to know about the entire resort."

Because they're rich, I think. The richer they are, the more power they have. The more they expect. I always thought Frank was rich, but although his house was in a great neighborhood and he didn't look at prices in the grocery store, he wasn't the kind of rich that could spend a hundred and fifty grand a year just to get a chance to book this place.

"There's no need to feel intimidated," Hazel says. "We'll role-play a lot of scenarios, and there are work-arounds to everything." Her smile is warm and encouraging, but I can't *help* feeling intimidated. Checking in cars for service at Frank's dealership was a job I'd done for two years. I could do it with my eyes closed. It was just a few clicks on a mouse, filling out a name and address, and asking the customer a couple of questions I read from the screen. This sounds much more complicated.

"Let's start here," Hazel says, her attention pulled toward the enormous flower arrangement on the round, polished table in the center of the lobby. "A member might ask you what flowers are in the arrangement."

Jesus, were we all going to be trained in floristry now too?

"We don't expect you to be able to keep up with the different arrangements here or elsewhere throughout the resort, but there's a full list in reception at all times. So all you would say is, 'We use a local florist. I can get you full details.' Then you would tell your supervisor of the request and either you or your supervisor would retrieve the details and bring them to the member. Reception will have the information on a beautifully presented card with a scannable QR code, which allows the member to order an arrangement with the same or different flowers for their accommodation. Does that make sense?"

I swallow as I realize the expectations these guests are going to have of us. Of me.

"What's the average length of stay for a guest?" Akira asks. "Will we get a chance to get to know them?"

Hazel smiles. "We refer to people staying here as *members*. Or *members and their guests*. So if you're staying in the resort, you're either a member or the guest of a member. We want people to feel they belong here. This is their home away from home. Indeed, some of the members will own lodges here."

We must look a little shell-shocked, because Hazel smiles. Again. Maybe a little too wide this time. "It will take some getting used to, but we recruited you because we know you're capable of providing the level of service we aim to provide."

"It's a lot," Eden says. "But no pain, no gain. We'll probably need to know about the owner of the place too, won't we?"

"We're not going to overload you on your first day. Today we'll be focusing on the tour so you can understand the layout of the resort."

"Sounds good," I say, before Eden can reveal her real motivation for taking this job.

"First on our tour are our four main restaurants. You'll get a sense of the difference in vibe. All three of you will be working primarily in Autumn, but it's important you know all the restaurants so you can advise our members accordingly. You'll be required to cover in other restaurants from time to time, depending on bookings and staffing levels."

We follow Hazel along the corridor, down some steps into the first restaurant of our trip—Blossom. Its booths are pink velvet and the color scheme somehow contrasts beautifully with the gray blue of the sky beyond the floor-to-ceiling windows. As we walk through the restaurant, I notice how the staff are dressed exactly like us. I guess we'll all fade into the background when the members are here.

It feels like a very different world to one I've ever visited before. If I'd married Frank, I wouldn't know places like the Colorado Club existed. I wouldn't understand that waiters and waitresses for the seriously wealthy don't dress the same as normal waitstaff. It feels like I've woken up on a different planet. It's certainly a world away from Oregon. I'm surrounded by people I've known for less than an hour, in a town I've been in just over two days. All I can think is how I was about to get married and cement my future when I knew so little of the world.

Eden's looking around, probably trying to spot the wealthy, gay owner of the Colorado Club.

"Here we are at Blossom. It's our fine-dining restaurant. Some members will want to eat here all the time, but we think most will come here once or twice a week."

The tables are very spread out and the space seems small. Then again, I don't have much to compare it to. I've only ever been out to dinner with Frank and he just wanted the best steak. Fine dining wasn't really his scene. Hazel keeps talking about the chefs and the menu, and I mentally rush to commit it all to memory. I wish I had my cell, so I could take notes, but it's strictly forbidden to have a personal phone while you're on shift.

"Did you see that guy in the suit?" Eden whispers as we

trail Hazel toward the kitchen. I was focused on Hazel, worrying about how I'll remember to pronounce *fois gras* correctly.

Eden turns her head and I follow her gaze. Three men head in the opposite direction, so all I see is their backs. Living next door to Byron has done a real number on me. I swear, I'm imagining him everywhere. It's just, the middle guy is about the same height and has the same broad shoulders.

"The guy in the middle?" I ask. As well as broad shoulders, he also has a nice ass. I haven't noticed Byron's ass, but I make a mental note to check it out next time I see him. Maybe that will be tonight. I don't know why he's filling up my head when I have so much else to think about. I keep thinking about how open he was, talking about his family. Like we're already close confidants or something. Mom always told us we should keep ourselves to ourselves—*keep it in the family*, she'd say. So while I've never before had the kind of bare-your-soul conversation Byron and I shared, with him, it felt entirely natural.

She shakes her head. "The one on the left. You think that's the owner?"

I shrug. I want to tell Eden that marrying a man because he's rich might not make her happy, but I know there's no point. Maybe it will be enough for her. It wouldn't have been for me. I don't know what *will* be enough for me, now that I've cut my tether to the life I thought I had to have in Oregon. But Star Falls might be the place where I start to figure it out.

NINE

Byron

I shouldn't be here. I'm playing with fire, dancing with danger—whatever the metaphor. I should stand up, take my hot chocolate inside and return some calls or watch the game. I should do literally anything but stand here on my front porch, waiting for Rosey Williams.

But here I am.

After I saw her earlier today at the Club, I asked my assistant to remind me when I'd signed off on the waitstaff uniforms. I hadn't expected a plain black pantsuit to be so provocative. Maybe it was just *who* was wearing it that made the uniform seem so suggestive. Rosey looked sexy as fuck, her hair swept up, giving easy access to her neck. Then there was the way the vest clung to her torso, emphasizing her curves and small waist. I'd never even noticed the uniforms until today. Until I saw Rosey in hers.

I don't know why I ended up telling her about my family background yesterday. For some reason, I wanted to share with her. Not that I've revealed the whole story. Like the fact that I'm the owner of the Colorado Club.

Will she be pissed I didn't tell her? Not that she'd have any right to be—I mean, we hardly know each other. Except it feels like we do. Or we... should. Maybe I'm hoping she'll feel like I *should* have told her. Like I owe her something because—because what? We shared a mug of hot chocolate and a conversation?

I'm being ridiculous.

I've never been one to question and second-guess myself like this. Not in business. Not with women. Why has Rosey managed to get under my skin?

The bus pulls up on the main road, to let me off at the end of the drive and I watch the door open with embarrassing eagerness. Rosey appears in the doorway, calls a thank-you back to the driver and steps down to the road. She's smiling to herself and that makes me grin. Two days ago she walked out on her fiancé and she's already smiling into the cold Colorado air. Is that the Star Falls Effect?

"Hey," she calls as she sees me, my boots resting on the balustrade of the porch. "More hot chocolate?"

"You've made me an addict," I say. "You want some? Milk's still warm in the pan."

Her grin lifts on one side and she nods.

I stand and throw her a blanket. I don't have a swing on my porch, just a bench. "Get under there. It's cold tonight."

When I return with her drink, the green plaid blanket is pulled up to her chin.

"I should have taken my coat off on the bus," she says. "So I'd feel the benefit."

"You want to go inside?" I ask her.

She reaches up for her drink. "No, this will warm me up." She glances at the mug. "No marshmallows?"

"I'm not asking for any favors tonight," I say, as I take a seat next to her. If she only knew I'd had my assistant arrange for the hot chocolate and milk to be added to my grocery order today. Gary got overexcited at the mild change in routine, and started suggesting other things, including marshmallows. He gets me the same order of groceries every week. When I told him I just wanted the hot chocolate and milk, it was like I'd just taken away his favorite toy. Poor guy is assistant to the most boring man in the world, apparently.

"We'll get you there." She shifts the blanket around so it covers both our legs, and I let her even though the air seems to have warmed several degrees since she got off the bus. "I've got a week before I move. You're going to be able to make the perfect mug before I leave."

My stomach tugs at the thought that she won't be my neighbor for much longer. I chastise myself. It's good she's moving. No more dancing with danger. No more taking stupid risks because the woman in the cabin next to mine is hot. I'm in Star Falls to work, not to fuck the staff. I've got to stay focused.

So why am I still sitting here?

"How was your first day?" I ask.

"A little overwhelming." She sighs, and I have the urge to fix whatever's troubling her—to extract every detail of what she's struggling with so I can make it better. "It all seems so complicated. I've never worked in a hotel—no, not a hotel, a *resort*." She laughs. "You know we can't call the guests *guests*, because it might make them feel like they're not at home? They're *members*." She squeals. "And apparently it costs *members* a hundred and fifty thousand dollars a year to... I don't really understand what that gets them, actually. The ability to pay more to stay there? It's wild. All that money." She shakes her head like she really doesn't get it. "Can you imagine?"

She turns her head in my direction when I don't answer.

"I think having a lot of money comes with its own challenges," I say, not wanting to outright lie. If I tell her the truth, it will change things between us. I'm her boss, after all. "Just like having no money."

"I guess. I mean, I suppose the super-wealthy have different worries. But I'd happily trade champagne problems for food insecurity any day." She says it like she has experience, which fills me with a deep urge to make things better.

She turns back to face the woods again, and we sit in silence for a few beats.

"I don't think money necessarily makes you happy," she says. "You know what I mean? I think you can be happy with money and sad with money."

"Right," I say, because I don't really want to say anything. I just want to listen to what she has to say.

"Frank—my ex-fiancé—he had money. Not Colorado Club money, but he was very comfortable. To me, and probably to most people in our town, he was rich."

"But he wasn't happy?"

"No," she says. "I think he was. I just don't think *I* would have been happy with him."

"And you were marrying him for the money?" I hope she can't hear the edge in my voice.

"No," she says, her voice bright, like she's not offended by my question. "Not for me, anyway. I think it was the safety for my family. Frank is kind and generous, and my mom loves him. I have three sisters who... let's just say I'm the oldest and the most sensible. Frank's given one of them a job. He represented a secure, dependable future."

"But you didn't marry him."

She pulls in a deep breath. "It wasn't enough. I didn't love him." She takes a sip of her drink. "And honestly, I think it was important for him to take care of me—in every sense. I was going to live in the home he bought years before we met. I worked at his garage. I slotted into his life. That worked for him. It gave him a sense of control."

"I think that sounds like it could be... constraining for you."

She gasps, and I feel her body shift beside me. "*Constrained*. That's exactly how I felt in Oregon. It was like I was living in a box and could feel every edge. Every corner. I knew every inch of that box, and if I married Frank, it was all I'd ever know." She takes a sip of her drink. "I sound ridiculous."

"I don't think you sound ridiculous at all." I can't say it to her, but I think the way she's describing her life is kind of poetic. And more than a little sad.

"My mom would definitely think I was being ridiculous. I guess that's why I'm in Star Falls and not back in Oregon."

"Because of your mom, not your fiancé?"

She pauses as if she's really considering my question—like what I've asked her is important and she wants to give it due consideration. The way we're talking, it's like we've known each other years rather than days. "Frank was a meal ticket for her. She knew she'd never have to worry about rent or bills as long as Frank was in the family." She glances down at her mug, like she doesn't like what she just admitted.

"She expected him to look after all of you."

"I think that was his expectation, too."

"And he was prepared to do that because he really loved you?"

Her eyes stay fixed on her mug. "I feel terrible. I just left. I should have looked him in the eye and told him what I was feeling. Instead, I sent him a text as I boarded my flight. I just knew my mom would force me to go through with it if I stuck around. Once I decided I couldn't marry him, there was no way back. If I had married him, I would have resented him and my mother for the rest of my life."

"Couldn't you just tell your mother you didn't want to marry Frank?"

She fiddles with the edge of her mug. "You'd think so, right? Problem is, my mom has a way of making me feel guilty unless she gets her way." She stares into her mug. "She would have told me I was being selfish and reckless, that I would never find a man as good to me as Frank was." She's chewing on the inside of her cheek like she thinks her mom might have been right. I have the urge to scoot closer, to tell her she did the right thing. But who the fuck am I to this woman?

"Sounds like she's more concerned with *her* happiness than yours," I say.

"It's weird, the farther I am from her, the more differently I see her. I always thought she was just doing whatever she needed to do to make sure our family made it. But now I think she was making *me* do whatever *she* wanted to make sure our family made it."

I set my mug on the railing. "Sometimes parents don't realize the pressure they're putting on their children," I say. "Or they don't think about it." For years after his death, I wondered how my dad slept at night, knowing he'd taken out loan after loan on the family farm to pay off his gambling debts. Eventually, I realized he wasn't thinking about us at all. He was only ever thinking about himself.

"Do you think I've been selfish?" she asks.

"No." My voice comes out with a gravelly edge. "It sounds like you escaped a future you didn't want. That's not selfish. It's self-preservation."

"That's exactly how it feels." She scans my face like she's committing it to memory. "You say that like you know how that feels, too."

I let out a breath. "Yeah, I know a thing or two about escaping a future I didn't want."

"And you didn't want Star Falls?"

"I didn't then," I say. "Right now, there's no place I'd rather be." Our eyes lock, and I want to reach across and press my lips against hers. Earlier today—even earlier this evening—it was clear kissing Rosey was the last thing I'm supposed to do, the last thing I'm supposed to want. But in this moment, all the clarity has gone and my mind is full of fog and *her*. I can't think of one single reason why I shouldn't be kissing the woman in front of me.

"Are you cold?" she asks, as I take her mug from her and place it next to mine.

I shake my head and cup her face. "Are you?"

She bites down on her lip. "This is probably a bad idea, but I want to kiss you right now."

"You're right, it probably is a bad idea." I let my hands drop from her face, but she places her palms over them and puts them back.

"But I want you to do it anyway."

We stare at each other for a few more moments. I try to remember why being here, staring into Rosey's blue eyes, is a bad idea, but my mind is blank. All I can see is her.

I lean forward. She smells of a pine forest after rain.

Her fingers smooth up my chest and my entire body clenches at the feel of her touching me. Part of me knows I should try to resist her, because if I let myself melt into her touch, I'm screwed. I can't ever remember feeling this way before. Maybe because in New York, it's easier. All the rules are laid out in front of you: You go on a date. You kiss, you don't kiss. And then you can disappear back into the city if it doesn't work out. Things in Star Falls aren't so simple.

Rosey lifts her face slightly, as if she's asking for me, and suddenly I remember why I shouldn't be kissing this woman. The Colorado Club. I'm her goddamn boss.

I'm her goddam boss and she doesn't know it.

I should tell her, say something. She needs to know. But I'm trying to lie low, stay focused. Kissing Rosey was never part of the plan.

A screeching yowl from somewhere interrupts us and we break apart, my hands falling from her face, our breath still mixing in the cold night air. Just as I begin to think I imagined the noise, Rosey—panting, chest already heaving —says, "Did you hear that? Was it a wolf?"

We shift to face the wilderness, but I can't let her go completely. My hand slides down her arm and takes her hand in mine. "It didn't sound like a wolf."

The yowl sounds again, just before a long-haired white cat lands from nowhere on the porch railing.

"Fuck!" I say. "Where did that come from?"

Rosey starts to laugh next to me. "Not a wolf, then."

"Way scarier than a wolf."

"Byron, it's the fluffiest cat I've ever seen. There's nothing scary about it." She leans forward, holding out her hand. "Here, kitty, kitty. Who do you belong to? Is she Beth and Mike's cat?"

"I have no idea. But Beth and Mike live on the other side of town, so I doubt it."

"Maybe we should feed it."

"That will just encourage it to stay."

She beams as I say it, like that was her exact plan.

"But it's someone else's cat," I say, as if that's the real reason I don't want to encourage its presence here. "I'm sure they'll miss it if you steal it away."

Rosey narrows her eyes at me. "I'm not sure your intentions are honorable."

I chuckle. "If you knew what I was thinking up until we got interrupted by that cat, you'd *know* they weren't honorable."

I enjoy the blush creeping over her cheeks. I glance back at the cat to find it staring at Rosey, like it knows she's the soft touch here. It's not wrong.

It jumps from the railing onto the floor by Rosey's legs and starts to rub itself against her jeans. I can't blame it. Wasn't I ready to do the exact same thing a minute ago?

"I've always wanted a cat," she says. "But there wasn't enough room for all of us in our trailer, let alone a pet." She scratches the cat under its chin and the cat starts to purr like a Bugatti.

"It's loud," I say.

Rosey laughs. "You jealous?" she asks. "You want me to tickle you under your chin?"

"You can do anything you want to me," I reply.

"I'm going to take a rain check on that," she says, letting go of my hand and standing. "I have an early shift tomorrow. I don't want to piss off my boss on my second day."

"Yeah, that would be a bummer."

She laughs, though I'm not quite sure why.

I don't want her to leave, but we barely know each

other. I can't expect her to stay. The cat follows her into the cabin, and all I can do is sit here and wonder how the fuck I almost kissed a near-perfect stranger, and why I don't know if I'll be able to stop myself next time.

TEN

Rosey

As Eden, Akira, and I file out of the locker room, ready to meet Hazel in the lobby for our second day of training at the Colorado Club, excitement fizzes across my skin. I hope I see Byron again after work. Less than a week ago, I was supposed to be walking down the aisle with another man. I know it doesn't make sense that I'm almost kissing someone else. Not just almost kissing him, but thinking about him, dreaming about him, seeing him in strangers at work.

It's just more evidence that Frank was never meant to be my future. In the two years we were dating, I never felt butterflies in my stomach the way I do when I see Byron. I have a list of questions I want to ask Byron, and I keep thinking up new ones. I never had that urgency to *know* Frank. Maybe whatever I'm feeling toward Byron is nothing more than childlike infatuation. But it feels good. It makes me feel alive. I'm excited for the new day. The fact that I never had that with Frank must mean I made the right decision by not marrying him.

"We're going to start off by touring the swimming, gym, and spa facilities," Hazel says. "We saw the Eat Well Café yesterday, but I want to get into the non-F-and-B aspects of the area. You'll notice we don't just say *sports* or even *indoor sports*. Indoor sports are divided into two areas. First swimming, gym, and spa, which are all on level one, and then the basketball, squash, racquetball, indoor tennis, and pickleball, which are all located on the basement level."

"Is spa a sport?" Akira asks. She does it in such a gently inquisitive way, it's like she was born a diplomat.

"It depends how seriously you take your relaxation," Hazel says. She smiles and adds, "It's not technically a sport, but as it's in the swimming pool and gym area, we include it when we refer to our facilities on level one."

We follow Hazel as she points out the entrances to the spa and gym. She explains that members will be able to order foods from various restaurants to be delivered to them wherever they are. "There's no such thing as no," she says. "If they don't want to eat the food at Eat Well, they can order from wherever they like. As waitresses, you might not be working at Eat Well, but you may well deliver food from the restaurant you are working at to guests in the basketball court, or who are seated at Eat Well."

"And if they want to eat in the swimming pool? Or want an order of fries in the sauna?" Akira asks.

Hazel nods like she's been expecting the question. "You need to use your charm and influence to persuade them to a suitable dining location. If they're on the basketball court and want a burger, that's fine. It's a big space, they're probably with a group of friends who all feel similarly. If they're in the sauna and order soup, you would say something like, 'I can certainly get that delivered to Eat Well to be ready for you as soon as you've finished your sauna.'"

"If they *insist* on soup in the sauna?" Akira asks, an expression of concern on her face.

"Speak to your supervisor. They'll be able to handle it. Bear in mind that while our members will be demanding and expect perfection, they're sophisticated travelers. It's unlikely they'll make a request for soup in the sauna."

Despite what Hazel says, I'm not convinced members won't make outlandish requests. Frank was by no means a billionaire, but he liked what he liked. And he didn't like people saying no to him. I can only imagine a billionaire will be a thousand times worse.

"The key thing," Hazel continues, "is not to get flustered or appear shocked. You have to act like you're taking it all in your stride—like you've heard this request a thousand times before. Even if you feel like a member's being unreasonable, you can never show it. They pay an awful lot of money to have every demand catered to by us. And we have to do our best."

For a second I can't catch my breath, because what she's describing reminds me of my relationship with Frank. He was paying, so he had all the power. Just like the members of the Colorado Club. It was my job to cater to his demands. At least as a waitress, I get a paycheck at the end of the week and not a ring. And I get to leave at the end of the day.

We come to the pool and stare through the glass at the inviting water.

"How come it's full? We don't have members arriving for a couple of weeks, do we?" Akira asks.

"Not my circus, not my monkey," Hazel says. "But I'm sure they need to test out everything thoroughly before we launch."

We file past the doors to the member changing rooms and, through them, enter the gym. It's huge and full of equipment I've never seen before. Not that I've ever been a member of a gym. There's a whirring sound in the background and I wonder if the air-conditioning is faulty, until I notice someone on one of the treadmills in the far corner of the gym. There's something familiar about the hair, and as I turn back to whatever Hazel is saying, realization dawns.

I snap my head back toward the runner.

It looks like Byron.

But it can't be. It doesn't make sense. My mind is so full of him, it's embarrassing.

Whoever it is faces away from us, so I can't see his face. He's shirtless, his muscular back shifting and bunching with each step. He's built like a Greek god. From what I've seen of Byron, there's no doubt he works out—but this guy has the body of an Olympic athlete.

I turn back to Hazel and she catches my eye, following my gaze to the runner in the corner. The runner who absolutely can't be Byron.

"Let's go," Hazel says, her voice hushed. "We don't want to interrupt."

She scurries out of the gym and we follow her.

"Was that a member?" Eden asks as we exit the gym and take the steps down to the basement level.

"We're not open to members yet," Hazel says. "The launch is February fifteenth."

"So staff can use the facilities until then?" Eden asks.

"Certainly not. I'm sure you know that use of any of the facilities by staff is strictly prohibited. That was one of the first things we covered yesterday."

"So who's that guy?" Eden asks. She needs to drop it. Hazel is clearly getting more and more irritated. It really doesn't matter who the guy is, does it? Unless it's Byron, in which case, it matters a lot.

"That's Mr. Miller," Hazel says, her voice hushed like we're supposed to know who Mr. Miller is. Clearing her throat, she resumes the tour. "This is the basketball court." She opens the double doors onto the full-sized court. I'm sure if I were a basketball fan, I'd be impressed. Given I'm not, I try to *seem* impressed. "There's a viewing gallery above that you can access from the hallway adjacent to the gym. You may well get food requests up there, although we expect most to be fulfilled by Eat Well."

I stare up at the viewing gallery, wondering if Mr. Miller is still running. It's impossible to make out any of the equipment from where we're standing.

"Next is the racquetball courts."

Eden rolls her eyes at me. "Will there be maps?" she asks.

"It's a good question," Hazel says, her tone returned to normal. "It's something we're working on."

We're waiting for an elevator by the entrance to the gym after finishing our tour of the facilities on this level, when the glass door of the gym opens. We all look around to see the shirtless guy with gray shorts coming toward us, a towel around his neck, his chiseled torso shimmering with sweat.

When my gaze finally lands on his face, I find myself looking straight at Byron.

Our eyes catch for a second, and then he looks to Hazel, nods, and takes the stairs by the side of the elevators.

"I'm pregnant," Eden says. "Like, all-the-way pregnant."

Hazel glares at her.

"When you said that was Mr. Miller," I say, as the elevator doors open, "should we know who that is?"

Hazel looks at me as if she can't believe I'm asking the question. She guides us all into the elevator, and when the doors close, she says, "Byron Miller. The owner of the Colorado Club, of course."

My knees weaken and I step back, hitting the wall of the elevator car.

Byron? The guy in the cable-knit sweater with a hilarious aversion to cats? The hot chocolate lover in the cabin next door? He can't be the owner of the Colorado Club. But Byron was definitely the guy running on the treadmill, shirtless, sweaty, and completely breathtaking.

"Told you he was hot," Akira says, but I can't answer her. I can't form words, I'm in such shock.

Why didn't he tell me? It makes no sense. Okay, so we barely know each other, but he knew I got a job here. I try to recall whether he told me why he was in Star Falls. Was he deliberately vague? And if he's the owner, why the hell is he staying in the log cabin next to mine? Surely there's a mansion somewhere on this mountain, ready for him to move in?

I have a thousand questions churning in my mind. I want to ditch this tour, run after Byron, and demand answers.

But I have no right to answers.

At least I didn't kiss him. Or he didn't kiss me. Something inside nudges at me. Maybe that's why he hesitated last night.

Hazel has moved on and we're led into a conference room. It's time to role-play some customer service scenarios.

I need some air. I need some time and space to think.

I almost kissed the boss last night. Of all the things on my to-do list at the moment—and it's a long list—almost kissing my boss is definitely not on there. In fact, it's on my list of things *not* to do.

Frank was the boss. I kissed him, and then he kinda

became the boss of my personal life as well as my professional life. Kissing him—or rather, when Mom found out I kissed him—was the beginning of the end of me being in charge of my life. He was my boss at work, and if I had married him, probably my boss at home too. He was the one with money and power and status. I became an adjunct to him, someone who didn't warrant her own opinions about anything that came with a bill. Where we ate, what movies we saw, what hand soap we bought for the kitchen sink—none of it was up to me.

And it all started with a kiss.

I don't want to get involved with another man who has all the power. Frank owned a car dealership. How much worse will the dynamic be if the person I'm kissing owns a resort for billionaires? My lack of control would just be amplified being with a man like Byron.

The excitement I felt this morning about seeing Byron tonight and maybe actually kissing the man I almost kissed last night fades into a pool at my feet. I can't let things between Byron and me go any further. I can't go on repeating my mistakes. I have to create a life for myself, rather than living in the shadow of someone else's.

ELEVEN

Byron

When the bus pulls up outside the cabins, I'm already on the front porch waiting for Rosey. The look of shock and confusion on her face today when I saw her at the elevators has been scorched onto my mind all day.

There's no doubt that she will know by now that I'm the owner of the Colorado Club. Maybe I should have told her before. It's just nice being the guy next door sometimes. Wherever I go in this town, I feel like I'm wearing a sandwich board.

The son of Mack Miller.

The kid from Star Falls who ran off to New York and never came back.

I guess I just wanted to be myself with Rosey.

She walks up to our cabins, avoiding my gaze.

"Hey," I say when she gets near enough to hear me.

She looks up and the disappointment in her eyes is like a sharp punch to the chest. *Did I cause that?*

"Hey," she says back. "I'm super tired. It's been a long

day. I'm gonna head inside." She pulls her mouth into a small smile, but it doesn't reach her eyes. All the promise has seeped away.

"Rosey," I say, standing, but I don't know what I'm going to follow it up with.

She shakes her head. "Everything's fine. I'm just tired is all."

I can't force her to stay and talk to me. I watch as she takes the steps up to her front door and lets herself inside. The lights in her cabin glow from the windows until, one by one, she shuts the drapes, snuffing out the orange glow.

"Fuck!" I kick the post at the end of the porch railing in frustration.

The post seems to respond with a yowl and a hiss. I turn and see the white cat that appeared yesterday has reappeared.

"Don't spit at me," I say. "I haven't done anything wrong."

The cat arches her back and shows me her teeth—like a snake about to bite. Last night with Rosey, the cat had been all cuddles and purring. Now it looks like she just found its prey—me.

"Go find Rosey if you want her."

The cat turns back, almost with a shrug, and marches along the railing, hopping off at the end and heading to Rosey's cabin like it understood just what I was telling it to do. It jumps up, leaning on its hind legs, scratching at her front door. In a few minutes, Rosey appears. She doesn't look over to me, she just bends down to greet the cat and lets her inside.

Lucky fucking cat.

Maybe I need to try the same tactic.

I go back inside and heat up some milk on the stove. If

Rosey won't come to me, maybe I need to go to her. With a peace offering. Not that I did anything wrong. Okay, so maybe I failed to tell her I owned the place where she worked. But she can't be mad with me forever about that. Can she?

When the hot chocolate is ready, I head over to her place with two mugs and knock on her door. I consider purring to get her to open the door, and then remember who the fuck I am.

She answers wearing pajamas. Pajamas with cats all over them wearing different kinds of hats.

"I made you some hot chocolate."

I wait the couple of beats of silence it takes for her to respond.

"Thanks, Byron." She takes the cup from my hand, our fingers brushing as I let go of the mug. I feel her warmth course through me. I don't know if it's the frigid air or the woman in front of me, but just being near her shifts every atom in my body.

I set my cup down on her porch railing. "Are you mad I didn't tell you about the Colorado Club?"

Her gaze flashes to mine. "Oh, you mean the part where you're my boss?" She doesn't deliver the words with any spite or venom. It's the resigned hopelessness in her tone that breaks me, and I feel awful.

"If it's any comfort, I don't even know who your boss is."

"Byron," she says, chastising, and her words echo in my chest.

I hold up my hands. "You're right, I'm your ultimate boss and I didn't tell you that. I wanted to be your neighbor. Not your boss. And I wanted to kiss you, and then I didn't because I..." God, I just rewound fifteen years and became an awkward teenager talking to girls for the first time. What the fuck is the matter with me?

I don't know why I said it. Why mention the kiss? Except I've thought about what kissing her would be like every second since I last saw her. We should both forget about it. Move on. But it's like there's a special kind of gravity in her, pulling me toward her. I'm helpless against it. I just can't step away.

She closes her eyes in a long blink, and I want to pull her close and make everything better. "I need to sleep," she says. "It's been a really long day."

She doesn't feel the pull like I do. She can't if she can shut the door.

I nod, accepting her decision. I might not want her to go, but I can't deny that it's for the best.

The last thing I need is to have a relationship with a member of the Colorado Club team. The gossip around Star Falls is bad enough, but no doubt it would spread like wildfire around the Club. It wouldn't work. And if it's not going to work, then why not cut things short now, when it's easier to walk away?

I push my hands through my hair. Why am I even thinking about *having a relationship*? I haven't even kissed this woman and I'm fast-forwarding. At the pace I'm going in my head, I might propose tomorrow night.

I'm a fucking idiot and I need to get a grip.

I take the steps down from her porch and head back to my cabin. It doesn't feel good, but walking away is the right thing. It was just a kiss and it will all be forgotten in a few days. I need to keep my focus on my business—the stakes are too high to get distracted.

As I'm climbing the steps to my porch, the door to her cabin opens.

I freeze as she comes out.

"Frank was my boss," she says. "And he had all the money and power, and I know we just shared a couple of conversations and an almost-kiss. It's not like we're getting married or even... having sex." Her voice skyrockets on the last word. "I just can't get into that. I can't have someone be the boss of me like that again. I need to stand on my own two feet and not be so dependent on someone else for... everything."

My insides curl up, hating that she felt so out of control and dependent on someone else. It's exactly how I felt when my dad died and I discovered we didn't own the farm anymore. That the loans were all being called in and we faced eviction. And even then we were left with the grief over a man who should have been a better father and husband. I ran *away* from Star Falls. She ran *to* Star Falls. But we both ran looking for the same thing—control over our own destiny.

She doesn't talk about Frank badly. There's nothing to suggest he abused his power. But it doesn't mean it didn't impact their relationship. I've never thought about the effect my money and power have on relationships. Partly because I've never been serious about anyone. I'm so thankful she told me—that she didn't just walk away leaving me with a thousand questions.

"I get it," I say. "I'm sorry I wasn't more open with you."

"We've known each other five minutes. It's completely understandable why you might not want strangers to know."

I've told her more than most, and I want to tell her more. What is it about this woman?

"Thank you for understanding. But I'm still sorry that it hurt you."

We stand, looking at each other from our respective porches.

And then the cat jumps onto the porch railings in front of her, ruining the moment. Again.

Fucking cat.

"Looks like you got the pet you always wanted," I say.

She laughs, stroking the cat along its back. "It's like she's adopted me. I have a day off on Saturday. If she's still around, I'll take her into town and see if anyone's missing a cat."

"There's a vet practice on Main Street. You can see if she's microchipped."

"Good idea," she says.

"I'm full of them," I say.

"I'm going to go to bed now before…" She pulls in a breath. "Before… before things get complicated."

She turns and leaves, and I have to use all my willpower not to ask her to stay.

TWELVE

Rosey

I take my morning coffee to the porch, breathing in the crisp Colorado air. I need to pick up some more clothes today, and I also need to take the cat into the vet. I'd walk if it was just me, but given my new feline friend, I've ordered a cab.

I glance over at Byron's cabin. I haven't seen him since our conversation on the steps. His truck is gone by the time I wake up in the morning, and I'm in bed every night when I hear him pull up. It doesn't mean I've done anything but think about him every moment since. More than once I've managed to convince myself that the connection we seem to share is worth pursuing. Then I remember he's my boss, the owner of the Colorado Club—and I remember why I need to keep away from him. It's a frustrating cycle of hope and disappointment.

I need to shake it off. Reboot. Move forward.

I need to get on with my day off. I have a cat to take care of. Part of me is hoping the vet will have details about an owner missing this kitty. Next week, I'll be moving into staff housing, where pets are strictly prohibited. Another part of me hopes I get to keep her for a few more days.

"Come on. You need to get into your pet carrier so I can take you to the vet," I say, like she can really understand me. "Please, Fluffball." I've been trying out different names. She certainly looks like a fluffball. But I'm not sure the name suits her. She's more Athena than Titania.

She looks at me and then sits down exactly where she is and begins to lick her front paw. It's like she's telling me to fuck all the way off. I can't blame her. I'm asking her to step into a plastic prison. She has no idea whether she'll ever get out. Why would she willingly do that? I'll figure it out once I've had my coffee.

A couple of sips into my drink, Fluffball/Snowy/Athena stops licking, looks at me, and saunters off in the direction of the cat carrier. I'm half expecting her to strike a match and burn the thing to the ground, but instead, she sniffs around the entrance and then heads inside, curling up into a ball as if it's her favorite place in the world.

If only every part of my life was that easy.

As if the universe wants to make sure I understand that is absolutely not an option, my phone vibrates with a text. A sense of dread shivers down my spine—a response that's starting to feel remarkably familiar whenever an alert arrives.

I'm going to take my wins while I can still get them, so I set down my coffee and lean forward to close the door on the cat carrier. "I'm going to take you into town to see if we can find your owner, Athena." Maybe that name will stick. She certainly has the attitude of a Greek goddess of war. When I take her to the vet, she'll probably be registered as Fluffy Bumpkins. And if she is, that's probably why she ran away from home in the first place.

The cab pulls up, so I abandon my coffee and head into town.

In a couple minutes, we're pulling up in front of the vet. I recognize the woman behind the reception desk. She was the person who came into Snail Trail when I was there on my first morning in Star Falls—the woman with red hair who was being taken advantage of. Donna, I think. I explain that I've made an appointment to see if the cat is microchipped.

"No problem," she says. "I can help you with that." She narrows her eyes at me. "You're not from around here, are you? But I've seen you before."

"From Snail Trail."

Her face breaks into a grin. "The girl in the wedding dress. How could I forget? And you got that coat," she says, nodding at my black puffer coat, also known as my most favorite purchase ever. "I'm Donna."

"I remember," I say. Then, pointing to myself, "Rosey."

"And now you have a cat," she says. "Looks like you're settling in nicely."

"It's not mine. She just turned up outside the cabin I'm staying in."

"Maybe." Her eyes twinkle, but I'm not quite sure what she means. "Let's see." She turns back to her computer. "We keep a register of missing pets." She clicks away at the screen. "Nope. Not on here," she says. "We'll check her for a chip, but honestly, owners that have chipped their animals usually register them as missing as well. And I don't recognize her. We usually get to know our patients pretty well here."

She opens her desk drawer and pulls out what looks like a remote control. "She seems pretty sedate." She glances at me, and I wince.

She laughs and pulls open the door. "Hey, kitty cat. Can I scan you, please?" She doesn't make a move to try and pull Athena out of the carrier. It's the right decision. She might lose a hand or at least a finger.

"So you're staying at Mike and Beth's cabins?" she asks. "I thought they were fully booked, just like the rest of town."

"Yeah, I managed to get in. How did you know that's where I was staying?"

"Oh, you know, small town and all."

The girl who arrived in town in a wedding dress. I'm never going to escape that particular label. Part of me wonders whether I should move on. I didn't arrive in town expecting Star Falls to be my new home. I just wanted a bed for the night, but the fact that I've been able to get a job and a place to live is more than I have back in Oregon. It doesn't make much sense to leave right now.

"I'll be moving up the mountain next week," I say.

"Oh, you got a job in the Colorado Club?"

"Yeah, I'm a waitress there. Or I'm going to be. I'm still training."

"I hear the training is brutal. There are tests and everything, right?"

"They're very thorough. They want you to be able to deal with any request from a member. You have to know the Club inside out."

"It's beautiful up there, huh? I know it's not finished, but like, it's super nice."

Super nice is the most lukewarm description of all time. The Club is more like a palace in the mountains. "I haven't seen any of the cabins or chalets yet, but the communal areas are... amazing. I've never seen anything like it. Carpets so deep you could twist your ankle in them, light fixtures twice my height. Fresh flowers on every surface. It's beautiful."

Donna searches my face like she's willing me to say more. She lowers her voice to a whisper, even though there's no one in the waiting room. "Every time I have a bad day here, I think about applying. I hear there are a lot of people from out of town there, though. I don't know how I'd feel surrounded by people I don't know."

"I guess you'd get to know them."

"You're right," she says enthusiastically. She switches on the contraption she has in her hand, just as Athena decides to exit her carrier.

Donna has the feline touch, because Athena sidles up to her like she's catnip. Donna strokes and fusses over the cat while she runs the tracker over her body several times. "You're so beautiful," she says. "But no one's looking for you. I think you found yourself a new momma." She smiles at me. "I can put her details down on our register so if someone does come looking, we can call you. It could be that her owners have gone off on a vacation and she's feeling a bit lonely. It's just odd, because I don't recognize her."

"I can't keep her," I say. "I'm moving into staff housing at the Club next week. They don't allow pets."

"We could take her, but if we couldn't find a home for her, we'd have to..." She drags a finger across her neck, like Athena is destined for beheading.

I take a physical step back. "Come on, Athena. Back in your carrier."

"Maybe put up some found posters around town?" she suggests. "And stop by at the diner and let them know. The post office, too. And the market. All around town, really. Ask around. If someone's lost a cat, people will be talking about it."

Athena steps back into the carrier and takes a seat. I shut the door before any heads can roll.

Donna takes my cellphone and taps away at the computer—presumably, Athena is now on the lost and found register.

"See you again," she says. "Maybe up at the Colorado Club." She smiles wide, and then holds her finger over her mouth, like it's a secret.

———

AFTER I EXIT the vet's office, I look up and down Main Street, trying to orient myself. Last time I was here, I was only focused on getting out of my wedding dress. I didn't bother figuring out the lay of the land. When I see a sign for pancakes, my stomach starts to rumble. It's fate, just like everything else since the bus dropped me off.

The Galaxy Diner is as cute as can be. The floors are black-and-white checkered tile and the chairs are cherry red. There are booths by the window and tables in the center of the restaurant. It's not busy, but a handful of patrons are scattered through the space, enjoying waffles and coffee and whatever that delicious smell is...

"Take a seat," a woman with a pencil in her hair calls over the counter. "I'll be over in a second."

I slide the cat carrier into a booth and follow it. "Be a good cat," I whisper. "I don't want to get thrown out before I get coffee and pancakes."

Athena gets the memo because I don't even get a meow in response.

I glance up at the ceiling and see lots of different-colored spheres hanging from the ceiling. I guess that's what gives the diner its name.

Rachel, if the name embroidered on her shirt is accurate, comes over, takes the pencil from her hair and asks for my order. I scan the menu and realize I've never ordered my own food at a restaurant, let alone dined on my own. Frank always ordered for me if we went out, and the two times we went out to eat as a family, Mom ordered for all of us.

"Are the waffles good?" I ask.

"They're great," Rachel replies.

"Maybe the pancakes..." I'm not sure. I could just do eggs. "What's the chef's specialty?"

Rachel narrows her eyes like she's not quite sure what I'm asking her. "The pancakes are good," she says. "And the waffles. It's all good."

I chew on the inside of my cheek. As I'm deciding, the bell over the door chimes. When I glance up, I lock eyes with Byron.

My breath catches, and I pull off my scarf, suddenly too hot. He was the last person I was expecting to see here. His hands are shoved in his dark blue jeans, his navy sweater fitted close to his torso. He looks even more handsome in the natural light of the diner's huge windows. Shouldn't he be at the Colorado Club, doing things owners of billionaire retreats do?

"I'll take the pancakes," I say, and hand her back the menu, unable to tear my eyes from Byron.

It occurs to me that he might be looking for me. Before I can second-guess myself, I smile at the thought. "Hey," I mouth.

He nods at me and heads to the counter, sliding onto a stool.

I glance back at Rachel, who's looking between me and Byron. "Syrup and butter on the side, please. And a cappuccino." Athena is going to have to carry me home.

"You want bacon?" Rachel asks. "Hash browns?"

"Just the one diabetic coma this morning, thanks." The truth is, I'm all maxed out on decision-making. Choosing pancakes was hard enough.

She shrugs. "You betcha."

She turns, swiping Byron over the head with her pad of paper as she passes him.

"Rachel," he mutters in response.

"Heard you were back in town." She rounds the counter.

"You heard right."

"It's been a while."

He sighs and ignores her comment. "Can I get a coffee and some scrambled eggs?"

He seems grumpy this morning. Maybe I should leave him alone, but I feel like I should ask if he wants to come sit with me and Athena. He's my neighbor and my boss; I don't like the idea that he's in a bad mood and doesn't have anyone to talk with about what's bothering him.

Once again, I shove down the voice of doubt inside. I slide out of the booth and head over to Byron.

"Hey," I say.

He flips his cell so the screen faces the counter, and turns to me. "Hey."

"Athena and I have a lovely spot by the window if you want to join us?"

He narrows his eyes. "Athena?"

"The cat."

"Oh yeah. For a moment there, I thought you were sharing your waffles with a Greek goddess." His expression is blank, like he's not trying to be funny. Is it weird that I find him hilarious?

I grin. "Uh-huh."

He shrugs. "It's a good name for that cat."

"*Right?*"

"Look, you don't have to invite me to join you because I'm your boss and you're worried you pissed me off. I'm not going to have you fired."

"The thought never occurred to me until just now, so... thanks? But for one, you need all the staff you can get. And two... I don't believe that's who you are."

Something passes between us. Maybe it's an understanding that we're not whoever's hurt us in the past. Maybe it's the clarity that we'll never be anything more than friends.

"I'm sorry," he blurts. His words pass through me like an unexpected static shock. Apologies were never readily handed around in our family. My mother wore the fact that she never apologized like a badge of honor. "I should have been more open about who I was—you know, that I own the Club." He's adorably awkward and suddenly seems ten years younger than the man who walked in here.

I sigh because I'm not sure he's done anything wrong. We had a couple of conversations and an almost-kiss. From the outside looking in, Byron never owed me anything. But maybe he feels our connection as strongly as I do, because I appreciate the apology. It feels warranted, despite the short time we've known each other.

"It must have been a shock. Given what you've been through with Frank—"

"Thank you," I say, interrupting him. There's no point in rehashing anything. There's a line in the sand that's been drawn and now we can both see it—there's no reason to make this bigger than it is. "I accept your apology."

His blue-green eyes draw me in, and I can't help but smile at him. Just being near Byron relaxes me, makes me more confident. I'm going to need to keep a close eye on that line in the sand.

I lift my chin toward my booth and Byron slips off his stool. We take a seat opposite each other.

"I haven't seen you in a few days," I say, trying to sound breezy, like maybe I saw him, maybe I didn't. Like I haven't been thinking about him every minute since.

"Busy," he says. "There's a lot going on. Like you say, we need more staff. We're trying to finish off the staff housing and implement health and safety protocols. Avalanche and storm procedures. That kind of thing."

"It's a lot of responsibility," I say. Byron always seems so cool, calm, and collected, but there's a lot resting on his shoulders. "How come you're not living up there? The cabin is cozy and everything, but I'm betting the chalets are a little more luxurious."

He shrugs. "I like the cabin. My chalet isn't ready yet. Anyway, sometimes it's nice to get away from the... pressure. Being the boss isn't always fun."

My stomach dips. The boss thing is an issue for both of us, it seems.

"I'll move up there eventually. Staff housing and the last few chalets are the priority at the moment."

"You're going to live in a chalet like a member?" I ask.

"Sort of." Before I can ask what *that* means, he says, "Did you find out who lost the cat?"

Rachel comes back with our orders, which are basically enough to feed the town for the rest of the weekend. I think I could get full just by inhaling the scent of the stack of pancakes. Each of them is as thick as my palm and the same golden color as the jug of syrup Rachel slides onto the table.

"Eggs," I say, nodding at Byron's plate. He furrows his brow like he's wondering whether there's more to that observation, or if I just like to state the obvious. "They look good."

"They are. Will makes the best eggs. Or at least he did fifteen years ago when I last had them."

"You never came back? Not even to visit?"

"You were talking about the cat," he says, ignoring my question.

"Yes, let's change the subject again," I say with a grin. If he doesn't want to talk about himself, that's fine, but I'm not going to let him think I didn't notice. "She didn't have a chip and no one's called looking for her. Donna said they don't keep lost cats, not unless..." I run a finger across my neck.

Byron bursts out laughing. "Fred's decapitating cats now?" he asks.

"Who the hell is Fred?"

"The vet."

"Oh, I didn't meet him. Just the receptionist. I'm pretty sure she didn't mean literal decapitation. At least I hope not. But the end result would be the same. Athena would be no more."

"Wow. Brutal."

"Right? So I need to find the owner before I move into the staff housing on Tuesday. Donna said I should make some posters and put them around town. Then tell people in the stores that I've found her."

"Sounds like a good idea. If you get me a poster, I can have my assistant make copies."

"You'd do that?"

He shrugs like it's no big deal, but I'm sure Byron has bigger things to worry about than a missing cat.

"Thank you. I guess I'm going to spend the rest of the day going up and down Main Street, telling people I've found a cat. I need a megaphone or something."

Byron laughs again, and I get a warm, gooey feeling inside at the thought that I've helped him relax. "It's a way to meet people, I suppose."

I shake my head. "Now I'm going to be the crazy girl who arrived in a wedding dress and tried to get rid of a cat."

He sighs, but he's still smiling. "Yeah, there's no escaping the town grapevine."

"I suppose it's nice in some ways."

"It is?" he says, eyebrows raised.

"You know, people looking out for each other, in and out of each other's kitchens, asking after each other's kids and health conditions. It's a community. I probably don't need a megaphone. I probably need to tell three people, and the entire town will know about dear old Athena in no time."

"It's a community with a long memory," he says, a look of resentment in his expression I just don't understand.

"I bet you remember just as well."

He shoots me a puzzled expression.

"Tell me about Rachel." I nod to where she's stacking sugar packets into bowls. Her pencil is back in its rightful place behind her ear. "She seems to know you. But I bet you know her too. Tell me something you remember about her."

Byron sighs. "I don't know. Her hair is a different shade of red every week. She never drinks apart from New Year's, when she really lets loose. One year, the town placed bets on which track on the jukebox would have her dancing on the bar at Grizzly's."

I glance over at our waitress, who seems far from the bar-dancing type. "Was it 'Sweet Caroline'?"

Byron chuckles, his eyes crinkling at the corners. "No. 'Brown-Eyed Girl.'"

"You know, that doesn't make me like her less. In fact, it has the opposite effect."

Byron takes a forkful of egg but doesn't respond.

"They must be really proud of you, though. The local boy who's bringing jobs and tourists to the area."

He takes a sip of his coffee. "They don't see it like that."

I wait for him to say more. I don't want to change the subject this time.

"People in towns like Star Falls don't like change."

"You think they don't like the idea of the Club? But you got the planning approvals and everything?"

"Sure. I'm bringing jobs and tourism to a part of the state that's kind of been abandoned. And the building is respectful to the local area. The building materials have been chosen because they're locally sourced and sustainable, and won't detract from the beauty of the place." He sounds resentful, like he's trying to convince me he's done something good. But I'm not the right audience for his argument.

"You're getting pushback?"

He sighs. "We're not seeing applications for jobs from townspeople like we thought we would."

"I suppose people already have jobs."

"Yes, but a lot of people have to travel to get work. When I was a kid, my best friend's dad had to travel two hours to get to work. I've lost count of the number of times I heard people talking about Aspen and Vail, how the opportunities there sucked the youth out of the town. The Colorado Club is a couple of miles out of town. I'm giving people what they've been saying they wanted for decades. Now it's here, and everyone's acting like I'm taking something away from them."

"Taking what away?" I ask.

"I don't know. Jim says he wants to be able to walk his dog on Club land."

"There aren't other places in the area to walk his dog?"

He sighs, moving the food around his plate without taking a bite. "I've bought up some of the federal land. Members of the Colorado Club have high expectations around privacy and security. They're not going to want to come across Jim walking his dog while they're on a hike."

"So people in Star Falls think you've stolen their land, while you're trying to buoy the local economy and give people jobs."

He goes to speak, but I interrupt him.

"You have two issues as far as I see it. First, you need to come to some kind of compromise around land access. There's no way around it. You're going to have to give Star Falls residents limited access. Maybe it's the first weekend of the month or every Wednesday or something, but you're going to have to let people inside the boundary lines."

Byron shoots me a look like I don't understand anything, but I get it. He needs to get his head around the facts.

"It's not going to be as much of a problem as you think. If Star Falls is anything like where I grew up, it's not reality people don't like—it's the idea that someone might be trying to take away their freedom. If you do open up the land in a limited way, people aren't going to take advantage. I bet you Jim didn't walk his dog up there *before* you bought the mountain. He just likes the idea that he can if he wants to."

"But I can't let Jim on the mountain. I just can't. The members are paying—"

"Hear me out, Byron." I probably shouldn't be interrupting my boss like this, but I don't have much more to lose in this life than everything I've walked away from. And anyway, he's short-staffed—he's not going to fire me. "This is all about presentation. When I'd had customers on the phone asking me when their cars would be finished, I'd tell them it was taking a little longer than anticipated because we were detailing the car before it was returned to them. People stopped complaining.

"I think if you tell your billionaires and centimillion-aires—thank you, by the way, for extending my vocabulary with that particular phrase—that you're respecting local culture by giving Star Falls residents limited access to the land on these days, in these areas, you're highlighting the Colorado Club as a company with a conscience. By exten-sion, that means your members have a conscience, too. Your generosity and consideration is *their* generosity and consid-eration. Your billionaires get something for nothing—a clear conscience. They don't need to know it's all a ploy to drum up local support, just like my customers at the garage didn't need to know their detailing was included in the service price and only took twenty minutes."

I hold Byron's gaze as he silently stares back at me. I try and read his expression. Am I about to wear a face full of eggs? Is he going to leave?

"You're really smart," he says finally, and I feel a little glow inside me at his approval. "We need to sell it to members like it's part of our offering. It could work if we open up the land on certain days, or certain parts of the land on certain days. During those times, we can just direct members to other areas. Or offer them additional security."

"Exactly," I say. "It's doable."

"I've got to sell it to Jim. He's going to want access whenever he wants."

"The limited access is the price they pay for revitalizing employment opportunities in town. If all the young people are leaving because there aren't any opportunities for them, the Colorado Club gives them something to stay for."

Byron nods. "It really does. Or it could."

"I agree," I say with a smile.

He holds my gaze, his stare intense. It heats me from the inside out, like he's trailing his fingers over my skin, bringing every goose bump to life. "It's a really creative solution, you know?"

I laugh. "I never even went to community college."

"Doesn't mean you're not clever. It just means you didn't go to college."

I glance down at my pancakes, full with his praise and the way he sees me. "Thank you." I take a bite of pancakes. "Now you have to help me find Athena's family."

"I'll make you a deal: If you don't find her owners, I'll take her in when you move next week."

I tip my head back and laugh. "She hates you!"

He smooths his hand over his stubbled chin. "That is true. But maybe we can acclimatize her before then." His eyes twinkle as he looks at me. One minute he's a grumpy, hard-nosed businessman—the next, my thoughtful, hot neighbor who makes plaid look like it costs a million bucks.

THIRTEEN

Byron

The weather forecast has injected the air with panic. Even Kathleen, the project manager, is jittery, and that makes me nervous. People who don't live in Colorado think tornadoes can't hit the mountains. The people of Star Falls know different.

"What's the worst-case scenario?" I ask Kathleen as we stand on the balcony outside Blossom. I can see the entire town of Star Falls from here.

The main building is finished. We have proper storm defenses built into the design of the place, from hurricane glass in all the windows to state-of-the-art generators. Any trees close enough to cause damage to the main building have been removed. It's not the main building I'm worried about. It's the buildings that aren't finished. There's a real possibility that if we can't finish weatherproofing before the storm hits, they'll be destroyed. That includes a block of staff accommodations and ten member chalets.

"Worst-case scenario is total power loss, two blocks of

staff housing totally or partially destroyed, and we lose half the chalets," Kathleen says.

The hits just keep on coming. I feel like I'm playing disaster Whac-A-Mole. Just when a plan to get the people of Star Falls fully behind the Colorado Club starts to materialize, I have to deal with the possibility that I'm going to have to delay opening. Founding members have already paid their fees. For the first six months from opening, potential members are going to come out and experience the Club in all its glory. That can't happen if parts of the site lie in ruin. The resort has the potential to turn into a gigantic money pit.

"I thought it was up to ten member chalets and one block of staff accommodation," I reply.

"That's the most *likely* scenario. You asked for worst case. But I don't think it will come to that. We're beefing up some of the storm defenses in the structures that aren't completed. Our aim is for everything to be standing at the end of it."

"You think some of the chalets with furnished interiors will go?" I ask. We've invested a lot of money into the soft furnishings. It's going to be a huge setback if they get destroyed.

"I really doubt it. Less than a handful of shutters still need to be installed, and some of the outside generators still need to be connected. Most of that's being done today. If everything goes to plan, completed chalets won't sustain major storm damage. The contractors are working around the clock. Some of them will be staying in the second block of staff housing during the storm, to address emergencies should they arise."

"How did you manage to persuade them to do that?"

"You're paying them a lot of money."

Money's always the answer.

"You either pay to anticipate the damage now, or more to fix it later," she adds.

"Right." I refresh the storm-tracking app on my phone. The *Severe Thunderstorms and Possible Tornado* sign is still flashing. "And it might not hit."

"Absolutely. This could be a nasty storm even without the tornado. It's January. We shouldn't be having tornadoes at all, so there's a lot... up in the air, if you excuse the pun."

I hate the unpredictability of the weather here. In New York, it's going to be cold as fuck in winter and meltingly hot in summer. You can depend on it and plan accordingly. It's my inability to plan that's a problem for me. I'm used to having a lot of responsibility. I'm used to there being a lot at stake. But it's usually down to me whether I succeed. My businesses have never put people in harm's way before. There's an entire staff here who are at risk.

"The most important thing is to keep people safe," I say.

"Hazel is dealing with that, as per the procedures. I believe everyone has to shelter in the main building. Which reminds me—are you going to ride out the storm up here with us or down in town?" Kathleen asks.

"I'll be here," I say. I don't want anyone to think I'm not in this with them. There's no telling whether the cabins will come off better or worse than the Club. It's not like I'm trying to dodge danger.

And Rosey will be up here too. There's no point in being down in the cabins by myself.

"Anything I can do to help?"

Kathleen pulls in a breath. "No, but I have a thousand things to do if you don't mind—"

"Get to it," I say, and she heads off.

I feel useless as I stand in front of the huge windows

overlooking Star Falls. Everyone's rushing back and forth, carrying things. I don't quite understand how there's nothing for me to do if everyone's so busy.

I spot Hart and stalk over to him. He's carrying a lamp. "What are you doing?" I ask.

"Emptying the chalets we think are the most vulnerable to storm damage. It's all hands on deck. I've got every member of staff on shift helping."

"Alright," I say. "Then let me help too."

"Okay then," he says, leading me out the main entrance. He glances up at the sky threatening to pour with rain at any moment. "Prepare to get wet."

As we head over to chalet four, a line of staff comes toward us, carrying blankets and mirrors, dining chairs and coffeemakers. It's like we're looting the place. I scan faces, waiting to catch a glimpse of Rosey, but I don't see her.

"Is everyone who was due on shift still working? We haven't sent people back to their families?" I ask, picking up one end of a huge antique oak chest in the primary bedroom of the chalet. Hart picks up the other end.

"Anyone who wanted to leave has gone already," he says. "Most people aren't local. Oh, and one of the waitresses had to find her cat."

My heart leaps out of my chest. Cat? Was that Rosey who left? She can't have thought leaving the protection of the Club to go after Athena was a good idea.

Hart and I get into a rhythm carrying the chest across the site. As nonchalantly as possible, I say, "I take it we have a list of everyone who's staying up here so we can ensure everyone's accounted for?"

"Absolutely," he says. Of course he doesn't offer me a look at the list. Why would he? I'm not known for micromanagement, but I frantically try and think of an excuse to see it. All the while I'm scanning faces, trying to find Rosey.

As we make it inside the main building, Hart calls out to Hazel. "Have we updated the roster since the last bus left?" he asks.

"Yeah, it was just Rosey Williams on the bus. I've taken her off."

My heart sinks.

Fuck. *Rosey.* I have no idea if she knows how to prep for a tornado. I can't imagine there are many tornadoes in Oregon. Does she even know about the shelter by the cabins, or how to use a weather radio?

There's no way she can be on her own in the cabins. I glance at the darkening sky. Hart and I put the chest down and I say, "Actually, there are a couple of things I'm going to need from the cabin. I'm going to head down into town."

It's the easiest decision I've made today. There's no way I'm going to leave Rosey on her own.

I step outside to find rain has started to fall. The staff emptying cabins are being called into the main building. This isn't the main storm, but there's no point in carrying stuff in this weather. The people of the Colorado Club are in good hands. But I need to get to Rosey.

By the time I get to my truck, I'm soaked to the skin. I slide into the driver's seat, wipe the water from my face and head down the mountain. As long as there are no fallen trees, I can get to her before the real storm hits.

I hope.

FOURTEEN

Rosey

All anyone has talked about at work today is the weather. The bus doors open and part of me wants to ask the driver to turn around and drive me back to the Club. But I can't. I have to make sure Athena's safe. She's an independent little thing, but she always comes home last thing at night.

The rain is so heavy, I can barely see the outline of the cabin. And apparently, this isn't the storm everyone's worried about. I like rain. I'm from freaking Oregon—rain runs through my veins. But the look of worry shadowing the locals' faces today has me on edge.

I hope Athena is curled up on the porch. I learned my first day with Athena that I can't keep her in the cabin all day. She clawed my leg and shot out the door when I showed up after my shift the first day I left her at home. She's not a cat who can be shut in. How she ended up in the cat carrier, I have no idea.

The short walk from the road to the cabin leaves me drenched. I don't think I've ever been so wet. Athena normally comes from nowhere to circle my legs before I have my key in the door. Today, there's no sign of her. I scan the porch, but I can't see any huddled-up bundle of white fluff anywhere.

"Athena!" I call. "Kitty cat!" I doubt she can hear me. The rain on the roof of the porch hits like a hammer on granite. I check the time on my phone. I wonder if Snail Trail is still open? I could use some rain boots. I glance up at the sky. No, rain boots aren't going to help. I need a freaking canoe.

All of a sudden, my stomach turns over. What was I doing, coming down here? I should have stayed up at the Club. At least I was with other people there. What happens if the tornado lifts the roof off the cabin? I might get buried under a pile of logs.

If I'd been at home, my mom would be telling me what to do. She probably would have told me to stay at the Club. I'm not used to ordering food at a restaurant and I'm not used to deciding where to ride out a tornado. I look out into the black sky. It's too late now to head back to the Club. The bus turned right around when it left me. Nerves tumble in my stomach. I don't know what I was thinking coming down to look for a stray cat.

Athena's probably safely tucked away somewhere—maybe even the home she escaped from. If she could see me, she'd be licking her paws with disdain, contemplating what a fucking idiot I am.

The shuttle bus is long gone. Maybe I could get a cab? I'd feel terrible bringing someone out here in these conditions, especially since they'd be returning down the mountain alone. I've left everything too late.

I just need to do the best I can. Nothing left for it now but to go inside and try to get warm.

I peel off my coat and hang it on the back of the door. "Athena!" I call again, just in case I locked her inside this morning when I left. She's used to her name and usually saunters toward me when she hears it. Maybe she needs a little incentive. I grab her cat food and put some in her dish. "Athena!"

Nothing.

I head to the bedroom to check in there. Opening the door, I hear the rain hammering against the window. It's fierce. I wish Athena were as eager to get inside.

I dip down to check under the white, metal-framed bed, but it's clear.

The rain is relentless.

Drip, drip, drip.

Wait. That's not rain.

I try and silence my breathing so I can hear better.

Drip, drip, drip.

That sound is definitely coming from inside the cabin.

Just then, the sound of creaking wood splinters through the bedroom. Shit, is that the ceiling? I don't know where I'm safe. And that's when I see the pool of water on my bed. I glance up to a ceiling bulging downward, dripping a steady stream of water.

"Oh no!" I cry out.

I go into the kitchen and grab the biggest pot I can find to put under the leak. It won't keep the ceiling from caving in, or save the mattress that's probably already soaked, but I need to feel like I'm doing *something*. Anything.

I really need to move the bed and save it from any further damage. The room isn't big though, and no amount of shifting left or right will escape the steadily worsening leak. I should call Beth and Mike.

And I need to find Athena.

"Athena," I call out, my voice strained as I push the foot of the bed frame with all my body weight. Once the frame hits the far wall, my suspicions are confirmed—it's not far enough to escape the leak.

Now the drips are hitting the edge of the bed and the creaking sounds louder. There's so much water. I bet it got through to the mattress. Maybe I should just pull the mattress off the bed and put the pot on the bedframe.

I pull at the mattress, but it's about a foot thick and feels like it's full of bricks. How is it this heavy? When I manage to move it down to one end, it gets stuck at the other. Maybe I can pull it from the other side? I clamber over the bed, my pants getting soaked from the pool in the middle of the blankets.

I get to the other side of the bed, but realize I can't get down between the wall and the frame.

Shit, I'm bad at this. I need to pull the bed back to where it was, or at least a couple of feet from the wall so I can get on the other side and push. I climb over the bed again, getting even wetter.

Is it me, or is the leak getting worse? Is the ceiling likely to cave in?

I start to pull the bed, first the head and then the foot.

A pounding at the door makes me screech in surprise.

Maybe someone found Athena and has brought her back? For a second I wonder if it's Frank, swooping in to rescue me. I suppose that's what his role was meant to be in my life—a man rescuing me from a future I didn't want. But he was just offering a different future. Not a better one.

As I make it out of the bedroom, the cabin door opens and Byron appears in the doorway. His hair is slick with rain and he's breathing hard.

"Rosey," he says. I've never been so happy to see anyone

in my life. I want to leap into his arms and bury my head in his chest.

"Byron!" I say. "I've lost Athena and it's raining in the bedroom and I shouldn't have left the Club. I don't know—"

He strides across the living space and holds me by the shoulders. "It's going to be okay."

I sigh with relief that he's here. Thank god.

He releases me and stands tall. "Don't leave my side," he says, heading into my bedroom. I scurry in after him.

He moves quickly, pulling the bedding from the mattress, then pulling the mattress off the bedframe like it's a pool float, rather than the heaviest thing I've ever had to move.

"Do you have a bucket?" he asks.

I hand him the pot I collected from the kitchen. He takes it from me and positions it under the leak.

The creak of wood sounds again and our gazes meet. "Is it the ceiling?" I ask. He grabs my hand and pulls me out of the bedroom.

"Get your coat on and let's take any supplies we might need. Water. Food. I probably have enough, but it doesn't hurt to have more."

I don't have a chance to ask him where we're going because he pulls out his cell and dials a number while he opens the refrigerator and starts tossing stuff onto the counter. I gather it all up and put it into bags.

"Beth, it's Byron. Cabin two has a leak in its roof." He listens. "Yeah, Rosey... No, I don't want either of you to come out in this. We've moved the furniture. Yeah... Agreed. No, that's fine. Keep safe."

He hangs up. "Nothing we can do about it until the storm has passed. Let's pack up your things. You'll have to stay with me."

Panic races through me. "What? No. I'll just stay on the couch."

Byron glances around, sees the bag from Snail Trail and grabs it. "Let's go."

"No, Byron, I'm staying here."

"No, Rosey, you're not. You have a leak in your bedroom now, but the entire ceiling could collapse. Water likes to travel. Without inspecting the roof, there's no way to know where the ingress started. The entire ceiling could be at risk. You're staying with me."

Tears form at the back of my throat. I arrived in town a week ago in a wedding dress with no place to stay and no job, having let down my entire family, but it's not until now that I feel truly vulnerable.

"We used to get leaks in our trailer all the time." My voice quivers as I finish my sentence. "We always had a couple of buckets collecting rainwater."

"This isn't a trailer. If this ceiling comes down, you'll know about it. And we could be facing tornadoes in the next twelve hours. You're not staying here."

"I can't stay with you. Maybe the inn—"

"The inn is still full, Rosey. I'm not asking you to move in with me. I'm telling you, you need to shelter at my place. There's a big difference."

His tone has darkened. I realize I don't have any other choices here.

Silently, I get to work gathering up the few belongings I have here in Star Falls. It's just toiletries and clothes, but it's nothing I can afford to sacrifice.

My Snail Trail bag full, we head out. "But Athena. I don't know where she is," I say.

"She'll turn up. Or maybe she went back to whoever she lived with before she turned up here."

"And maybe she's frozen and vulnerable, hiding somewhere."

"Shit, Rosey." He pulls out his phone and starts to type. "There. I messaged a couple of people to keep an eye out. Bring her food in case she comes back. We gotta go."

I hand him my bag of belongings and grab the cat food. We both brace ourselves for the storm as we head to Byron's cabin.

FIFTEEN

Rosey

Byron's cabin is an exact replica of mine, but it still feels weird being here. With him. He's my boss, but it doesn't *feel* like he has all the power. It feels more like we're at the end of a date—minus the tornado threat. That can't be a good sign. I need to focus on the impending disaster rather than the guy who came down the mountain just in time to... rescue me?

"Help yourself to whatever you need," Byron says, as if an incoming tornado is a regular occurrence. "There's hot chocolate on the counter. Should I make us some?"

"You think we're going to be safe?" I ask, glancing out the window. The rain sounds less like it's falling and more like it's attacking the cabin with pickaxes.

He catches my eye, holds my gaze and says, "You're safe now. It's going to be okay."

My stomach lurches. Does he mean tonight or forever?

But of course, I know the answer.

I break eye contact. "I'll make the drinks," I say. The least I can do is make myself useful. "Thank you so much for helping me," I call out as Byron heads into the bedroom. "And letting me stay here."

He reappears in dry clothes with a towel in his hand. "It's not a big deal. This is the pre-storm. It's going to get worse." He rubs a towel against his wet hair, leaving him looking adorably mussed.

"Of course it's a big deal. I'd be completely on my own if you hadn't shown up."

"I didn't expect the rain this early," he says.

"I didn't think I'd need to worry about tornadoes in Colorado." I pour hot milk into mugs and try not to think about Byron's worn gray joggers, or the way their low-slung position on his hips should carry an R rating.

"Was that part of your criteria when you were deciding where to come to after the wed— You know?"

I smile at him trying to say the right thing, which is impossible when talking about how I ran out of my wedding. My situation is so ridiculous. He's not the one who should feel awkward.

"Honestly, I just got on the first plane out once I got to the airport. I didn't care where I was headed. But Colorado... I don't hate it. Star Falls, I mean. It's not like I've seen anywhere else in the state other than the airport and whatever I caught through the bus window. But it's beautiful here. It must have been nice growing up with the mountains in the background."

"I guess," he says, in a way that makes me think he doesn't feel lucky about any aspect of his childhood. He scrapes his fingers through his hair, his biceps flexing as he does.

"Whereabouts in Star Falls was home for you?" I ask, glancing back at the milk in the pan so I don't start drooling.

"The family farm was at the foot of the mountain."

"Below the Club?" I ask, handing him a mug of hot chocolate. We both take a seat on the couch, the rain echoing determinedly off the roof.

"Yeah," he says. "The outer perimeter of the Club's land on the southeastern side was the boundary of the farm."

My eyes widen and I lean against the counter. "Oh, so the farm doesn't exist anymore?"

"The apple trees are still there. Mainly. We took the diseased ones out."

"Oh, Byron, that's amazing. So the farm's stayed in the family in its own way."

"It's *back* in the family," Byron says. "When my dad died, the farm was taken by his creditors. But I bought it back." His eyes are hardened, the boyish smile I see from time to time disappears completely. This is businessman Byron—steely and determined.

"I bet you did."

"No marshmallows?" he asks, in his least artful subject-change yet.

"Apologies, in the rush to escape the potentially collapsing cabin, I forgot to bring them."

He puts his arm out toward me, and for a moment, I think he's going to cup my face, lean in and kiss me, but when his gaze flits behind me, I realize he's reaching for something on the table behind me.

Was I thinking about kissing this man?

My boss?

The really rich, powerful guy who is exactly the type I'm supposed to be staying away from?

I know all the reasons I shouldn't—each one is categorized and stacked up neatly in my brain. The problem is, the reasons I want to kiss him are mounting up, too. The more I get to know him, the more I want to know.

He holds up a bag of mini marshmallows. "You used to get a lot of leaks where you lived?" he asks, as he shakes the packet of marshmallows into my mug, then his.

I stare into my mug, avoiding staring at him. Even though the rain is trying to break in and the wind has started to howl, I don't know if I could put up any resistance to Byron if he touched me. And I know I need to.

"We lived in a thirty-year-old trailer," I say, gazing into my mug. "We were used to leaks. Bits of the ceiling used to collapse every now and then, but I guess it wasn't solid wood coming down on us like in this cabin." All of a sudden, it feels like we're sitting too close. I don't know if it's the sound of the storm, or the way he seems so comfortable, but it feels like this cabin is half the size of mine next door.

"Who is us? You said you have *three* sisters?"

"Yeah, three sisters. I'm the oldest. What about you? Is Mary older or younger?"

"Younger. She just finished college in California. Four siblings must have been..."

"A lot," I finish for him. "There was a lack of everything except people in our family. Not enough money, or clothes that weren't worn through, or food that was edible, hot water, privacy, respect. You name it."

"You never wanted to escape? I mean, before..." he asks, his eyes searching mine like I'm the most interesting person he's ever met.

"Sure. Ironically, that's why I was getting married." I can hear something outside—a tapping, scratching sound. I put my mug down and cock my ear. "Can you hear that? I think there's someone outside."

Byron stands and heads to the door. He pulls it wide and in jumps Athena, straight onto my lap. I don't know where she's been, but she looks bone dry, like she's been hanging out in the pet spa all day.

"Athena! You're back!" I ruffle under her chin and she closes her eyes, pushing her head against my fingers. "Are you hungry, kitty?" I ask. "Let's get you some yummy food. You can stay here with us and keep dry, okay?"

I set about fixing her some food. She doesn't wait until I've finished dishing it out before she starts eating. Wherever she's been, she's worked up an appetite.

"How worried do we need to be about the tornadoes?" I ask.

Byron pulls in a breath. "I have no idea. I would say usually in January you wouldn't need to be worried at all, but here we are."

"Is there a town storm shelter?"

"Beth and Mike put one in on the other side of the drive," he says. "We'll get an alert if anything comes through. It will give us ten minutes or so to get inside."

My heart begins to thud. This is starting to feel like a situation where I need to panic. But I don't want to give it away. "Should we put some food and supplies in there?" I ask.

"I've got a box ready to go," he says, nodding toward a crate by the door I didn't notice before. "We can just take it with us."

"And by *us*, you're including Athena, right?" I grin and glance over at him, then wish I hadn't as the room shrinks. I swear I can feel his body heat from here.

"I suppose I am."

"It's a bonding experience," I say, trying to lighten the

mood. "You two need to get to know each other if I have to move into staff housing before we find her owner."

"As long as she keeps her claws to herself."

He grins at me, his boyish smile back with a vengeance. I wonder if I'd be safer next door with a collapsed roof after all, rather than here, with Byron.

SIXTEEN

Byron

The rain has stopped, but it's only a temporary reprieve. The next time it starts raining, we know it will be the beginning of the big storm we've been preparing for.

I've been in near-constant contact with Kathleen. I need to do something to distract me from the fact that Rosey is naked at this very moment, taking a shower. I don't want to think about how she looks in nothing but water and bubbles. Or how she'd taste, straight out of a shower.

Kathleen texts that most construction work had to be abandoned due to the heavy rain. We're going to have more damage than I would have liked. We're going to have to prioritize the staff accommodations and the already furnished chalets. If necessary, we'll have to delay marketing visits. It just depends on the extent of the damage when all this is over.

I'm going to have to brace myself for the worst-case scenario. I'm impatient to know where we're going to end up. It's only when I know what we have to fix that I'll know how to get us there.

I groan and collapse on the couch, Athena yelping as I catch her tail on the way down. "Sorry, cat," I say.

"What happens when you move up to the Colorado Club?" Rosey says from the door of the bedroom. "Will you be able to take Athena?"

I glance over at her and wish I hadn't. Her cheeks are pink from the heat of the shower. The tank top she's wearing fits snugly over her breasts, and rides a little high so I can see a couple of inches of the golden skin on her stomach.

"Let's not borrow trouble." I look away, shaking my head, like I'm trying to empty all the dirty thoughts I'm having about Rosey. The weight of her breasts in my hands, the heat of her skin, how wet she'd be if I slid my fingers into her right now. I need to take some of my own advice. I don't know why I can't just let things take their course. There's nothing I can do to change the direction of a storm. I push my hands through my hair.

"You're stressed," she says.

"A little," I admit. Her being here is making it worse, but I don't say that. Having to control myself around her is more difficult than I expected. She's filled up this space with her infectious smile, her chatter, her goddamn cat.

"Will it affect the opening?" she asks.

"Don't know yet." I hope fucking not. There's way too much money at stake. "You should get some sleep," I say. "In case the storm keeps you awake tonight."

"I don't have work tomorrow," she says. "Don't worry about me."

"You can take my bed," I say. "I can stay out here on the couch."

She sighs. "There's no way I'm taking your bed when you've already given me a place to stay and rescued me from a collapsing roof. Athena and I will be good on the couch."

"I need the kitchen. You take the bedroom."

"You need the kitchen? Why?"

"I like to cook when it's like this."

"When it's raining?"

"No, when... when it feels like life's in limbo. Like the coin has been tossed and it's up in the air and I'm just waiting for it to land."

"You *cook* in these situations?"

"I do. Comfort food. Beef ragu is my first port of call."

"Nice!" she says enthusiastically. "Are you good? Am I going to love it?"

Did I say I was cooking for her? Typically, I have the urge to hide away when life gets difficult. I have a tight friend group back in New York. I know they'd do anything for me—listen to my problems, help me find solutions, lend me money, introduce me to all the right people. The problem is, when things get difficult, I always retreat. I pull back from reality, figure it out and then come out guns blazing.

Rosey being here is forcing me to stay engaged with the world.

"Yeah," I say, shooting her a look. "You're going to love it."

"You want a hand?" she asks, pressing a kiss to Athena's head.

"I don't. Turn on the TV. Let's listen to the weather report while I get started."

The kitchen area's small, which is something I'm grateful for when the world seems too big. All the prep surfaces are against the wall, so I'm facing away from Rosey while I dice onions and press garlic. I listen as she talks to the cat and makes the odd comment on the local weather map.

"Oh, that sounds promising, doesn't it?" she asks.

"What does?" I ask. I haven't been listening to anything but the chop of the knife and Rosey's chatter. It's oddly meditative.

"They think wind speeds are coming down."

"They can just as easily climb back up."

"Let me check outside."

"Rosey—"

"I'm just going to stand on the porch to see if the rain has started up again."

She closes the door behind her, but not before a cold swirl of air whooshes inside to curl around my ankles.

She comes back inside. "It's very black, but it's not raining."

"It's not due to restart until around five tomorrow morning."

"Star Falls has been good to me so far," she says. "I have faith this place will come through the storm okay."

I hope she's right.

When all my ingredients are in the pan and the hours-long simmering process has begun, I turn to find Rosey staring at me. Has she been watching me the entire time I've been cooking? Our eyes lock, and a bolt of energy passes between us, like she knows I've been thinking about how she'd taste if I kissed her... everywhere. Like I know she's thinking about how hard my chest would feel if she pressed her palm against it.

Her mouth parts. She runs her tongue across her bottom lip.

I'm mesmerized.

I'm good at compartmentalizing—like how I keep New York and the Colorado Club separate. How I don't think about how I'm missing Monday nights with the guys while I'm in Star Falls. I don't let myself think about how I walked away from everything I knew when I got to New York. I should be able to put Rosey in the box marked "employee" and move on.

But if I'd done that, I'd be up in the Colorado Club now, not down here in the cabins. I wouldn't have been there when her ceiling started to leak. I wouldn't be here now, wondering how I'm going to resist her for a full night.

"You want a drink?" I ask.

She nods, not taking her gaze from mine.

I don't move to make her one. "Anything else you want?" I ask.

She nods again.

I know what she's thinking. I know *exactly* what she's thinking. I want it too. I want to be in front of the fire, naked and under her, over her, inside her. I want to be kissing and sucking and licking and biting. I want to be exploring and wondering and making her moan.

I want *her*.

I push a hand through my hair. "I'll get you a drink." I grab a glass from the cupboard and turn on the faucet. I need some iced water over my head right about now.

When I turn back to the living room, Rosey's right there in front of me. I hand her the drink. Her fingers circle the glass, but I don't release it. I can't move. Don't want to.

I scan her face, looking for signs that she doesn't want this. All I see is her desire. Want. Need.

I pull the glass from her hand and put it on the counter behind me.

She's stayed stock-still.

"Rosey," I say. It's a question. *Do you want this as much as I want this? Can I kiss you? Can I have you?*

"Yes," she releases on a sigh. Then she nods, in case there was any doubt.

I close the distance between us and dig my hand into her hair, holding her in place. My eyes flit from hers to her mouth.

"Tell me no," I say. It would be easier if she did. It would be far simpler if I didn't have any entanglements here in Star Falls. The only label I want here is owner of the Colorado Club. I want any labels I've had in my past—son of Mack Miller, the kid whose father gambled away the farm, the boy whose father died—I want them all to dissolve until it's just me and the Club, one entity, zero tragic backstory. I certainly don't want to be the guy who fucks his employees.

But I can't walk away from this moment unless Rosey tells me to.

She shakes her head. "I'm telling you yes."

I close my eyes in a long blink, accepting my fate.

Her fingers sweep over my jaw when I press my lips against hers. She moans, and I take advantage of the moment, sliding my tongue though her lips. I want to know her. I want to explore every inch of her.

I pull her closer. I don't want any space between us. No gaps. No secrets. Nothing unsaid.

"I want to feel you," she whispers, pulling my shirt from my waistband and sliding her hands up my chest, just like I knew she was desperate to. Her touch makes me shudder, makes me hungry for more. I pull my sweater over my head and her fingers fumble for my hem of my shirt. I take her face in my hands, deepening our kiss with every breath. I wonder if I'm being too rough. I haven't shaved for a couple of days.

I pull back.

"Don't stop," she says.

"Your face is red," I say, reaching out with my thumb. "My beard is—"

"I like it. It feels good." Her voice is a breathy whisper.

Blood races to my cock so fast I'm light-headed.

"I want to kiss you everywhere," I choke out.

She takes a half step back and pulls her shirt over her head. "I want that too."

Her bra is plain white. I can't pull my gaze away from the way her breasts push up over the edge, begging to be set free.

My breathing is frantic and I don't know where to start. My mind is whirring. I want everything to slow down so I can think for a minute. I take a breath, turn back to the stove and shut off the heat.

When I turn back, her eyes are filled with confusion.

She needs to know I want her. I *definitely* want her. I can't remember wanting anything more.

She starts to say something, but I don't give her a chance before scooping her up and striding into the bedroom.

Something switches in me, and I'm filled with the clarity of knowing exactly what I should be doing right now. I lay her back on the mattress and inch down her sweats. Pressing a semicircle of kisses from one hip bone to the other, I revel in her softness, her sweet scent, her fingers in my hair. She writhes underneath me and I have to hold her at the waist to keep her still.

So soft. So sweet. So needy.

I pull her waistband down a little lower and my lips

follow. I'm teasing, but I want to draw this out. I want her to be crazy for me by the time I taste her.

I take off the rest of my clothes and crawl over her. My erection is hard against my stomach. I settle between her thighs, my hardness pressing against her leg. It's all for her, but she can't have it. Not yet.

I dip, pulling her nipple into my mouth, flicking and licking before slowly tightening my teeth and biting.

She arches her back on a scream and digs her fingernails into my shoulder. I swirl my tongue, giving comfort, while I take the other nipple between my fingers and squeeze.

Her knees come up either side of me as she groans.

"Feels good, huh?"

Her eyes open. Her face is flushed and her chest heaves between us. Her eyes flit over my face like she doesn't know what to say.

"Tell me," I say. "I want to hear you say it."

She nods. "It feels good."

"You want more?" I ask. "Tell me." She's used to being controlled—to being powerless. She has all the power now, over me, if only she'd use it. "I want to hear what you want."

She grabs my hand and slides my fingers between us, down, down, down, until I'm touching her pussy.

"I'm so wet," she says. "I don't know how—"

My groan interrupts her. I can't help it. Her juices coat my fingers and I'm dizzy with the need to feel more. To slide into her and have my cock coated in her. To fuck her until we both forget our names.

But first, I want more. More of everything.

I bite down on her other breast and soothe the opposite nipple between my thumb and finger, rolling and pressing.

I kiss the soft fresh of her breasts over and over, then suck the side of one, knowing I'll leave a mark. It will take a week for the bruise to fade, and every time she gets in the shower until then, she'll think of everything we did tonight.

"Byron," she whispers.

I press up on my palms to admire my work. Her fingers skate over the spot I just marked.

"I haven't had a hickey since..."

"Don't tell me," I say. "I don't want to hear about anyone else. Only us. Only now."

She presses her palms on my cheeks. "There's only us. Only now."

Her words make me feel raw. Like she's stolen my invisible shield. She's unhooked my armor, unmasked me. She's seeing through to my soul. The real me, not the guarded, careful strategist. Everything that's left is hers.

We stare at each other like we're newly glued together, waiting to set. We can't move or we'll destroy everything.

"I want you so badly," I confess.

She widens her legs in response, inviting me to take what I want. My heart thumps in my chest, trying to wake me from a lust-induced coma.

I'm desperate to slide into her, but at the same time, I don't want to move. I don't want to undo anything. It's like a spell has been cast over us and I don't want it to break.

Her gaze falls on my mouth and she trails her finger over my lips, sweeping her tongue over her bottom lip. How can just the tip of her finger feel so good?

"Tell me what you want," I say.

"Kiss me," she whispers, her eyes fluttering shut.

I crash my lips to hers and shift my erection between her legs. All I feel is hard and soft, need and desperation. All I want is her.

Twisting my hips, I rock over her slick folds, coating my

cock in her wetness, my heart thudding—a warning that it doesn't know if it can survive this. Survive Rosey.

Pulling away, I grab a condom and fumble with it, my fingers working too slow for the rest of my impatient body.

Rosey whimpers as I roll the condom down my shaft. "Now, Byron. Please."

"That's right, Rosey. I want to hear you. I want to know you, know what you want. I want to give you what you need."

I pull in a breath, trying to steady myself, trying to regain some kind of control of the situation, but it's futile. Something has taken over my body and I have no conscious choice left. I'm being driven by desire, and it's pointless trying to wrestle the wheel away.

I position myself on top of her, my gaze flitting between where the tip of my cock rears toward her entrance and Rosey's desperate expression. It's not just her words that are begging me to fuck her. Her ripe, hard nipples, her hips undulating underneath me, the eyes that tell me she'd do anything to have me right now.

I've never recorded sex with a woman, but for a second, I wish there were cameras all around us. I can't remember sex ever feeling this intense, this necessary, this important. I want it to go on forever, and then I want to replay it every day for the rest of my life.

I slide in slowly. Rosey's eyes widen—half pleasure, half disbelief—and I swear to god, if the tight clench of her wasn't about to kill me, her expression would finish the job. It's too much. I can't take it. I still, squeeze my eyes shut, try to focus on something outside this bedroom.

The rain has started again. The wind howls around the walls of the cabin, like it's trying to get in. This is it. The storm. The big one. We should be listening for tornado warnings so we can get to the shelter, but at the moment, I know that's impossible for both of us. There's no going back now.

I breathe and slide deeper, never taking my eyes from her face. Her mouth falls open and she lets out a silent cry. I hear it in every cell of my body. This isn't sex. This is some kind of transcendent, spiritual experience. My entire body is vibrating. I don't know where I end and she begins.

"Okay?" I whisper.

"Byron." It's more than my name she's saying. She's asking me a question—is this as good for you as it is for me? She's wondering whether she's going to survive this. She's asking for more.

Yes. Yes. Yes.

I drive into her, slowly at first. Sweat already sheets my skin. My heart rate is already at max. I'm already too close to coming. I just want to circle the mountain, make this last, but I'm not sure I have any choice.

Her fingertips dig into the skin on my shoulders and I gasp, pushing up into her. Deeper. Deeper. Deeper. She's tight. *So* tight.

She bucks underneath me. I pin her down, her elbows at her waist, so I can fuck her. Hard. Fast. Deep.

She feels so delicate beneath me. I slam into her, desperate to show her how I own her now. I need her to know that I'm going to fuck her like no one else ever will. She's going to remember this forever. She whimpers underneath me and her sounds power something new inside my chest. I feel like a fucking god with her under me, vulnerable and exposed. I feel like I rule the world right now.

I drive deeper into her, and she tenses before seeming to accept her fate. Like she's let me in. Completely.

She comes hard, her back arching, her pussy milking my cock. It's too much.

I can't hold back any longer. I push in one last time, as deep as I can go, and empty myself into her.

All I can think is how I wish I wasn't wearing a condom. How I need to be closer. How I wish I could fuck my seed into her.

Shit. Where did that thought come from?

I'm usually ready to nominate the person who invented condoms for sainthood. But not tonight. Not with Rosey.

I collapse on top of her and she trails her fingers over my back.

"You're incredible," I mumble.

"You make me feel incredible," she says.

I move off her, get rid of the condom and rearrange us so we're covered in blankets. Rosey snuggles into the crook of my arm.

"The rain has started," she says. "I only just noticed."

"We were focusing on other stuff."

She tenses. "Did we miss the tornado warning?"

I reach across her for my phone. "No notifications."

"Can you put that thing on loud?" she says. "You're sure we'll have enough time to get to the shelter?"

"I'm sure." My thoughts start to wander to the Colorado Club.

"You think you should check in at the Club?"

I pull in a breath. "I might just do a quick call. Do you mind?"

"Of course I don't mind."

Thunder rumbles above us. The rain is coming harder now. And this is just the storm before the real storm. I swipe my phone open and dial Hart.

"Just checking in," I say. "There storm is over the town now. But no tornado warnings so far."

"Everything is fine here," he replies. There's a lot of background noise. Voices calling out among background chatter. "All the staff are here in the main building, hunkered down for the night. I just spoke to the sheriff, and he says that tornado activity has lessened. Thinks the warning might be withdrawn."

"Okay, keep me posted. I'll check in a bit later." I end the call.

"Everything okay?" Rosey asks.

"For now."

"How worried are you?"

I huff out a laugh. My entire fortune is on the line. Everything's at stake. "Not worried enough that I don't want to fuck you again." It's true. My entire future might be destroyed in the next hour, and all I can think about is how ripe Rosey's breasts look. I want to sink my teeth into her.

She slides her legs over mine and my cock springs to life. "It's good to stay distracted in a crisis." She pushes up and straddles me. "I don't know if I can do this," she says. "You turn me to Jell-O."

A grin tugs at my mouth. "Oh, I'm going to enjoy having you try." I tuck my arms behind my head as she arranges herself over me, her folds hugging my dick as it hardens beneath her.

"I think I might do anything you want," she says.

She didn't need to say the words, though they're nice to hear. I can see the truth in her eyes, but it makes me groan just the same.

"I want you," I whisper. "Any which way."

Unexpectedly, she slides down the bed, leans over and takes the tip of me in her mouth. She suckles on the end of my dick, and I think I might have died and gone to heaven until she takes me deep, to the back of her throat—then I know I have.

She pauses, controlling her gag, and I groan, trying everything I can not to push my hips up to see that expression again. Fuck, she's so sexy.

I can't watch for long because I'm overloaded with sensory input. I'm seconds away from coming for a second time, but I'm not ready for this to be over. My mind wanders to how I can make sure this happens again. How can I convince her to take my cock in her mouth every damn day for the rest of my life?

She works her mouth up and down my shaft, her fingers coiled at the bottom of my cock, gripping me tight, showing me she's in charge. So hot. So fucking hot.

She pulls back and releases me with a pop. She pumps her fist up my length a couple of times.

"This is selfish," she says, reaching over me, her sharp nipples grazing my chest. She grabs a condom. "But you're so hard. So big." She groans, tipping her head back. "I'm so wet. I want you inside me right now. Do you mind?" She holds up a condom.

Do I mind that she wants to feel my cock inside her? Do I mind that she wants to feel me where she's soft and warm and wet? Do I mind that she's so fucking desperate for me?

My skin is so hot, we could toast marshmallows on my abs. I've never wanted anything more than to feel her on my cock again.

I go to take the condom from her, but she rips open the packet herself. "I want to."

She rolls on the condom and my mind wanders to the real possibility that I might come, just from the feel of her fingers sliding on the condom. Fucking *condom*.

I push up on my elbows, ready to flip her to her back, but she presses her palm against my chest.

"I want to," she repeats on a smile.

She kneels up, reaching for my sheathed cock, positioning it so I can feel her heat, her wetness.

"Oh god, Byron. What are you doing to me?"

"Fuck," I splutter as she lowers herself onto me.

"I'm so wet," she says. She smooths her hands up her body to her heavy breasts, cupping them, before taking my hands and replacing hers with mine. "How can I ask for what I want so easily with you?" She's not looking for a response.

None of this makes sense. Not for either of us. There are so many reasons why this shouldn't be happening, but I can't think of any of them right now.

I squeeze her breasts and pinch her nipples hard and mercilessly before releasing her as she groans.

She starts to move, her hips rolling forward and back, working my cock in a mesmerizing rhythm that pulls the air from my lungs. I can't move. The rumble of my orgasm twists and circles. I don't dare do a thing to encourage it. I just want to take in the glory of this woman on top of me, fucking me, making me see stars.

She slumps forward, her hands on my chest, bracing her body, but she doesn't stop moving. "I'm so close," she gasps.

I wait a second, two. Does she need something from me? I want her to ask. I like that she knows she can. She knows I like her asking for what she wants. "Tell me what you want," I hiss out from my tensed jaw.

She grabs at my hand. "Touch me," she gasps out. "Please."

My hand slides between us, fingers finding her clit. It's all wetness between us, and I growl at how undone she is with me. How turned on she is. It ratchets up the desire, knowing it's mutual.

"Byron," she cries out. "I'm so, so close."

She moves quicker now, like she's racing to the finish line. I don't know how long I can hold off for. I'm so ready to come, but I want to wait for Rosey. Her fingers dig into my chest and I can't resist any longer. I push my hips up, our bodies slamming together until my vision blurs and my orgasm crashes over me. Rosey starts to shudder above me. I pull her over me and hold her close as her entire body convulses, worried that she might shatter if I let her go.

I don't release her. I keep her pressed to me as our climaxes rocket through us and we start the slow float back down from heaven. Her face is buried in my neck, and I breathe in her scent of wet pine and lemons.

Her heat against my body, her legs tangled with mine. It's all fucking perfect.

"Byron, what is that?" she says finally. "What is this?"

"What is what?"

"That," she says, like I should know what she means. "The sex. I'm not even sure we should call it that. Or at least, I shouldn't. I've never... it's..."

I pull in a juddering breath. "Intense."

"It feels like my entire body is on the brink of breaking into a thousand pieces. You're the only thing holding me together."

I'm used to holding back, dealing with everything—good or bad—inside my own head. But with Rosey, I can't seem to fight the urge to share. "It feels like what's happening between us is the only thing that matters."

"Yes," she sighs. She wiggles in my arms, but I want her to stay put, lying over me like this. It feels so good.

"You keeping me prisoner?"

"Yeah," I say. "I think I might."

She laughs. "I might let you."

I press a kiss to the top of her head, then release her. I get rid of the condom and we settle down into the covers, listening to the rain.

"It's still raining." She says softly while trailing patterns on my chest. "You have a really good body."

I laugh. "It *is* still raining, and back at you." Rosey doesn't just have a good body. She has a body designed for *me*. She's all soft curves and smooth skin, pouting lips and eyes that show me exactly what she's thinking.

"There are a lot of reasons why we shouldn't be doing this." She picks up my phone and hands it to me. "Please check the weather again. I think we're in real danger of missing the tornado warning."

"Rosey, we're in real danger of missing this tornado if it passes right through this fucking cabin."

She laughs and snuggles in closer. I bring up the weather on my phone.

"It's a lot of rain," I say. "Even without the threat of tornadoes, it could be a problem."

"You think it will affect opening?"

I sigh. "I don't know. I hope not."

She sweeps her hand over my chest. "It will be okay."

I close my eyes. I hope she's right. All I know is that with Rosey lying next to me, everything feels like it's going to be okay.

SEVENTEEN

Rosey

It's possible the storm has just given Byron and me a time-out from reality. I'm no longer the runaway bride and he's not my boss. He's just a hot guy and I'm just a girl who's hot for him. Maybe we're both just trying to get through the night.

Part of me thinks that's what this is—just a night suspended in time. Then the other part of me, deep down inside, whispers *this guy is different. This man makes you different.*

I never asked Frank for what I wanted—in bed or out. It didn't occur to me that I could. And he never asked what I wanted. It didn't seem to matter to him. But with Byron... with Byron, it feels completely natural to tell him everything. What I want. What I don't want. Who I am. Maybe it's because no one's depending on my relationship with Byron. With Frank, my entire family was behind me, pushing me forward, willing me to do everything right so

Frank would want me. So Frank would become part of our family and, therefore, responsible for us all.

Here in Star Falls, the only ones who care what I do with Byron are me and Byron. And I've never wanted anyone more.

I scoop up two mugs of hot chocolate and pad back into the bedroom.

"That shirt looks sexy on you," he says. I'm wearing his navy plaid shirt and his socks.

I pause and cock my head to the side. "How sexy?"

His eyes grow hooded, instantly renewing the wetness between my legs. Byron makes sure I'm more than satisfied, but I can't help wanting more of him. Part of me wonders how long we have left before either we have to make a quick exit to the shelter, or worse, the storm passes and life goes back to normal.

I slide the mugs onto the bedside table and undo the buttons on his shirt, letting it fall open a couple of inches.

He shakes his head disbelievingly, then leaps out of bed and wraps his arms around me from behind. With his face burrowed in my neck, he asks, "You ready for more?"

In answer, I twist my hips against his hardening cock. In one swift movement, he shoves me down to the mattress, my feet still on the floor and my ass still pressing against his thick length. "You like to tease, don't you?" His hands press on my back to keep me in place and he lifts up the shirt, then smacks a kiss on my ass. A waft of fresh air follows before he lands his palm on my cheek with a sharp slap.

I squeal at the unexpected contact. It kinda stings, but not in a bad way. Actually, it's kind of hot.

"You have such a perfect ass." He sinks to his knees and positions me so I'm over his face.

Really?

This is new for me. Frank never went down on me and no one has ever done it like this. It feels... I'm so on display this way. But if that's what Byron wants, that's what I want. Not because I want him to like me—although I do. And not because I'm submitting to him because I have no choice. I want what Byron wants because being desired by him is the sexiest I've ever felt. I choose to give him what he wants.

He circles my thighs with his hands and his thumbs nudge at my entrance. My knees weaken at his touch. He can see how wet I am. If I wasn't so turned on right now, I'd be embarrassed. His breath is hot on my skin, and when his tongue lands in my folds, I struggle to keep my weight on my legs. I grab on to the covers on the bed, trying to stay in place.

His tongue darts into me, swirling and pushing, and I press my face into the mattress and cry out. I'm laid out for him and he's devouring me. It feels so good. The vibrations from his moans travel up my spine and my breasts push into the quilts. I've developed one hundred million more nerve endings than normal. My entire body buzzes with feeling. The clamp of his hands around my thighs, the insistent push of his tongue, his stubble everywhere. It's all too much.

He pulls away, and before I have a chance to figure out what's happening, he's over me. He flips me to my back, spreads his shirt wide, then my legs. "You taste fucking delicious. I'm hungry for you."

He sinks to his knees again and buries his head between my thighs. My fingers find his hair as he brushes and strokes me with his tongue, over and over, while I get wetter and wetter. His beard scratches against my thighs and the contrast between the softness of his tongue and the sharpness of his beard is almost unbearably good. I arch my back and begin to float up, up, up. He circles my clit before sliding first one thumb in, then a finger, working them together, making my hips lift off the bed.

My orgasm tears through me like it's been held captive for a decade and has just broken free. My body shakes and I cry out. I chant Byron's name like it's the answer to every question I didn't know to ask.

Finally he's lying next to me. "I'm here, baby," he whispers. "I'm here."

I turn into him, hiding, scared at how distant I feel from who I was before I walked into his cabin tonight. How close I feel to him right now. How I never want tonight to be over.

He scoops me up in his arms and pulls me closer. "I'm here," he says. "I'm here."

I inhale and let myself sink into him. Eventually, I drift off to sleep.

I don't know how long I've been out when a blaring alarm wakes me.

"Quick," Byron says. "We need to get into the shelter. It's the tornado warning."

I bolt upright and scan the room for clothes. Even if Byron's the only other person in the shelter, I still want to be wearing panties. We both dress quickly, pull on our boots and coats, and head out. Byron grabs the crate by the door and leads me outside with his other hand.

"Wait!" I say. "We need Athena."

Like she heard me say her name, she's at my feet. I scoop her up and we head out.

It's almost impossible to notice the rain because the wind is so ferocious. The silhouettes of the trees that line each side of the road are swaying like a crowd with its arms outstretched, raging against the sky. We crouch and head across the porch and behind the cabin. Thankfully Byron's here. I wouldn't have known where to go. I've never faced a tornado before. Never worried about the weather, other than to wonder whether I'm ever going to see the sun again after days of relentless Oregon rain.

The shelter is only ten yards from the cabins, but it's far enough to get covered in mud from the rain-soaked grass. The shelter has been built into the ground. He flips open the doors and nods for me to go inside. The doors are at an angle, but rain sluices inside in sheets. I don't have time to ask all the questions I have: Are we going to be able to breathe in there? How big is it? What happens if a tree falls on the door?

My feet slide on the steps as I find myself inside the dark hole. Byron flicks on a light.

He must see something in my expression, because he moves to cup my face and presses a kiss against my forehead. "It's going to be fine. We're safe here."

"It's cold," I say, glancing down at the two wooden benches set opposite each other, running the length of the shelter. It feels like a prison cell.

"We have plenty of blankets and hats and gloves in here." He starts pulling things out of the crate. "And food." He hands me a thermos. "Homemade tomato soup."

"You make soup?"

He chuckles. "I can't take the credit. Nancy French makes the best tomato soup in the state of Colorado. She dropped some off yesterday."

"And you know that it's the best soup in Colorado because you've tasted everyone else's?"

"I haven't," he replies, "but Nancy's won the county soup-making championship five years in a row."

I grin. "Are you serious?"

"I never joke about soup. And neither does Nancy."

This guy.

He pours me a cup and I take a seat on the bench. He huddles next to me and puts a blanket over our knees like we're on a camping trip and this is no big deal.

"How long will we be in here?" I ask. "And will we be able to get out if a tree or something falls on the door?"

"Sheriff Altaha knows we're down here."

"He does?" I ask. "How? He'll probably think we're both at the Colorado Club."

"I texted our location in. We're going to be fine."

"Can we get a phone signal down here?" I ask.

Byron pulls out his phone. "Nothing at the moment."

"Then how will we know when to come out?"

"We have an NOAA radio." He pulls it out of his crate and sets it on the bench opposite before turning it on.

"You came prepared."

He nods and squeezes my knee.

"I don't know what I would have done if you weren't here."

Despite the small space, I don't have the sense of being hemmed in and constrained that I did in Oregon. Byron's organized everything, but his instructions don't feel controlling. It feels caring. I didn't know the difference until right now. He's looking after me. He's thinking about me. That's the difference.

He slings his arm around me. "But I am. There's no need to worry."

It's impossible not to hear the rain and the wind. It sounds like there's a war being fought beyond the doors of the shelter. The occasional crash rumbles against the other noise. Athena is curled up sleeping on the opposite bench like this is her home away from home. I try not to think about how it feels like we're in a big metal coffin. Like Byron says, emergency services will find us if we can't open the doors. Won't they?

"The soup is good, right?" he says, like he's trying to distract me. I know he doesn't want to know about the soup.

It's been warming my hands, but I haven't been drinking it. I bring it to my lips and take a sip.

It's so good. Fruity and spicy and exactly what I need right now. It trails down my body, warming me from the inside out. "It's really good," I say. "It could even be the best tomato soup in the state of Colorado."

He grins, and for a second, I forget we're sheltering for our lives. "Told ya."

He slides his hand over mine and squeezes. I want to ask him what happens now. When we come out of this bunker, do we go back to how things were before? Do we pretend tonight never happened? That we haven't seen every inch of each other, heard every cry and moan? Do I pretend he doesn't make me feel like I'm a woman who knows her own mind, rather than some kind of income-generating add-on, responsible for funding her family?

Byron's changed everything, and he doesn't even know it.

Whether the tornado strikes Star Falls or not, my life beyond this bunker will never be the same.

EIGHTEEN

Byron

The cab of the truck is thick with worry. Phone lines are down, so I haven't been able to speak to anyone at the Club. I don't know what I'm going to find when I get there. In the end, the tornadoes burned themselves out before they got to Star Falls, but the storm still brought high winds and driving rain. I'm hoping for the best, but given everything that's on the line, and how tight our deadlines are, I might be facing serious changes to our opening strategy. It would cost me millions.

Rosey's nibbling her bottom lip. Athena's missing. As soon as we opened the doors of the shelter, the cat bolted like she'd been freed from jail. I slide my hand onto Rosey's thigh, wanting to reassure her. "I bet she finds her way back by the time we're home. There's not as much damage as there would have been if a tornado struck. She'll be okay."

I glance over at Rosey and wonder what happens now. Last night felt so seismic between us, like things have shifted completed. But maybe that's not how Rosey sees it. All the reasons why neither one of us wanted to get involved in the first place still exist. The storm didn't take them with it as it passed through Star Falls. Does that mean there's no way forward, or did last night make all the concerns lighter somehow—like they're no longer bold and underlined?

I still need to focus on the Colorado Club. I still don't want the town gossiping about me and the runaway bride.

At the same time, I don't want to give up Rosey.

Does she feel the same?

I don't have an answer to any of it, and I shouldn't even be thinking about it, given the enormity of the issues I might be facing when we arrive up the mountain.

"Cats don't like the rain," Rosey says. "Where could she have gone?"

"She's probably found herself a tree to climb up," I reassure her. I feel like an idiot for obsessing over what happens next for me and Rosey when that's the last thing on her mind. "I'm sure she's fine."

"Maybe," she says.

I'd offer to buy her a new cat if I thought that would help. It's probably insensitive. I'm just not a cat person.

"I'm sorry," she says. "You've got more important things to worry about."

"I'll figure out the extent of the problems at the Club soon enough. And we'll find Athena. I promise. Anything else... we can work out," I say obtusely, giving her room to say something about what happened between us last night and what might happen in the future.

She meets my gaze, nods, and gives me a small smile.

We can figure this out, I think, hoping she hears me somehow.

The road is passable so far, but the wind has taken its toll. Trees are down either side of the road.

"What's that?" Rosey asks, gripping my arm.

Ahead there's something blocking the road. I slow the truck to a stop. "Looks like an old oil drum." I could drive around it, but I don't want another vehicle to come along this road and run into it if they're not paying attention. I put the car in park and grab my gloves from the door pocket.

I don't know where the hell the oil drum has come from. I give it a push. It's heavy—definitely not empty. I slide on my gloves and give it another push. It refuses to roll. I circle the drum, trying to see what's stopping it. There are a couple of dents in it, but nothing that should stop it rolling. I push it again and it moves a few inches, then stops. It must just be the way whatever's inside is moving inside the barrel. It's resistant. Eventually, I get a rhythm going, one hand pushing after another. It creates momentum and I manage to push it off the side of the road.

I jog back to the truck, take off my gloves and slide into the driver's seat. I catch Rosey's eye as I slam my door shut.

I narrow my eyes, and she blushes. "What?" I ask her.

She shrugs. "You're hot. That's all."

I chuckle. "You like watching me doing manual labor, do you?"

"Sue me," she says, lifting her chin defiantly.

"There are plenty of other things I'd prefer to do to you," I say, because I can't not. I put the truck into drive.

"Maybe later," she says and keeps her eyes on the road.

My heart inches in my chest at her words. I'm half tempted to pull over again and bend her over the hood of this truck. I shake my head and try to get my head back where it needs to be. I can't think about any of that right now. I just want to get to the Club and work out the damage.

We pull into the drive of the Club and everything looks fine. It's a good start, but no more than I would have expected. This area around the main building was fully finished.

As we get out of the cab, Hart comes out, followed by Kathleen.

"I've been trying to call you," Hart says, his gaze flitting between me and Rosey.

"Phone lines are still down," I say. "How are things here? Everyone safe?" I watch Rosey as she disappears into the main building. I don't get to say "see you later" or "thanks for the best night of my life." I need to focus on the Club.

"Yeah, everyone was fine in the main building," Hart says. "We barely heard the rain and wind. Head of construction is doing a full walk-through now, but we think the peripheral buildings have fared a lot better than expected. The chalets are all fine, except one where the shutters weren't installed."

I raise my eyebrows. I don't need to ask why a shutter wasn't finished. Kathleen can see my question in my expression.

"I know, I know," Kathleen says. "But there are always going to be mistakes made in these circumstances. That's the nature of human beings. One chalet isn't bad. The only other real damage is a leak from the roof of the second block of staff accommodations. The temporary fix for the roof couldn't withstand the amount of rain."

At that moment, Ralph, our construction foreman, rounds the corner followed by a couple of other men I recognize from his team.

"Ralph. How are things?"

"Not bad. The main thing is we've had no significant mudslide and that's because we kept as much of the existing trees and vegetation as possible. Then we've got some damage to one chalet and the roof of the second staff housing block."

"Kathleen said as much. How long will it set us back?" I ask.

"The roof is a problem. That'll cost us at least a week."

"I want you to prioritize that over the chalet." Repairing staff housing first means one of the marketing visits will have to be pushed back. "We can't run this place if we don't have the staff."

"We're on it," he says.

My cell starts to ring. "Looks like we have service back." It's Worth, one of my closest friends. "I'll catch you later, Hart."

"How are you?" Worth asks as I accept the call.

"Fine. Spent most of the night in a tornado shelter, but it didn't hit in the end."

"I still don't believe you can get tornados in the mountains," Jack says. "It doesn't make any sense."

"You're on speaker, in case you hadn't guessed," Worth says. "We just finished a run and thought we'd check in."

A pang of loneliness catches me off guard. After last night, it would be good to go to Worth's for a beer tonight. It feels like there's been so much pressure leading up to last night, that all my adrenaline is seeping away and I'm not sure what's going to take its place. "I miss you guys," I say. It's not something I'd normally admit—to myself, let alone them.

"We miss you too," he replies.

"I don't miss him," Jack says. "If he prefers Colorado to

New York, he's not the sort of friend I want. He can go live out his cowboy fantasy without me involved in any of it."

"Don't worry, you're not in anyone's cowboy fantasy," I say with a grin.

Jack chuckles. "You never know, we might come out and visit sometime. What's there to do out there? Lasso some cows? Catch some fish?" Jack was born and raised in New York City. He's more likely to go to St. Tropez than Colorado. There's no way I'll be able to get him to come out and visit. He doesn't even go to Aspen—he prefers Chamonix. But I love him anyway.

"When this place is finished, I'll figure out a way to get you all here. Fair warning, if you try and lasso cows, you're going to get arrested, Jack. And just so you manage your expectations, there's not a spare room in the entire town at the moment."

"It will be worth the wait," Worth says. "We're proud of you."

"I'm not proud of you," Jack says. "I think you need to get your ass back to the city and stop fucking around."

"Well, this has been fun," I say. "But I have my ass to save right here in Colorado. Speak to you soon, guys. Send my love to Sophia, Worth."

I hang up the call, but I can't wipe the grin from my face. No, I can't go to Worth's tonight and ask my friends about the right move after a night like the one Rosey and I shared. Still, it's good to know they're on the end of the phone if I need them. It's good to know they're there.

I'll have to figure the Rosey stuff out on my own. Or maybe—and this is a big maybe—I'll get to do it with Rosey.

NINETEEN

Rosey

I stay on the bus until the stop in town after my shift. The first place I'm going to check for Athena is the vet's office to see if she's been handed in. Then I'll go check at home, do laundry, and figure out what to do about the ceiling in the cabin. Byron said he'd call Mike and Beth, but he's got bigger things to worry about. The truth is, I want to make sure I have a place to stay tonight without having to rely on Byron. He shouldn't feel any obligation to put a roof over my head, despite the way things have... *shifted* since last night. I want to be able to stand on my own two feet. I don't want to have other people solve my problems. I want to figure this out for myself.

As I arrive at the vet, Donna is just putting up the Closed sign. She opens the door for me anyway.

"Hey, how was the storm for you?" she asks.

"Okay. A leaky roof. You?"

"A few things in the yard got tossed around. I've seen worse."

"Athena—you know, the cat that adopted me—disappeared. She was with me during the storm but fled right after. I wondered if someone had brought her in."

"Oh no. I'm sorry. No, no one brought her in. Honestly, we haven't had any animals brought in at all. I thought there might be some injuries." She shrugs. "Fred had some callouts to the ranches farther out of town. That's it." She closes the door behind her and locks up. "I'll let you know if anyone brings her in tomorrow, though."

"Thanks. You off work now?" I ask.

Her eyes grow wide and she smiles conspiratorially. "I am. I'm headed over to Valley Park." She says it like I should know what that means. "Apparently a huge RV parked up there, just showed up out of nowhere. Marge says it's so big and fancy, it must have cost more than a million dollars. I want to see it for myself."

"Tourists?" I ask.

She leans forward. "No one knows. No one has seen anyone come or go from there. Marge says it's the government, but I don't see why it can't be someone just wanting to spend some time in this beautiful town of ours."

Her phone rings and she answers. We start to walk toward the market.

"Are you serious?" she says. "There are two? I'm definitely coming. I might just knock on the door and see who the hell is in there. Okay, I'll see you in ten minutes." She hangs up. "Did you hear that?" she asks. Before I can answer, she adds, "There's two of 'em now. Two million-dollar RVs. Another one pulled up right next to the first."

"That's weird," I say. "Could be tourists passing through on some kind of cross-country trip."

"Right. But maybe *not*," she says conspiratorially. "You wanna come see?"

A warm feeling nuzzles inside me at the thought of going with her. She likes me. And from what little I know of her, I like Donna, too. "I can't," I say. "I have to fix up the cabin. But thanks for asking. You'll have to let me know what you find. Be careful."

"Oh, I'm going with Marge. She's used to hunting wild boar. I'll be completely safe with her."

Wild boar? Is that... a thing around here? I make a mental note to ask Byron when I see him.

"You don't know where I might buy a dehumidifier, do you?" I ask.

"Go see Betty in the hardware store." She nods her head to the left. "She'll fix you up."

RON THE TAXI driver helps me bring the dehumidifier up the steps. Before I go inside, I check around the outside of the cabin for Athena.

"Athena!" I call. Maybe I'll set out some food for her on the porch and see if that entices her back. "Athena!"

I wrestle the dehumidifier into my bedroom, which thankfully still has an intact ceiling, then check the pot I left under the leak. I emptied the overflowing pot this morning, before I went to the Colorado Club. There's been no rain since, but I expected residual water to drip through the morning.

But the pan's almost dry.

I glance up at the ceiling. The wet patch is still there, but it doesn't look as bad as it did this morning. Maybe the dry mountain air is speeding the process along.

I plug in the dehumidifier and it hums to life. Then I drag the bedding from the pile on the floor, put it in the washing machine, and start a cycle. There's too much bedding to fit it all in one load, but I'm sure I can get enough washed and dried for me to have something for tonight. Maybe I should have bought a sleeping bag from Snail Trail.

I'm not sure I want to sleep right under the leak, even if it has dried up. Like Byron said, there's no telling if the entire ceiling is going to collapse. But there's no room for the bed frame to fit somewhere else in the room.

I lived in a trailer with four other women; I can figure out how to make the most of this space. I can sleep on the couch if necessary, but... I check out the mattress propped against the wall, running my hands up and down each side. Where I expect to feel sodden fabric, I only find dry softness.

Huh.

That unexpected piece of luck means I can sleep on the mattress in the living room. I maneuverer it away from the wall and pull it along the floorboards. It's heavy, but it's moving. My muscles are still sore from doing... everything with Byron last night. Images flash through my mind. It was so incredible and dirty and freeing. I half expected people to stop me and ask me what happened, because I'm sure I look different to how I looked yesterday. Sex with Byron altered my biology—I'm just not sure how yet.

I pause and pull down the neck of my shirt to reveal the hickey that he left me. It's still there. I shudder at the image of his determined mouth over my breast, his large hands holding me in place.

I don't want what we started to stop, but I don't know how we can keep moving forward either. I don't want to jump from the frying pan into the fire. Byron and Frank are completely different in so many ways, but they also have things in common. They're both much more established, powerful, and wealthy than me. For all the ways Byron made me feel amazing last night, I don't like the feel of an uneven power dynamic. It's uncomfortably familiar, even in the afterglow of what we shared.

I give the mattress a tug and slide it into the living room. There's not enough space to lay it down, so I spend the next hour configuring and reconfiguring the couch, dining room table and chairs, and side tables. Partly, I want the mattress to fit, and also, I like that I can decide where. Our trailer was too small for anyone to have a choice about where things went, but even if we'd lived in a mansion, Mom would have made all the decisions. Frank was very particular about his place, too. I was only ever a guest at the house that was meant to become my home. It never felt like a place where I could move the furniture around.

Finally I settle on putting the dining room table flush against the back of the sofa. It's not like I'm throwing any dinner parties anytime soon. I really only need to use one chair. Then I put the side tables either side of the sofa, leaving me plenty of room for the mattress against the wall of the living room.

I put my hands on my hips and survey the new arrangement. My chest lifts with pride. It feels good to solve a problem on my own, even if it's just a problem of interior design.

Someone knocks on the front door, and I jump.

"It's Mike," a man's voice says through the front door.

"And Beth," a woman's voice calls.

Shit. I just moved all their furniture around. I hope they're not mad. I pull in a breath. I can move it back easily enough. I open the door. "Hi. I'm Rosey."

"Hi, Rosey!" A woman with long dark hair and a really

tall guy with blond curly hair grin at me. "We're here to have a look at the roof. What a lot of rain, right?"

"For sure. Though I'm from Oregon, so..."

Beth laughs. "You thought you'd escaped, but you brought it with you." She laughs again, but something about what she says makes me want to remember it later. "We're going to take a look. That okay?"

Mike has a ladder, which he moves around to the side of the house. He holds it while Beth goes up. I hang back on the porch, scanning the area for Athena while I wait for the verdict.

"It's stopped dripping inside," I say. "I bought a dehumidifier since the ceiling's still a bit damp."

"Mike, you're going to have to come up here," Beth says. "Rosey, has someone been up here today?"

"Up on the roof? I don't think so. I've been working all day, so I haven't been here, but who would have been up there?"

"Maybe the damage just isn't visible," Mike says, climbing the ladder.

"No, someone's put a membrane up here and sealed it. Look."

Both of them move out of sight, but the sound of their voices suggest they're happy with what they find. Maybe I'll be able to sleep back in my bedroom before I have to abandon this place for staff housing.

I hear a cell going off and Mike answers. "Yeah, we're just here. Ohhh, that's real good of you. I appreciate that. Can we pay—" He listens to whoever is on the end of the phone. "Yeah, we have buckets all through our house at the moment. We really need a new roof. Maybe we'll get to it this year. Okay then. I might swing by with a pie for you later. Thanks, Byron."

My heart skips in my chest at the mention of Byron's name.

Mike and Beth descend from the roof, all smiles. "Your neighbor there sent some of his men down from the Club to fix the roof."

"Byron?" I ask.

"Said he had a few construction guys who weren't busy, so he directed them to fix the roof of the cabin," Mike says.

Byron's trying to launch the Colorado Club on time. I can't imagine his construction team has a bunch of free time, especially after the storm. I wonder if Byron just saved Mike and Beth, or me. In reality, he saved all of us. Though I'm grateful, worry pulls in my chest. I don't want a man who feels like it's his job to save me.

Beth grins. "I told you. He was always the nicest guy in high school."

"I don't remember him," Mike says. "He's been away a long time."

"You went to high school with him?" I ask Beth.

"A thousand years ago," she says on a smile. "He had a rough time of it by all accounts, but you'd never know it. Nothing ever seemed to ruffle his feathers. He was always the sweetest."

"Well, he's saved us a few days' work here," Mike says. "And a bunch of money."

"Which means that we can focus on our house," Beth continues. "You should run a pie up to him later." She turns to me. "Mike makes the best apple pie."

"Don't tell Nancy," Mike says with a wink. "She's the town cook. No one dares compete."

I laugh. I'm going to have to get someone to point out Nancy to me.

"Did your home get badly damaged?" I ask.

"The roof leaks every time it rains," Beth says. "We need to replace it. The tiles lift in the slightest breeze. It's crazy."

"We'll see about it this year," Mike says.

"You said that last year," Beth says.

"Can I get you a coffee?" I ask. "You're welcome to stay."

"Thank you so much," Beth says. "But we'd better get going. Will we see you at Grizzly's tonight?"

I look at her blankly.

"Everyone goes to Grizzly's after a storm," Beth says.

"Why is that?" Mike asks. "I know we do it, but I've never thought about why. To celebrate not dying?"

Beth laughs. "I guess. It's a way for the town to come together. Or something. And I want to hear the latest thing about those two government RVs in Valley Park. Donna and Marge said they were going over there to check them out. I want to know what they found."

"There are three of them now," Mike says.

"*Three?*" Beth asks.

"Apparently. That's what Jim told me."

"Someone's screwing with us," Beth says. "It's either the government, or someone wants us to *think* it's the government."

"I think our government has enough to do without parking RVs in Star Falls," Mike says.

"You know that. I know that. But Marge certainly doesn't. She won't rest until she knows who the hell's in there."

"I think Donna has it covered," I interrupt. "I saw her in town earlier. She said she was going to knock on the door. But maybe she'll have second thoughts, now that there are three of them." I stop when I realize I'm getting sucked into this RV drama, when what I really need to do is sort my laundry.

"Let's go," Beth says. "What if something happens to Donna?"

Mike turns to me. "Wanna come?"

The warm feeling from earlier returns. It's so nice to be asked. "Maybe later. I have a few chores to do. I can't wait to see what these RVs are all about."

"See you at Grizzly's later!" Beth calls as she heads back to their truck.

The RVs *are* a bit odd. I add it to my mental list of things to ask Byron about. Maybe he's organized them to be in town to house more construction workers?

I shake off the thought. I probably won't see him tonight. He's going to be busy. And am I really going to head to Grizzly's on my own? Last time I was there, I was wearing a dirty wedding dress. I'm not sure I'm ready to show my face there again so soon—or ever.

TWENTY

Rosey

I hear Byron's truck pull up in front of the cabins just before seven. I spot him out of the window and try to ignore the flutters of god-knows-what in my stomach. I need to get perspective. This man is just the guy next door. Someone who knows his way around a woman's body. Someone who happens to be my boss. And it's not like he's pulled up to see me. He lives next door.

My laundry is finished and my bed, in the corner of my living room, looks super cozy. I go to the refrigerator to pull out the milk for cocoa, when I hear Byron's footsteps coming up the steps to my porch. My stomach lifts higher and higher with each step.

He raps on my door, and I call out for him to come in.

"Hey, how are you doing?" he asks as he appears. "Sorry, I lost track of time and realized just now that you didn't have a key to my cabin and—how is this place doing?" He comes in and shuts the door. I feel the pull of him so deeply, it's like he's the moon and I'm the sea. His hair is mussed, and I have to hold myself back from reaching up to rearrange it with my fingers. I have to stop myself from circling my arms around his waist and drinking in his cool, fresh scent.

And then I remember who he is. Who I am. How things are... uneven. Difficult.

"I'm good. Someone had my roof fixed, so thanks for that." I hold his gaze, waiting for his reply. I'm grateful, but I'm also wary. He didn't talk to me about it. He just went ahead and did it. I've spent my life being told what to do and what's expected of me. I don't want to slot into someone else's way of doing things anymore.

He shrugs. "Mike and Beth don't have much money. I knew they'd do the repairs themselves and it would take a couple of days, but they've probably got damage to their place they need to focus on. I figured it would be easier and better just to get it done."

He did it for Mike and Beth, not me. Why didn't I see that before? The muscles in my jaw unclench. I breathe a little more deeply. He's not trying to take over or exert his control. He was just being kind to a couple without much money.

"But you needed the workers for the Club," I say.

"Nah, most of the day was spent opening shutters and rearranging fixtures and furniture from the chalets."

I laugh at I don't know what. A weight has lifted off my heart. I'm more carefree than I've felt in... as long as I can remember.

He rubs his stubbled chin with his palm. "It's set us back, but I really think we've got a shot of being ready. We just need some more kitchen staff. And— Never mind." He checks his watch. "Have you eaten?" he asks.

"Not yet, I was—"

"Let's go to Grizzly's," he says. "Eat wings and drink beer. Relax. It's been a weird twenty-four hours." He shoots me a grin, and I can't help but smile in response.

Weird is one way to put it.

"Everyone's going to be there," I say.

"Right," he says. "Everyone goes to Grizzly's after a storm. Or when the first snow falls. Or whatever other occasion people think up." He laughs. "Some things never change." He seems lighter. Happy. His mood is contagious.

"So you think we should go... together?" I ask. I don't know if this is a date or if it's just one neighbor giving another a lift to a bar.

He narrows his eyes. "Did you have an alternative suggestion?"

I transfer my weight from one foot to the other. People are going to see us. I guess that's fine. We're neighbors. But in the bar, I'm not going to know anyone. Is he going to be off talking to his friends while I nurse a Coke at the bar? Is he going to slide his hand into the back pocket of my jeans and...

"We don't have to go if you don't want to."

I want to go. I *really* want to go. I want to feel the atmosphere at Grizzly's after a storm, when the entire town is celebrating, rather than looking at a girl in a dirty wedding dress. I want to see if Donna went to the park. I want to meet the famous Nancy, of soup and pie fame. Most of all, I want to stop worrying about every little thing and just hang out with Byron. I want our time-out from reality to go on a bit longer.

"Let's do it," I say, before I can change my mind. "Wings and beer sound good to me. And as a bonus, we get to find out whether the RVs in Valley Park are a government conspiracy."

He brushes his hand through his hair. "Now you've lost me. Tell me in the truck."

TWENTY-ONE

Byron

Rosey has confused me from the moment I laid eyes on her, but never more so than as she explains Donna's theory about three RVs in Valley Park.

"But why would the government send RVs into Star Falls?" I ask.

Rosey shrugs and pushes the door of the truck open. "No idea. I thought maybe they were *your* RVs. Apparently, they're pretty fancy. I wondered if you'd had them brought to town so you could get more construction workers or something."

I slide out of the truck and slam the door shut. "Wasn't me." I shake my head. "I hope that rumor doesn't get picked up. Next thing you know, I'll be *part* of the government conspiracy, and the Colorado Club will be my spy headquarters or something."

Rosey laughs, and the sound travels down my spine like cool water. I've been so wrapped up in everything today, I haven't had the chance to think about what happened last night. All I know is, I couldn't wait to get back to her today. At least we're on safe ground at Grizzly's. I'll have to use every bit of willpower I have, but I'm going to be forced to resist her. I don't want the entire town gossiping about me. Again.

There's no music playing, but Grizzly's is loud. Every table is full of people and excited chatter fills the air.

"It's busy," Rosey says, turning back to me with a grin.

We make our way to the bar. There's one seat open and I gesture for her to sit.

"Tequila?" I ask.

She shoots me a puzzled look that says, *Did you remember from the first night we met or are you just guessing?* But of course I remember. How could I forget that night?

"Sure," she says.

"Tequila," I say to the bartender. "On the rocks. And I'll take a beer." I can feel her gaze on me. Eventually, I give in and look at her.

"That night feels like a thousand years ago," she says, almost too quiet for me to hear.

I chuckle. "In a good way? Or a serving-time-in-a-Thai-prison kind of way?"

She smiles up at me. "In a really great way."

The bartender slides our drinks across the bar and I lean back on the mahogany while Rosey sits beside me.

"Everyone's so happy," she says.

"Sure. They all survived the storm."

"It was pretty terrifying having to go into the bunker," she says. "I can't imagine you ever get used to it."

"Not living in the mountains in Colorado."

"Were there many storms when you were a kid?" she asks.

I don't look at her, because I don't want to feed the rumor mill. I'm not convinced I can pretend I'm not completely enthralled by this woman if I give her all my attention.

"Plenty of storms," I say, staring over at a table with a couple of faces I recognize. "But not many tornado warnings."

One of the girls at the table glances over at us and waves. I raise my beer in response.

"Who's that?" Rosey asks.

"I think it's Juniper French. I went to high school with her, but she looked a little different back then." Juniper French had been a little kooky in high school, to say the least.

"Juniper French. Sounds like a movie star or a pastry or something. She's pretty. Did you two date?"

I chuckle. "No. I'm not sure Juniper dated in high school. Thinking back, she was pretty, but not to a fifteen-year-old boy. She had that baggy-sweatshirt, glasses-and-braces thing going on." As we're talking, Juniper slides out of her booth and wanders over.

"Looks like she grew up," Rosey says, as Juniper approaches wearing a huge smile.

"I heard you were back in town," she says, flinging an arm around me. She's all long limbs and pouting lips. If it wasn't for her powder-blue eyes and the same blunt bangs, I wouldn't recognize her.

"Hey, Juney," I say.

"It's so good to see you. I'm hearing all the things about the Colorado Club."

"What a ringing endorsement," I reply.

"Actually, I wanted to talk to you about it." She glances

at Rosey, then back at me. "But I don't want to interrupt your date."

"Oh, we're not dating," Rosey says before I get a chance to respond. "We're neighbors."

I shift my weight from one foot to the other, slightly uncomfortable. No, we're not dating. But we did have sex last night. I'm not putting a ring on her finger, and I know she just got out of a serious relationship, and it's not like I'm out here looking for love, but last night was... it shifted things between us, didn't it?

My thoughts are running away from me. I just want a beer and a good time. Overthinking never ends well.

"Maybe I can come and see you up at the Club," Juney says. "I don't know if you know, but I do a bit of painting in my spare time. Some pottery, but mainly painting. I wondered if you wanted to see it."

My heart sinks. My designer is in charge of sourcing all the artwork for the Club, and I know she's not going to want me purchasing stuff she can't use. Maybe I can buy a couple of pieces to put in staff housing or something. "That would be great."

"You paint?" Rosey says. "I can't draw a stick figure."

"Oh, I bet that's not true," Juney says. "You probably just haven't practiced very much. I've been doing it a long time now." Her smile is warm and genuine. Rosey's too.

"Have you?" I ask. "Was that always your thing? I can't remember."

Juney laughs. "Really? I was a mess in high school. You don't remember I always had paint in my hair and under my fingernails?"

"It's been a while," I respond. I just remember Juney being quiet. It seemed like she was in a world of her own.

"You were too busy playing sportsball."

I chuckle. "Yeah, *sportsball* was a big thing back then." I used to take out all my frustrations about everything out on whatever field I was playing on. Sportsball was what the kids that didn't play sports called any sport that involved a ball.

Juney pulls out her phone from the back pocket of her jeans. "Do you have your phone? I'd love to share my digital business card." She holds up her phone, which has a QR code on it. I scan it and hold up my phone so she can see that I have it. "I won't take up any more of your time. Take a look at my work and if you think you might be interested, give me a call. I won't hound you, I promise."

"You can hound me. I have a lot going on, so I might forget—"

"He won't forget," Rosey says. "I'll make sure he remembers."

My eyes widen in surprise. She's going to be moving up to staff housing soon. How does she think she's going to remind me if we're not neighbors?

Juney makes her excuses and heads back to her table.

Rosey mutters under her breath, "This is perfect."

"What's perfect?" I take a swig of beer and turn to face her on the stool. No one's taking any notice of us anyway.

"*Local art.*" She says it in a way that suggests I should know what she's saying. "The Club can start supporting a local artist. You're trying to make the town less hostile to the Club, right? This is another way you can encourage local support."

"I can't put up art that isn't any good. If I refuse to support a local artist, that could have the opposite effect— people might start to hate me."

Rosey holds out her hand. "Let's have a look at her stuff."

Our gazes lock, and for a second, I wonder why the hell I insisted on coming to Grizzly's. I can't do anything I want to do to her with all these eyes on us. Rosey breaks eye contact first and clicks on Juney's website.

"Whoa," Rosey says. "This is *not* what I was expecting."

I hadn't really thought about what Juney's art might look like. I guess I'm expecting intricate paintings of birds and bears and deer—local wildlife landscapes, that kind of thing. I get a sinking feeling. I should not have come to Grizzly's tonight. I should go back to avoiding town and Star Falls residents in general. It just gets me into trouble. The last time I was here, I ended up with a neighbor. Now, I have to buy art I don't want and can never display.

"I don't necessarily understand it," Rosey says. "I'm not an art person. But this looks... fresh. She's had some exhibitions in Denver and Aspen."

She pushes the phone into my hand and I take a look. There's not a detailed wildlife painting in sight. Instead, there are huge abstract canvasses. I glance at Rosey, whose gaze is fixed on my phone. Her lips are mere inches from mine, and I can't do a damn thing about it.

"I think some of these would look amazing in the chalets. In the main building as well, though I'm not sure you have room for them."

"I'll send the site to Rosalind and see what she thinks."

"Rosalind?" Rosey asks.

"The designer. She's in charge of all the interior decoration."

"Tell her it's a local artist. I think they're beautiful." Rosey's cheeks are flushed with the heat of Grizzly's and her enthusiasm for Juney's paintings. She's beautiful all the time, but lit up like this, she's radiant. Maybe I should buy her a painting.

"You came!" someone screeches from behind us. Donna appears and grabs Rosey by the hand like they're long-lost sisters.

"Did you complete your investigations?" Rosey asks. She's clearly intrigued.

She grabs my elbow and stands close, pulling the three of us into a circle. "I knocked on the doors," she whispers. I'm not sure if she's drunk or just overinvested. "No freaking answer. It was six thirty. If it was a tourist, there's no way they wouldn't be in their RV at six freaking thirty."

She looks between us like she's a trial lawyer who's just presented a smoking gun.

"So you think it's the government?" Rosey asks, her eyes wide.

Donna lifts up her palms. "What else could it be?"

I'm about to give her at least a dozen possible explanations that don't involve federal agencies, when suddenly the door to Grizzly's crashes open and three very unexpected faces appear.

TWENTY-TWO

Byron

I slide my beer onto the bar and try to focus on the three men who've just come through the door. I glance back at my drink. How many have I had? Is it enough to start hallucinating?

"You know those guys?" Rosey asks.

"If the mountain won't go to Mohammed," Worth says as he saunters toward us.

"Then the New Yorkers have to come to the mountains," Fisher finishes.

Fisher gets to me first and pulls me into a hug. I still can't believe what I'm seeing.

"What are you guys doing here?"

"Heard this place was banging," Fisher says, glancing around at the timber-clad walls and stone floors. "Had to come check it out for ourselves."

Jack offers me an effusive handshake and back slap, always the most formal of our group.

"Fuck," I say. "It's going to be a tight squeeze in the

cabin tonight." I glance over at Rosey. She'll probably need to stay too. I'm not sure if her place has dried out, and I'm not sure I care either way—I just want her near me. "This is Rosey, by the way."

Each of my friends greets Rosey with a handshake.

"Known Byron for long?" Fisher asks.

"I only got to town a couple of weeks ago," Rosey says. "Are you local?"

The four of us laugh. "These guys are from New York," I say. "We've been friends a long time."

"And we miss Byron," Worth says, ruffling my hair like a sitcom dad. "So we thought we'd drop by. Anyway, we want to see what's been keeping our friend in Colorado so long." He shoots me a look that asks, *Does Rosey have something to do with it?* "This *Club* better be good."

"It's beautiful," Rosey says. "Billionaire beautiful."

The guys laugh, we order drinks, and no one asks who Rosey is to me. Instead, the guys sweep her up in conversation, asking her where she's from and whether she's enjoying Star Falls.

"Valley Park is beautiful," Jack says. "Even before we left the RVs, there were so many stars out. I swear we can see fucking Saturn from where we are."

"Did you say RVs in Valley Park?" Rosey asks. "Like... the three million-dollar RVs that arrived today? That's where you're staying?"

"We couldn't get a bloody room anywhere," Fisher says. "Worth got us an RV each."

Rosey dissolves into giggles. "This is perfect," she says through her laugh. "I bet it takes all of five minutes before someone wanders over and accuses you of being from the FBI."

"Am I missing something?" Jack asks.

"The whole town has been talking about the RVs," I explain. "No one understood why they were there or who they belonged to. It makes sense now."

"Donna said she knocked on your doors earlier. You didn't hear her?"

"We only got here. Dumped our stuff in the RVs and came right over. It was the only place where there were lights. None of us could get a phone signal. I asked a guy where you were living and they told us we'd find you here."

"Small towns, right?" Rosey says. "Ever watch *Superman*?"

"Conversational whiplash," Fisher says.

Rosey shakes her head. "I know you're not clad in black leather or anything, but I bet the three of you looked like those Zod villains walking down Main Street."

"Day made. I always wanted to be a comic book villain," Jack says.

"I think that's Leo's kink, isn't it?" Worth says.

"He just got there before me. There's no way I would have let Mystique out of my sight if I'd met her first."

I raise my eyebrows. "You have a crush on Mystique, or you have a crush on Jules?"

Jack shakes it off. "Nah. Well, not now anyway, she's my sister-in-law."

We all exchange glances. I never picked up on Jack having a crush on Jules, Leo's wife. Maybe I'm reading too much into what he's saying.

"I'm lost," Rosey says, breaking through the awkwardness of the moment.

"Me too," I confess.

"Come on," Fisher says. "Let's play pool." He nods at the table in the back.

"I'll leave you to it," Rosey says as everyone moves off.

I turn back to her. "Come with us."

She shakes her head. "You should have time with your friends. It's so nice they came all this way to surprise you. It's the kind of thing you expect brothers to do. But not the reality of what brothers would *actually* do. These guys care about you." There's a sadness in her tone I'm not used to.

"The way brothers should act?" I ask.

She shrugs and glances away. There's something there, but she clearly doesn't want to talk about it.

"I want you to hang out with us." I say it because I don't want her to be sad, but also because I want her around. I like her. She's fun and so are my friends. They'll all get along.

Our gazes lock as she decides what to do. I don't want her to stay if she doesn't want to. But I think she does.

"Okay," she says. "But I can't play pool."

I sling my arm around her shoulders before I can second-guess myself or worry about what the town grapevine will say. I just want to be myself tonight. When New York comes to Star Falls, I just want to soak it all in and enjoy.

We head over to the table where Jack and Fisher have already started to play. "Maybe I'll teach you."

She slides her hand into the back pocket of my jeans. "Has anyone ever told you, you have a really nice ass?"

I chuckle and catch Worth's eye as we head towards the back.

"Just neighbors, huh?" Worth says, handing us both pool cues. We take them and separate—reluctantly.

"Tell me about New York," I say. "Remind me what I'm missing."

"My wife called me an asshole before I left, and she wasn't even the first that day. That honor goes to the person behind me in the line at the coffee shop, because I accidently brushed her coat with my elbow."

I chuckle. "God, I miss the place. How is Sophia?" I ask. "How's married life?"

"You're newly married?" Rosey asks. She beams like she thinks it would be wonderful to be newly married. Ironic, given how she arrived in this town.

"I am," Worth says wearing a shit-eating grin. "Sophia and I got married in Vegas the second time we ever met."

Rosey's hand slaps against Worth's arm. "Are you serious? And you're making it work?"

"I would have asked her the first time I met her if I'd thought she'd say yes."

"When was the first time you met her?" I ask.

"At the brunch where we were discussing Leo and Jules eloping."

"What are you three gossiping about while I whip Jack's arse?" Fisher asks.

"Worth was just catching Rosey up about how he fell in love with Sophia at the brunch where Jules was trying to set *you* up with Sophia," I reply. "I wasn't there but I heard about it. A lot."

"It sounds like you're all very... family style with your dating," Rosey says.

"Family style?" Fisher asks.

"No," I say, a rush of protectiveness surging in me. "We're not. There's absolutely no sharing."

Fisher chokes on his beer. "We're close, but we're not *that* close.

"It's not like that," I say, looking Rosey straight in the eye. I'm not sure if it was just an offhand remark or whether she's wondering if we're just a bunch of playboys who hand women around like hors d'oeuvres. "None of us would ever.

You're safe." I don't want her to think I'd ever try to take advantage of her or treat her like a thing rather than the insightful, kind, sensitive woman she is.

She offers me a small smile. "I've never been to New York. I imagine things are very different there compared to Oregon or Star Falls."

"People are people," I say. "There are assholes every-where." The guys have moved over to the pool table, debating which shot Jack should take next.

"I haven't met any in Star Falls yet," Rosey says. "It seems to be filled with the best kind of people." She shoots me a smile. "But maybe that's because of you."

"Me?" I ask, confused.

"Maybe you attract the best people. Maybe the assholes stay away when you're around."

I huff out a laugh. "Wouldn't that be a good superpower to have? Asshole repellant." I lift her chin between my thumb and finger. I don't know why I don't care if my friends see me with Rosey, or if I feel so comfortable with her *because* they're here. "Is this okay?" I ask, my voice low.

She sighs. I feel any tension in me or between us ebb away. She brings her hands up over my shoulders and nods. I brush my lips against hers in a half kiss, release her, and turn back to the game.

TWENTY-THREE

Rosey

We pull up in front of the cabins and I can't shut up about the RVs. It's like someone's turned a tap on inside me and words are just pouring out. To think that I almost thought it was too cold to go back and see the stars from Valley Park. "I didn't expect them to have actual tile on the floors. Did you see Worth's? What's an infrared sauna, anyway?"

Byron chuckles. "I'm gonna risk a guess and say you were impressed with the RVs."

"I thought they were kidding when Donna said they were 'million-dollar' RVs. I've lived in a trailer most of my life and hated every second of it. But I'd have loved a place like that."

"Did you live with Frank?" he asks. "What was his place like?"

I shrug. "I had a drawer at his place and some stuff in the closet. I was due to move in after the wedding. But it never felt like mine... or even like it *could* be mine someday."

"Did you think about leaving him before the wedding day?"

I pull in a breath. "Yes. Obviously I knew I didn't love him. But he wasn't a bad man. I knew my family would always be comfortable if I went through with it, and that was... enough. We'd never had money. Even when I started working, almost all my money went to Mom for rent. So the idea of not having to struggle was... great." I pick at the skin on my fingers.

His expression is full of sympathy, and I exhale, relieved that I don't hear any judgement in his voice.

I turn in my seat so I'm facing him. "Your friends are super fun. You must miss them, being so far from New York."

"I do. I miss my life there, but the Colorado Club is important." His brow furrows, and he looks so serious that I get the urge to tickle him.

"Wanna give me a piggyback ride to the cabin?" I ask.

"A piggyback ride?" he asks, like he thinks I might have lost my mind.

I shrug. "I haven't had a piggyback ride for a very long time. I want to remember what it feels like."

He slides out of his side of the truck and opens the door to my side. I grin at him, wondering if he's going to follow through.

He turns and bends, encouraging me onto his back. I squeal as I climb on, and he grips my legs tight before he stands. I tighten my grip around his neck and he strides over to my cabin. His neck is warm and solid. I slide my fingers into the neck of the t-shirt under his plaid button-down. He groans at the contact.

He turns his back to the stairs and I hop off. Then he faces me. "How was it?"

"The best I ever had," I reply. How could it not be? Byron is hot as holy hell, but he's also kind and funny. He has the kind of friends who are only friends with good people.

He grips either side of the porch railings and grins up at me.

"It's cold," I say. "We should go inside." I grab him by the shirt and pull him up the stairs.

I want him. It's as simple as that.

He climbs up the stairs, and I keep pulling until my ass hits the door. He keeps walking until our bodies are pressed together. He cups my face and dips down for a kiss.

I moan as his lips press against mine. It's different from the half kiss he gave me at the bar. Not that that kiss wasn't good. It was better than good. And it was surprising because it was as if he was claiming me in front of all of his friends—letting them know I'm off-limits.

It was cute and territorial and made me melt.

But this kind of private, desperate kiss is my favorite of Byron's kisses.

I sweep my hands up the sides of his chest. He's all hard muscle under the soft plaid.

"What a day," I say dreamily, when he releases me from his kiss.

"It's not over yet." He rounds his hands over my ass. "Let's go inside."

I fumble with the keys and let us in.

"You moved things around. I didn't notice earlier."

"Oh yeah, the mattress is on the floor. I'm going to sleep in here tonight to give the bedroom ceiling a chance to dry out."

He doesn't answer. When I look around, his eyes are full of heat. "You won't do much sleeping tonight." He tugs me to him with his fingers tucked into the waist of my jeans. He presses kisses down my neck, and instantly it feels like last night never ended.

We shrug off our coats and I pull at his shirt, my hands trembling with need for him. Why the hell did we waste time going to the bar tonight? We could have been here doing this. All night.

I don't know how I've managed to retain my self-control all evening. Right at this moment, I'd be happy to drop to my knees and take his dick in my mouth even if all his friends were watching. I just want to feel him. I want him to feel me.

As if he can hear what I'm thinking, he pulls open my jeans and shoves his hand down my pants. His fingers find my folds. I know I'm wet.

"I fucking knew this is how I'd find you. Tell me it's for me, Rosey. Not Fisher or Jack. Tell me that all this delicious wetness is for me."

"Of course," I choke out. "I'm crazy for you."

He works his fingers hard and fast. I grab at his arm, trying to get him to slow down. I'm so wound up, I know if he keeps going like this, I'm going to be orgasming in a matter of seconds.

"If you want me to stop, tell me to stop and I will."

I shake my head. He can't stop. I think I'll die if he stops touching me. "I'm going to come," I say, my voice tight and high.

"I know," he says. "I want you to come. And then I'm going to fuck you on the couch and against the door and in the shower. Come for me, so we can get to all that."

I whimper. I want that so much. I want to give myself to him. Surrender.

He flips us around, pressing me against the door, and

drives his fingers into me. It's hard and rough, and all I think about is his hand shoved in my jeans, his lips on my neck, his growl in my ear, saying all the things he wants to do to me.

His fingers press against my flesh, and the scrape of his stubble against my skin sends every sense into hyperdrive. Sensation shoots from me and I convulse around his hand.

"That's right, Rosey. Come for me."

Stars explode in my vision. I feel like I'm floating and melting and disappearing.

I cling to Byron's shoulders as my orgasm ebbs away.

I'm panting, my body weak. Byron slides his thigh between my legs to keep me from falling. I'm unable to catch my breath. I'm lifeless.

"It's like I'm addicted to your sounds when you come. I can't get enough."

My cheeks flush with embarrassment. I have no control over the sounds I'm making when I'm with Byron. I have no control around him, period. But it's not just when we're having sex. I simply can't resist him. I don't want to take my power back from my mother and Frank and give it to someone else—especially not a man as powerful as Byron. But I can't seem to say no. I don't want to.

The more time I spend with Byron, the more I wonder if he even *wants* my power. A voice inside says the answer is no. Maybe it's because this—whatever this is between us— has a natural end date. I'll move into staff housing next week, and things will naturally fade out. They're bound to.

Byron scoops me up and I hook my hands around his neck. "You don't want my power," I whisper against his chest.

"I want your body," he growls.

He lays me on the bed and steps back, like he's considering his options. "There are so many things I want to do to you."

"I want all of them," I say.

He strips off my jeans and top. When I'm completely naked, he pulls his clothes off, not taking his eyes from mine as he does. When he takes off his boxers, my gaze drops to what's between his thighs.

I've always thought penises were weird. They serve a purpose and all, but really, I always found them a little off-putting. But Byron's penis is gorgeous. Flat against his stomach, it's rigid steel covered in smooth velvet. I lick my lips at the thought of my hands around it, my tongue over it, pressing it between my thighs.

"I love your dick." It slips out before I can think what I'm saying. I cover my face with my arm.

"It loves you back," he says on a chuckle. "Come here," he says, nudging my thighs open and standing between them.

I push myself up so I'm sitting in front of him, his dick level with my face. I glance up at him, and he's grinning. He lifts my chin and shakes his head like he's seen something he can't quite believe.

I start at the base of his cock. My tongue flat, I lick in one long, slow movement up, teasing out a groan from that dirty mouth.

It's beautiful. I glance up at him, and his eyes are dark—fierce, like he's on the brink of war. I take him in my fist, starting at the top and pushing down in another slow movement.

"Are you trying to kill me?" he growls.

I think it's me who has all the power now, and I like it. I bite back a grin and get to work. I lick, suck, pull, and push, and he cries and moans, fueling the sense of power washing through me. Sucking him makes him feel good. I know that for sure. But it makes *me* feel good too. It makes me feel sexy and powerful that a man like Byron can be so weak for me.

I take him so deep, I reach around to his ass to keep him in place so I can take him to the back of my throat. He cries out my name like a chant. It's such a thrill to be able to drive him mad like this. My nipples are so hard, they hurt. The wetness between my legs is borderline embarrassing.

I'm losing focus. This is meant to be all about him, but I'm so turned on, I might be able to come like this. His dick in my mouth. I moan at the thought, and Byron curses and steps away.

"Fuck, Rosey. You might just be about to kill me."

I glance up at him, confused. He bends, presses a kiss to my forehead and pulls us both back onto the mattress. We lie side by side on our backs.

"I need a couple of minutes," he says. "I want us to come together."

I prop myself up on my elbow, watching him, wondering if I just heard him right. I want that too, but I also want him to come in my mouth. I want everything from him.

I take his hand and guide his fingers between my thighs.

"Fuuuck," he groans. "You're not making this easy for me, are you?"

I shake my head. "I thought I was going to come when I was sucking you."

He groans again, flips me to my back, and rolls over me. "I want to feel this." He pushes his cock through my folds. I'm so ready, there's no resistance.

He pauses, the tendons in his neck tight, his jaw set. "You're fucking everything."

I set my palm on his chest. He exhales and our gazes lock. We hold each other's stare like we don't want to move in case something spoils this connection. We've tried to fight it. We've tried to resist. But whatever there is between us keeps pulling us back.

Eventually, he grabs a condom, rolls it on, and plows into me, pushing me up the bed with the force of it.

My orgasm is awoken immediately. The way he stretches me, fills me up. The way he looks at me. It's all overwhelming. I feel the best kind of weak with him. I have a deep urge to give myself to him. To give him everything. Not because I'm forced to, not because it's the right thing to do, but because it's what I want.

"Byron," I whisper, his lips on my neck as he drives into me. I lift my legs, skirting either side of his torso. He fits deeper like this.

I've never felt so free. So entirely myself. I've spent my life doing everything everyone expects of me, but here in Star Falls, Byron on top of me, for the first time in twenty-eight years it's about nobody but me. And Byron.

I've been engaged before. I've stood in front of a mirror on the morning of my wedding, and I've never felt more committed to a man than I do right now with Byron.

"Rosey." My name on his lips is what breaks my final thread of control.

My orgasm curls around every muscle and sinew, rearranging my brain chemistry, changing my DNA. Byron's rewritten my history and is changing my future, and he doesn't even know it.

We lie there, our bodies pressed against each other, for what seems like hours. His heat, the weight of him, the way he intermittently says my name, like he can't believe I'm real—if I stay like this until the end of time, it won't be long enough.

I trace patterns on his back, memorizing every line, dip, and curve on him. He's beautiful. And for the moment, he's mine. I can't let myself think about the future. Not even next week, when staff housing will be ready. I don't ever want to think about a time when I won't be able to feel him like this. When he won't be mine to touch. To taste. To enjoy.

"Rosey," he says again.

I push my fingers into his hair and sigh.

"I think I'm addicted to you."

I know exactly what he means. Life changed forever when Byron walked into my world, and I can't imagine him walking out. I block out the fact that his three best friends arrived today from New York. He clearly has a life there—a life he'll go back to when the Club is up and running, and I'm still here.

TWENTY-FOUR

Rosey

The staff break room is noticeably fuller at lunchtimes now. I guess once the Club is open, fewer people will be having their lunch at the same time, but while we're all training, we're all coming and going at similar times.

There are long dining tables set out like a canteen at one end of the room, with more comfortable seating at the other end, gathered around low tables. Windows stretch along one side of the room, but they're set in close to the ceiling, so you see out to the treetops and the sky. The room still has a faint smell of fresh paint along with the food everyone's eating. There's the odd person reading and a few more scrolling phones, but most people are just chatting.

I take a seat at the long tables with the salad I just grabbed from the kitchen. Eden and Akira are taking calls outside and said they would meet me down here. I've gotten familiar with a lot of faces this last week, but I haven't eaten lunch with anyone apart from the other waitresses I started with.

"Hey, Rosey! Wanna sit with us?" Patricia, one of the waitresses who's been here from the beginning, calls from the long table closest to the wall. She seems to know everyone here, including all the managers.

A guy I recognize from reception takes the seat Patricia was indicating.

"Thanks," I mouth. "I'm okay." Honestly, I'm happy to have a few minutes to myself. I'm used to carving out space in noise and chaos and taking some downtime. Hell, that's been my life for a long time. We lived on top of each other in the trailer. I would have been driven mad if I hadn't been able to find a way to create some peace for myself along the way.

I stab at my goat cheese salad when my phone buzzes with the arrival of a text. I know it's not going to be Byron. He's so focused on a thousand things when he's at work, and on top of that he's got his friends here. That doesn't stop my heart lifting in my chest at the thought that I might get a message from him. I hold my breath as I pull the phone out of my pocket to check.

My stomach lurches at my youngest sister's name on my phone.

Shit.

It's been a couple of weeks since the wedding—since I got on a plane in a white gown and Lydia's gray hoodie. I've been able to block out what's going on in Oregon for the most part. I've been focused on Star Falls: my new job, the storm, Byron. Anything but what I've left behind.

After I've swallowed my mouthful of salad, I swipe open the message.

I miss you. Mom says we can't contact you. Don't tell her I'm messaging you.

I have to fight the urge to call my sister immediately. I

don't want to get Marion into trouble. If someone sees my name flashing up on her screen, it will probably cause a huge argument.

It makes more sense now why I haven't heard anything from my mom or any of my sisters. Mom has decreed the punishment of silence—an old favorite of hers, probably because it normally works. Before I ran away, being cast out of our family would have been my idea of torture. I went along with things that made Mom happy because I didn't want to upset the family dynamic—didn't want to lose her good grace, or my only place in the world.

The difference between when I've previously been given Mom's silent treatment and now is distance, and the little bit of history I've carved out over the last few weeks that doesn't involve her. Memories and experiences where she's not the center of things.

Maybe it was the understanding that doing what my mom wanted was going to cost me any kind of control over my future that's allowed me to hold my nerve and stay here. Mom played her hand, dished out my punishment, but it didn't work this time. The stakes were too high.

I type out a text.

I miss you too, Marion.

I do miss her. But I don't miss being responsible for her. For our entire family. I feel lighter here in Star Falls, with nothing but possibility in my future. I don't know how I stuck it out in Oregon as long as I did. Looking back, I don't understand how as a twenty-eight-year-old woman, I still felt I had to do everything my mother said.

Another text appears almost immediately.

You're so lucky you escaped.

My heart clenches in hope and pity.

I am lucky. I'm lucky I found Polly Gifford outside the

hotel, and even luckier that she was heading to the airport. As I watched myself in the mirror the morning of my wedding, I knew I didn't want to get married, but I didn't see a way out. Not until Polly offered me a ride. If it hadn't been for her, I'd still be in Oregon, either begging forgiveness from my mother or married to Frank. Neither one was a future I wanted.

What happened?

Marion must have hit call right away, as her name flashes up on my phone.

I tuck the cell between my cheek and shoulder and scoop up my salad before heading out for some privacy.

"Hey," I answer, as I make my way along the corridor to one of the back exits.

"I miss you so much," she repeats. "Mom's been a complete monster since you left."

A dull ache radiates from my stomach. I can only imagine how difficult it's been.

"I just want to move out, but you know what she's like."

"Yup," I say. She would make us feel so guilty if we even thought about leaving. She seemed to have a sixth sense when any of us were fantasizing about life beyond the trailer. "Could you and Kitty find a place to share together?" I know as I say it, it will feel impossible to Marion. When you're in it, under Mom's watchful eye, it's like being a prisoner. And because we had no experience of our own to compare it to, we accepted it as normal.

I press the exit button and hit the fresh, cold Colorado air. The sky's blue and the sun's shining. I don't know what it is, but the blue sky makes everything feel a little bit more hopeful. I step out onto the gravel that surrounds the main building and lean against the pine shiplap.

She sighs. "I made the mistake of suggesting that to Kitty. She went and told Mom on me."

Mom used to encourage us to tell on each other, even when we were little. We could win her favor by complaining that someone had smashed a glass or wasted some of the new shampoo. Looking back, it was like a constant war; we were either on Mom's side against each other, or we were on defense, fighting our way back into her camp.

She was a puppet master. We were just a game to her.

A huge bubble of grief and pity forms in my chest, and I start thinking about ways Marion can escape. And then it becomes obvious. The Colorado Club needs staff. And they're offering accommodations. All my sisters could come here and get jobs.

But I can't get the words out.

For some reason, I don't want to give Marion my escape route. But I want her to find her own.

"Have you thought about what your options could be? What happened to working your way through community college?" Marion was always an excellent student. Looking back, we all had been. But Mom never encouraged college. Instead, she wanted us to go to work as soon as we could. *We're a team*, Mom used to say. We all had to play our parts and contribute as soon as we'd left school. Boyfriends were strongly discouraged. Mom had her eyes on the prize, and the prize was her daughters providing her with an income.

"There's no way she's going to let me go to community college." I want to say, you're an adult, Marion. You can make your own decisions, but I don't because I know it won't help. Even if she knows it's true, it won't feel like she has the power or control. I know because I lived it.

"Do you have to tell her?"

"I wouldn't be able to hide it. I'd have to study and—"

"You could study in the library," I say. "Do they have lockers at community college? You could just keep everything there."

Silence comes from the other end of the phone.

"It seems impossible, right?" I ask.

"Right."

I know that feeling.

"Could I come and stay with you?"

I exhale. The old me would have said yes right away. I would have seen it as my duty to look after Marion. "Let me think about it. I'm not really set up at the moment. It's not like I have a place for you to stay. And—"

"I'll pay my way. You know I'm a hard worker."

"It's not that," I say. "It's more that I want you to find your own path out. I want to help you. But you can't just do what I'm doing. You have to create your own future. Your dream is community college. Let's try and figure out a way for you to do that."

She sighs. I know how hopeless she feels. Like there's no way out. Like she's trapped. I've been there. But somehow I found a way. Marion will too, especially if I help.

"You should look at scholarships," I say. "Maybe you should think about a college that would offer financial assistance for your room and board."

"What? You think I should apply to Harvard or something?"

"You made good grades. Did the guidance counselor not talk to you about applying anywhere?"

"Once or twice. She thought I should apply to the University of Oregon. She thought I had a good shot at a full scholarship."

"But you didn't apply?" I ask.

"Mom said I'd end up in a ton of debt, with the same job I'd have without a college degree."

My heart breaks a little more. Shouldn't a mother encourage her child's dreams, rather than focus only on herself? I wasted so much time trying to please a woman who didn't see me as a human. Just someone to serve her.

"Mom *would* say that."

"She's got a point. College isn't meant for everyone."

"But you're not everyone—you're you. College is made for people like you. Hell, I would have liked to have gone to college." I say it without thinking, but it's true. I got good grades. I never even considered college because I knew Mom expected me to get a full-time job as soon as possible. A future other than one she'd planned never even occurred to me.

"You used to love poetry, didn't you?" she asks.

I'd spend hours in the library creating poems. I mentioned going to college for English to my mom once and she'd just laughed. I didn't bring it up again.

"Yeah. But I gave it up. I shouldn't have. Mom isn't going to support you, but it doesn't mean you shouldn't apply to college. And you have nothing to lose. The worst that happens is you apply and don't get in."

"But Mom would be so mad."

"She won't ever have to know." I remember something Byron said to me. "Let's not borrow trouble. I can help you apply and then we can see what happens."

"You'd help?" There's a lift to her voice.

"Of course. And we have some time," I say. "Deadlines are nine months away. Why don't you go back and see the guidance counselor at school? I bet she'd help you, or knows someone who could. I can help you put together a plan and we'll keep it between the two of us."

"Mom won't find out?"

"Believe it or not, she's not a mind reader. You need to make sure you don't tell the others. Keep it to the two of us."

"But what would happen if I actually got in somewhere? Would I just move away?"

"You were ready to come stay with me."

"Mom would kill me."

"Not if you went out of state. You'd be too far for her to reach."

"But she really does need the money."

I swallow. There's no doubt Mom doesn't have a lot, but that isn't Marion's fault. There's no reason Mom can't get a job and start supporting herself. The realization that I own the trailer dawns on me. I need to find a way to transfer it back to Frank. It was a wedding present for a wedding that never took place. I can't possibly keep it. "I know she doesn't," I say. I want to tell Marion it's not our responsibility to financially support our mother, but I'm not even sure I believe that. "If you got a great degree at a fancy university, imagine what a great job you'd get. You'd be able to support her much more in the long term."

"That's true," she says.

"But you gotta keep this secret. And don't tell anyone you spoke to me either."

Marion agrees she's going to research who can help her identify scholarships and colleges, we say our I love yous, and hang up.

I'm exhausted. I gaze up. It's a Colorado sky I'm looking at, not an Oregon one. But Oregon feels closer to home than it has since I got here. Darkness settles over my heart like a cloud passing across the sun. I left Oregon in a wedding dress because I didn't want to get married, but what I really escaped wasn't Frank—it was my mother.

All the cuts and bruises from a lifetime there have been brought back by my conversation with Marion. My body aches. I feel the bruises on my soul. But this Colorado air is helping them heal.

Maybe helping Marion will help me too. I might have gotten out of Oregon, but there are some things I need to face before I can truly escape.

The first is transferring the trailer back into Frank's name. I just don't know how to start the process.

Probably with a call to Frank.

It feels like I've kept Oregon at bay for as long as possible, and now it's seeping in at the sides. I need to face it—clean up the mess I left. Be the adult I've been waiting to become.

TWENTY-FIVE

Byron

I'm not often nervous, but showing my three best friends around the Colorado Club is as close as it gets.

"Now that's what I call a money shot," Fisher says as we come down the stairs into Blossom. "You're just above the trees."

"Right," I say. "That was the plan. So we get the view into the valley."

"It's really beautiful, Byron," Worth says.

I push my hands into my pockets.

"Not so much the mountain-man look," Fisher says, nodding at my jeans and flannel shirt. "Are those... steel-toed boots?"

I shrug. "You want me to put on a Tom Ford suit?"

None of us are in suits. Worth, Fisher, and Jack are wearing what they'd normally wear on the weekend in New York. We're not dressed *so* differently.

"I guess we're not in Kansas anymore," Jack says. "This is Star Falls, Colorado."

"I'm impressed you remembered," I say. "I didn't think your brain would retain anything outside the 212 area code."

"Oh don't worry," he says. "As soon as I reach thirty thousand feet, I will have forgotten all about this trip."

I chuckle. "Should we eat? You can give me your honest opinion on the food."

We slide into one of the pink booths overlooking the valley, and a sense of pride rushes through me. I like showing my friends what I've built here. It's so different from when I was growing up. The farm wasn't a place I brought my friends. It was a place to work. A place that felt like home until it wasn't.

"I'm guessing it's not going to be as good as the wings we had at Grizzly's."

"They were heaven on a plate," Jack says. "Almost worth living outside of Manhattan for."

"We can try all the restaurants. This one is fine dining."

"As long as we can go back to Grizzly's tonight," Fisher says. "I wonder if we can take some wings back to New York with us."

"What about you?" Worth says from opposite me. "You think you'll come back with us?"

I grin, sliding my hand over my stubble. "Not tomorrow. Not until after this place is open and settled."

"Do you miss New York?" Jack asks.

Before I can answer, I see Rosey out of the corner of my eye, coming toward us.

Whenever we've seen each other at the Club, we've always given each other a small smile and carried on with whatever we're doing. But I know that's not how my friends roll.

Fisher is out of his seat as soon as he spots her.

Rosey's eyes widen in shock before her gaze flits to me. I smile, trying to be reassuring, but I'm not sure if she sees it because Fisher envelops her in a hug.

"The pool hustler herself. Good to see you."

Jack and Worth both stand and pull Rosey into a hug. I can see some members of staff behind us at the service station watching. We're going to have to figure out an explanation. Rosey and the guys exchange greetings and promises to see each other later, Rosey says she has somewhere to be, and I push down my disappointment at her not being able to stay.

I stay seated and offer a wave, then chastise myself. Am I being a dick by pretending not to be happy to see her? Should I have hugged her? Kissed her cheek like Jack did?

"See you later, Rosey," Fisher calls as he slides back into our booth next to me.

"Does she play a part in you being here?" Worth asks.

The question throws me for a loop. "What? I've known her for five minutes."

"I knew the first moment I laid eyes on Sophia," Worth says.

"Leo would probably say the same about Jules," adds Jack.

"Hardly," I scoff. "It took him years to realize what was right under his nose."

"Not really," Jack says. "You know he came home talking about Mystique that night after the party, saying how he might have met the love of his life."

"So you're asking if I've fallen in love with Rosey?" I mean to sound like it's the most ridiculous question anyone's ever asked me. But it doesn't.

My three friends all look at me, waiting for an answer.

"She's not looking to get into a relationship. And neither

am I. We don't see... whatever it is we're doing as... It's just not like that."

Words are coming out of my mouth, but I'm not really saying anything.

They all stay silent. Waiting.

"I like her, okay? I'm not denying it." Rosey has a way of making everything feel like it's going to work out. I don't know how she does it. "She's got a lot of shit to work out."

"Have you got shit to work out?" Worth asks. "Where was your family's ranch in relation to this building?"

I sigh. "It was a farm. An apple farm. It was down in the valley. It was demolished a long time before I came back."

"And building this is healing?" Fisher asks.

"A members-only resort is a really good business idea," I say, my voice a little guarded.

"Right," Worth says. "And you could have done it anywhere in the US. But you bought back the land your father gambled away and have built your kingdom in exactly the same spot."

I let his words settle.

"So sue me," I say. I don't understand why this is a problem for any of them.

"I'm asking whether or not it's helped. I'm your friend, Byron. It's not a criticism. I want to know if you feel better. If you've laid ghosts to rest. If you're ready for your future."

I lower my defenses. Worth isn't trying to hurt me. I know he isn't. But he's telling me truths I've been avoiding. I could have built the Colorado Club anywhere. But I settled on Star Falls.

"I think it's only now that I'm righting some of the wrongs in my brain," I say. "I avoided going into town for a long time. Last time I was here, my father's gambling habit was the center of all the gossip, and I hated the place for it. Now I see it a little differently."

"Differently how?" Jack asks.

"I think the people of Star Falls care about each other. I think they must have been horrified when the farm was repossessed. They weren't being malicious. Not most of them anyway. I labelled myself as Mack Miller's son as much as they did. I was running from something I couldn't get away from. I'm always going to be his son."

Fisher pats me on the back in a silent show of support. "So a place you've been running from has welcomed you back with open arms."

"And I'm back older and wiser."

"Are you back for good?" Jack asks.

I shake my head. "I don't know," I confess. All I can think about is what Rosey's plans are. Where does she see herself this time next year? Is she going to want to spend her life at the Colorado Club? We've never talked about her future. Only about her past. But I want to know. I want to know everything about her. At first I thought I had to resist her, but now I'm craving more and more of her. She's not a woman I *want* to resist anymore.

Since I'm not ready to get into all of that with the guys— at least not yet—I tell them, "I'll always need to spend chunks of the year here unless I sell the place."

The guys exchange looks.

"It's a damn good job we submitted our membership applications, then, isn't it?" Jack says.

"What?" I ask. "You guys didn't need to do that."

"We absolutely did," Worth says.

"You had me at *private powder*," Jack says. "Even if it's not Courchevel."

"My sisters will probably want to come, so it's a place

we can spend time together. I'm looking forward to it," Worth says.

I don't know what I did to deserve friends like this, but I know I'll never take these guys for granted.

"After I gave all that input into the recording studio here, there's no way I'm not bringing artists out here," Fisher says. "This is going to be the new Abbey Road. Except the view is better. I have an artist lined up, actually. She wants guaranteed privacy. This is the perfect spot."

"As long as she resists the call of the chicken wings at Grizzly's," Worth reminds him.

"Fuck," he replies. "My plans are in tatters. She'll have to break cover."

"I'm going to finance a delivery service between here and Grizzly's," I say, before making a note on my phone.

"That place should be nationwide," Jack says.

"Maybe I'll have a chat with them," Worth says.

I chuckle. "If there's a business opportunity there, I'm claiming it. This is my town." For the first time in a long time, I can say that about Star Falls, and feel good about it. *My town*. It has a nice ring to it.

TWENTY-SIX

Rosey

I head back to Autumn from Blossom, part thrilled to have seen Byron and part terrified. Gossip around here spreads like wildfire. I knew Miranda from concierge had changed her hair color before I even laid eyes on her this morning. There's no doubt the other waitresses in Blossom saw me embracing Byron's friends. By the end of the day, everyone will know. I need to come up with an explanation that doesn't include the words *I'm banging the boss*.

As I navigate the stairs to reception, I almost run into Patricia, who's scurrying toward me at lightning pace.

"Rosey," she says. "I heard you're tight with the owners' friends."

Wow. Move over wildfire and make room for the speed of sound. That was quick.

"Oh, not at all. I ran into them last night at Grizzly's—the bar in town. I gave them some change for the pool table." Both these things are true.

"Grizzly's?" she asks. "Do you go there a lot?"

"No, it's just kinda the thing to do after a storm. Everyone was going, and I've become friendly with the girl from the vet's office. She suggested it." I'm talking too fast, giving her too much explanation.

"Alright," she says, eyeing me suspiciously. "That's cool."

"Didn't expect to see them up here," I say. "Are you going to this all-staff town hall meeting?" I ask, trying to distract her.

"Of course I am," she says, and nods back in the direction she came from. We both head off together, and I can't help wondering if Patricia was just coming to find me to ask about my connection to Byron's friends. "Wouldn't miss it," she says. "I hear they're updating the move-in date for staff housing. The storm damage hasn't set them back as much as expected. I bet you're up here by the end of the week."

I should be excited about getting a space of my own—a place that's close to work that will provide an instant friend network. But there's one thing the staff accommodation won't have.

Byron.

I'll miss him. Yeah, the sex is great. Scratch that—the sex is spectacular. But I've never felt so open with someone. So free. It feels like I can't help but show him my entire soul, and he doesn't want to look away. It's a kind of intimacy I've never experienced before, and it's going to be difficult to say goodbye. For me, at least.

I'll get to see glimpses of him from time to time when I'm on shift. But I won't be able to trail my fingers all over his body. I won't be able to watch his ass as he cooks ragu.

The move will be the clean break I need. And what Byron needs too. It may not have been spoken between us, but we both know that whatever we have comes to an end when I move up the mountain.

"You okay?" Patricia asks.

"Sure," I say. "Just nervous about this meeting. They don't ask us questions, do they?"

Patricia laughs. "You've been quizzed by Hazel one too many times. No, this is a chance for us to ask *them* questions. I want to know if staff can expect our own gym facility soon. I figure it's good to have a healthy work force. It will benefit them in the long run, right?"

"Right," I say.

"Are you going to ask anything?"

I shake my head. I'm going to focus on not imagining Byron between my thighs, making me come. I'm going to try not to think about drinking hot chocolate with him, playing pool with him, the way he calmed me when we had to evacuate to the shelter. I'm going to try to imagine a time when we're not sleeping together. When we don't know each other anymore. And I'm going to do everything in my power to keep it together.

The ballroom has been set up with a raised platform and a row of chairs at the front, with folding chairs in arced rows for staff. Some managers are already on the stage, but I don't see Byron. Maybe he doesn't participate in these things, since he's not part of the management team. Patricia explained the other day that the managers all report to Hart, and Hart reports to Byron.

Hart comes to the microphone at the front of the stage and thanks everyone for coming. I'm half relieved Byron's not here and half disappointed I won't see him.

"First, we want to give you an update on the storm damage and how that impacts our opening schedule."

Various people come to the microphone and explain

how things will go over the next few weeks. There's furniture being stored in some of the conference rooms. This ballroom will be out of action for a period of time.

My mind wanders back to Marion, and how she's so brave to be talking about breaking free from living under Mom's strict rule. At her age, I wouldn't have even dreamed it was possible.

I feel a shift in the room, like someone is watching me. I glance up and my gaze catches on Byron, standing by the door, looking right at me.

My heart hiccups in my chest. I'm going to miss him more than I should when I move. I have to remind myself that we—whatever *we* are—only worked because there was always a time limit. I didn't feel he had power over me, because we weren't anything serious. If we'd ended up dating, things would have changed. Byron would have had expectations, and I would have had to comply. He's nothing like my mom or Frank, but it would have been inevitable. I was never going to be on equal footing with a man as rich and powerful as Byron—especially not while working for him.

Except as I look at him, I wonder if that's true. My heart tells me Byron's not that guy.

But even if controlling me and exerting his authority wasn't his intention, that's bound to be how it ends up. How could it be another way? He's the owner of the place where I work. I'm dependent on him for my paycheck. I don't want to be dependent on anyone.

Hart starts talking about staff housing, and I pull my gaze from Byron to focus on the stage. There's been another setback on some of the units, but most staff will be able to move in on Saturday. A little cheer goes up at the back of the room. Hart reiterates that not all units will be available.

They're looking for volunteers to delay their move-in date, and will pay some compensation to incentivize people.

More time at the cabin. Is that what I want?

I glance at Byron, whose steady gaze doesn't seem to have wavered. My body heats at the thought of more nights with him. In so many ways, I want that. I love spending time with him. I enjoy our time together. It was so unexpected, not what I was looking for at all. But with Byron, I feel like I can be myself for the first time... ever. There's no pressure. No expectations.

It's because there's a natural end date, I remind myself for the hundredth time. Things have been so good between us, I don't want anything to sour my memories of him. Byron's shown me what might be possible for me—what life could be like when I'm not simply there for everyone else's needs and desires. He's shown me I can be independent even while being with someone. I have to hold on to that idea, even though I can already feel my heart breaking at the thought of ending this.

I can't be a volunteer. I can't risk keeping Byron and me on simmer too long, and the pot burning. Better to walk away now, when I still have so much hope about what my future might hold.

Byron and I have hit our expiration date.

TWENTY-SEVEN

Byron

I've tried to stay focused on work today, but it's been tough. Rosey not volunteering to delay her move into staff housing was a surprise. It threw me off-balance a little, so I pushed it to the back of my mind to focus on the various problems that have been thrown at me all day. Now, as I drive back to the cabin, Rosey's decision comes flooding back.

Maybe I'm an arrogant asshole, but I thought she'd be the first person to volunteer.

I've always known things would shift between us when she moved up to the Club. It was bound to happen. I just didn't expect her to be so eager to make that shift.

I didn't come to Colorado expecting to find the kind of connection Rosey and I share. I've tried to resist it, but I've got both feet in now. I thought she felt the same way.

I pull up in front of the cabins and Rosey's sitting on the porch wrapped in a blanket. It's so cold. Why would she be out here on her own?

I get out of the truck and our gazes lock. I wander over

and she stands. I get to the top of the stairs and she opens her arms, stretching the blanket wide, and envelops me in a hug that shelters both of us in its warmth.

She rests her head on my chest, and I lay my cheek against the top of her head.

I sigh. I'm really going to miss this. I'm going to miss the way she smells like spring in the middle of winter. How she feels warm on the coldest of nights. She's so calm and considered in all the madness of the Colorado Club.

I lift my head. "I thought..."

She tips her head back to look at me. "I know. I just don't want to tempt fate. You know?"

I wince. No. I don't know.

"This is so good," she says.

"Agreed." So why change it?

"But it can't go on forever, right?"

I pull in a breath. I wasn't suggesting forever. But a few more days would have been good. Maybe from where she's sitting, that would just be delaying the inevitable.

"The guys said to tell you goodbye," I say.

She grins up at me. "They really love you. I can't believe they came out here and stayed in RVs."

They really do love me, and the feeling's mutual. I'm a lucky guy. I need to focus on all the incredible things in my life, rather than why Rosey doesn't want a few more days of what we have together.

"So Saturday morning, I'm losing a neighbor," I say.

"I'm really going to miss this," she says.

I nod, slowly. So will I. I don't know if I've ever walked away from a relationship and regretted it. I don't know if I've ever thought about an ex once they fit into that box. Maybe because what Rosey and I have doesn't feel done? I get the feeling Rosey is all I'm going to think of after Saturday.

"Wanna go to Grizzly's and eat wings?" I ask her.

"No," she says resolutely. "I want to stay here and drink hot chocolate." There's something about the tone in her voice I can't place. Maybe it's me, but she seems a little sad. "I'm going to miss our nights drinking hot chocolate on the porch." Yes, there's definitely a note of sadness in her voice.

I don't get it. If she's going to miss this, why didn't she volunteer?

We go into her cabin, make me a drink and refresh hers, then go sit on the porch swing.

"I heard from my sister today. She graduated high school nearly a year ago. She's desperate to go to college."

"That's great," I say.

"Yeah," she replies, but her *yes* says more than yes.

"Yeah?" I ask. I want to hear what she's thinking.

"My mom doesn't want her to go. She wants her to get a job so she can contribute to family expenses."

"You feel guilty because if your mom had your salary from the job at Frank's garage, your sister would be able to go to college?" I ask, trying to figure out why Rosey seems a little reserved tonight.

"No, I doubt she'd let Marion go either way. But if I were there... maybe she'd be focused on me and Frank, and what she could get from him. Her attention wouldn't be on Marion."

I don't know what to say to that. It's fucked up that she feels the need to shield her sisters from her mom. That she feels guilty for not taking the shots so they can escape.

"You want me to help with anything?" I ask.

She shakes her head. "No. I'll figure it out."

I want to help somehow. I want to make her feel better. Doesn't she see that?

She must read the disappointment in my face. "It's kind of you to offer," she says, "but I can't rely on other people for things. That's how..." She doesn't finish her sentence. She just shrugs.

I shift to face her. "That's how what?"

"I've never been independent. First my mom, then Frank. I've never made my own decisions about anything. I've never taken action that wasn't approved by my mom. I need to give the trailer back to Frank. I've made that decision and it feels like a big one." Her voice cracks and I want to pull her into a hug. This is clearly a huge deal for her.

"I'm not trying to influence your decision."

She nods. "I know. But I'm terrified that if we keep going like this, or if I let you fix my problems, I'm going to slip into a role where... I'm not myself."

"I don't want you to be anyone but yourself," I say. "I like you too much to want you to change."

"I know. The thing is, I feel like a toddler out in the world. I've spent my life trying to please my mom or at least avoid making her angry. I've bent and changed myself so much to fit her needs that I don't know who I am when I'm standing tall. I need to learn that."

"And you're worried you're going to bend for me if you talk to my lawyer, or if you spend a few more days in the cabin?"

She holds my gaze. We both know that her not volunteering to delay her move is circling our conversation like a hawk.

"This isn't about you wanting me to be different. I know you don't—you wouldn't. This is about me trying to second-guess what you want and make myself fit without being asked. I'm not saying I'd deliberately do that. It wouldn't even happen right away. But little by little, I think I'd change myself. To make you happy."

My heart sinks right into my boots. I hate that she feels this way. And although it's the last thing she wants, I want to scoop her up and make her feel better. I want to take all her years of hurt and put them back on the person who created them—her mother.

"You're a wonderful woman, Rosey," I say. "You shouldn't change for anyone."

She offers me a small smile. "You're the best man I've ever known."

I slide my hand into hers and we sit in silence, looking out into the dark.

A chill burrows beneath the blanket and I wonder if it will ever leave me. Rosey has been just what I need. She's helped me see the good in Star Falls. She's helped me fall in love with all the wonderful things about this town. That was the healing I didn't know I needed. There's a voice in my head that says I need her, too.

But life doesn't always give you want you want. I should have learned that lesson by now.

TWENTY-EIGHT

Rosey

My apartment in staff housing is clean and comfortable. Some people are complaining about the size of the rooms, but having spent most of my life living in a trailer, I feel spoiled having a bedroom to myself. There are built-in shelves and closets running along one side of the room, with the door to the bathroom and a double bed against the opposite wall. Between the two is a small green armchair, complete with a cushion shaped like a daisy and a low table beside it. The floors are polished wood, the view out the window a climb of a grass verge and the bottom of pine trees. It's not the view from Blossom, but I'll take it.

Is it weird that I can't shake the feeling that Athena disappeared just before I moved so I didn't have to feel bad about leaving her. Cats can't read minds, right?

I set my weekend bag on the floor by the chair and unzip it. It was Snail Trail's smallest size, but it's not even full. Everything I own is in this bag, plus one thing I don't. I pull out a Ziploc where I've put Frank's ring. Now that I've moved and it's clear I won't be returning to Oregon, I need to return this to him. That, and transfer the trailer back into his name.

I reach to place the ring on the small table near the chair, knocking the cushion off-center as I do. A small, white envelope with my name on it peeks out from behind the daisy.

I sit on the chair and pull open the envelope. It's a greeting card, illustrated with a picture of a cabin nestled among pine trees, a swing on its porch. My heart squeezes at the memory of sitting on just such a swing, on just such a porch, at just such a cabin, drinking hot chocolate under a warm blanket with Byron.

I open it tentatively, unsure whether I want it to be from Byron or not.

Happy memories. Be happy. B

I'm flooded with senses of loss and comfort at the same time. Byron must have snuck in here at some point this afternoon and hidden the card behind the cushion. I can't help but smile at the thought of him in here—risking being seen because he wanted me to have this card. From him. It makes the place feel more like home.

That's what it is now.

I work quickly, putting my toiletries in the bathroom and the few items of clothes I have in the drawers and the closet. I'm about done when there's a knock on my door. I snatch the card from where I've put it on the windowsill and slide it under the pillow on my bed before I take the four steps to the door and open it.

"Hi!" Eden squeals. "We're neighbors. Come see."

Eden's room is set up just like mine. Only the view out of the window is different—a slightly different stretch of knoll, and different tree trunks beyond.

"Aren't they nice rooms?" Eden asks.

"Really nice," I say. "Cozy."

"Have you seen the kitchen?"

Before I can answer, she pulls me out of the bedroom and leads me down the corridor to a room at the end. It's larger than I expected, and includes a pine table under the window and six chairs. "Six of us share the kitchen. There are two refrigerators though, and we have a cupboard each, along with shared pots and pans. Only one dishwasher."

"I'll take it," I say.

The blinds at the window are covered in pictures of daisies. The cabinets and counters are bright white.

"Should we have a cooking schedule?" she asks. "So one of us cooks every six nights?"

I wince. "I think that might get complicated. Maybe you and I could cook for each other once a week and the rest of the time we figure it out as we go?"

"Yeah, you're probably right. We'll all want to eat different things at different times because of our shifts and all. I got overexcited there for a minute. It's just I never had a big family, and it feels like this is what I'm getting being here," she says.

I laugh. "I was one of four sisters. Big family mealtimes were... not always fun." There was always a lot of arguing about everything, from who got the fork with the bent tine to who got drinks for the table. But there were some good times too. Mostly when Mom wasn't there. Every now and then we'd share a joke or reminisce about a funny memory—like the time Kitty decided she was going to make pottery ornaments and sell them to the fellow residents of the trailer park to earn enough money for a family vacation. Things hadn't gone to plan because she'd only made twelve dollars.

But the fun times never lasted. We were always squabbling soon enough, always trying to avoid Mom's accusa-tions of misconduct or pass them on if they landed on us. It was constant conflict.

"Well, let's make sure our mealtimes are fun," Eden says.

"I like that idea," I say with a nod. I like the idea of turning the negatives into positives. Of changing the future so it's nothing like the past, of unbending myself so I can stand tall. At last.

TWENTY-NINE

Byron

I sit on the porch, fixated on the empty swing next door.

I miss her. Maybe I needed a trip back to New York sooner than I thought I did. The opening of the Club is in less than two weeks. Maybe I could squeeze in a weekend back to Manhattan, catch up with the guys, shoot some bourbon. Have fun.

A meowing from underneath the cabin catches my attention. "Cat?" I ask. It couldn't be, could it? Just as Rosey leaves the cabins, Athena comes back? The creature probably feels sorry for my pathetic ass.

"Athena," I call.

Out of nowhere, a white ball of fur flies onto the porch railing, nearly giving me a heart attack.

"Jesus Christ, Cat, you know how to give me a scare."

Athena just meows, giving me a look that says, *You've mistaken me for someone who gives a shit about you and your heart.* My first thought is to text Rosey to tell her Athena is back. But I can't. I need time and space to move on. I'm sure she does too. Starting a conversation will pull us both back in, when what we need is to relearn what it feels like to stand on our own.

A car pulls into the driveway, stealing my attention. Nancy French emerges from the driver's seat.

"Hey," I call, hoping my voice hides my surprise.

"I brought you a pie," she says, lifting the edge of foil on a covered dish.

"Wow, that's great," I say, standing to greet her. I swear she's worn the same dark jeans and bright red bow in her hair since I was born. She probably dressed the exact same way since high school. "Thank you." I'm not sure what I did to deserve a pie, but I'm not going to complain. Hers is the best in the state of Colorado, regardless of what Mike says.

"Well, I do make a good pie, if I do say so myself. And I heard the girl next door moved out."

I chuckle. So the Star Falls grapevine is at it again. The pie is probably to soothe my broken heart.

"Can I get you a cup of tea? Or hot chocolate?"

"I'm not stopping," she says, sliding the pie onto the bench. "I just came to drop this off." She shrugs. "And check on you," she says. "It's been a while."

I nod. "Yeah, I've been in New York."

"Made something of yourself if you're building things like that." She nods up the mountain in the direction of the Colorado Club.

"I've been lucky."

"You've been more than lucky. You always were a hard worker. Never looking for a fast buck. Not like your dad."

The comparison presses against my chest. "I'd like to think I'm not much like my father at all."

She nods. "He wasn't all bad. Loved your mother and you. Loved this town. He just... had his demons. We all do.

They take over some of us. And some of us conquer them."
She says it in such a matter-of-fact way—like my father
didn't ruin our family when his "demons" meant we lost the
family farm.

"So we just chalk it up to demons and that's it?" I ask. It
comes out sharper than I wanted it to.

"What's the alternative, Byron? Stay angry with him
your entire life? Let that anger rule you? He's dead. Let him
stay dead."

"I'm not angry," I mumble. Even to me it doesn't sound
convincing.

"Is that what this *Club* is about? Proving to your father
you're better than him?" Her question hits me like a physical blow.

"No," I reply, with the tone of a surly teenager.

"You could have built that billionaires' playground
anywhere in the world, but you chose the town where you
were born."

She sounds like Worth. Don't they all know that I'm
rich enough to pay for therapy? I don't need it for free. "I
don't need to prove anything to my father. Like you said,
he's dead. Has been for a long time now."

"Let him rest," she says. She turns and heads down the
steps back to her car. "It's good to have you back, Byron."
She winks at me. "You might have run away from this place.
But there's no escaping a town that loves you. Don't be a
stranger, now." She slides into her car, toots her horn, and
then she's off. I didn't even get a chance to thank her for her
pie. Or the words of advice.

I stand on the porch, watching the driveway long after
Nancy has left. Athena is twisting and turning through my
legs like she doesn't actually hate me. Maybe she knows just
how good Nancy's pie is and she's hoping for a slice. I sigh

and pick up the pie before I lose it to the cat. I glance up in the direction of the Club, whose lights twinkle in the distance. It's as if it's saying hello to Star Falls, and the lights of Star Falls reply. They peacefully and harmoniously coexist.

I'd always kept track of what happened to the farm after I left for New York. I tracked it after it was put up for sale after my dad's creditors took ownership. It was run as a farm for a couple of years and then bought by a developer who didn't seem to get any of the necessary permissions to do anything with it. When I had the money, I approached the developer and bought it. I didn't even think about it. Maybe it was nostalgia. Maybe it was some kind of reach for a legacy. I just knew I wanted it—had to have it, actually. But maybe subconsciously I'd been wanting a home. Perhaps that's what the Colorado Club is for me—a home. Or maybe an excuse to come back to the one I've always had.

I grab my phone from beside the pie and dial Gary. I know he likes to catch up on everything once I've left for the day. It's one of the reasons I make sure I leave early— because he won't go home for two hours after I do.

"I have an idea," I say as he answers. "I want to throw a party."

There's silence from the other end of the phone. "You know we have a launch party in less than two weeks? You've been in on those meetings." He clearly thinks I have some kind of memory issue.

"This is a different party. And it's going to have to come together fast because I want to do it before the launch."

"Before?" His voice comes out strangled, like he might be mid-panic attack.

"Yeah. Like next weekend."

"And who or... what... is this party for?"

"For the people of Star Falls. No need to worry about invitations—I'll tell a couple of people in town, and everyone will know in no time." I chuckle to myself. I might not have been here in a long time, but some things in Star Falls never change.

THIRTY

Rosey

It's the first time I've been into Star Falls since I left the cabins and moved into my apartment. I haven't had a day off since. Even though the Club runs a shuttle bus into Star Falls every half hour, it feels like a long way away.

And I know it will remind me of Byron.

There's no escaping him. He's in every brick of the building I live in. He's in the diner, at Grizzly's. There are memories of him everywhere.

A few of us get off the bus at the same time. We're all starting to work shifts the closer we get to opening, and a few of us have a day off today. I recommended Galaxy Diner to a few of my co-workers, and some of the bar staff are going to check it out. I point them in the right direction as we get off the bus, and I head to the post office. Frank's ring is in my pocket. I need to mail it back to him. I haven't prepared a note or anything. I can't think of what to say. But mailing the ring to him still leaves the issue of the trailer. I don't know where to start with that. My mom has probably burned all my stuff by now, including the deed Frank gave me.

There's no line at the post office. I explain I'm mailing jewelry, and the woman behind the counter, who seems to be wearing a dead yellow bird in her hair, tells me how to package and insure the ring.

I fill out Frank's address on the padded envelope she hands me.

"Don't forget to put your address on the top left-hand corner on the front." She smiles at me like she's being helpful. But it's not helpful.

"Do I have to do that?" I ask. "Or can I just put down my name? I'd really prefer him not to know where I am."

She offers me a sympathetic smile. "You don't have to, but the postmark is going to give the town away. And there's no hiding anything in this town."

It's probably fine. Frank won't think twice about the postmark. He'll be so happy to get the ring back, I'm sure he'll just trash the packaging.

"You want the PO box?" she asks.

"It will be fine. I'll just put my address." It's not like he's going to get on a plane and try to change my mind. I humiliated him in front of his friends and family. Frank's not a monster. He's not going to send a hitman after me, either. And it's not like I'm alone in the woods. I'm living among loads of people. Putting my address on this package is no big deal.

Before I can second-guess myself, I scribble out Frank's address, my address, and stuff the Ziploc containing the ring into the mailer. I pay the bird lady and head out.

I exhale as I step out into the fresh Colorado air. I look up into the bright blue sky and smile. Sending back that ring feels powerful. I made that decision. Not out of fear—

which is what drove me to bolt from the wedding—but because I don't want to marry Frank. I never did. And he deserves the ring back.

I stuff my hands back into my pockets and head to the diner. As I pass by Snail Trail, I glance in, see Marge, and give her a wave. Her face brightens and she waves back.

I don't think I've ever felt so at home somewhere, despite living in the trailer park my entire life.

I get to the diner and slide into the booth closest to the door, avoiding the one I sat in with Byron, even though the view of the mountain would be better from there.

Rachel comes over, and I order a hot chocolate and the waffles with fresh berries without thinking twice. The description on the menu reads, *Because if it comes with fruit, it can't be bad for you, right?* I'm getting better at making my own decisions, though in fairness, waffles at the diner are an easy choice.

The door behind me opens, and I know without having to turn around that it's Byron. I close my eyes. Will he come over? Say hi? I so desperately want him to slide in opposite me and make me laugh. Make me see myself the way he sees me—someone with potential. A woman who could be with a man like him.

He places an order for hot chocolate, turns, and sees me. Our eyes lock and energy jolts through my body like I'm touching a live wire.

"Hey," I say.

His eyes search my face, like he's looking for instructions on what he's supposed to do now.

"You wanna join me?" The words are out of my mouth before I can think of the consequences. Do I want him so close by? And with staff from the Club in town, I don't need people to see me chatting with the owner like we're friends.

"I actually have to get to the vet to pick up Athena."

My eyes widen. "She came back? When? Where's she been?"

He grins at my tumble of words. "She's been pretty secretive about her movements since we last saw her. Can't get her to talk about it." He smooths his palm over his stubble, and I close my eyes in a long blink, remembering what he feels like.

We grin at each other like the other person is chocolate and we're desperate for a bite. I wonder how many people know this funny side of Byron.

Then the rest of his words register. "But she's at the vet. Is she okay?"

"She's fine," he says. "I got her checked out, vaccinated, and microchipped."

A smile tugs at the corners of my mouth. "You're going to keep her?"

"I made a promise," he says. "We'll figure it out."

I let his words seep in, staring at him as he stares at me.

Rachel calls Byron's name for his hot chocolate, interrupting us.

He takes his cup and raises it. "Have a good day, Rosey."

I watch him go and can't ignore the ache in my chest. I want to burrow deep in his plaid shirt and snuggle into him. I want to kiss him for so long, the skin on my face gets chapped and raw. I want to share hot chocolate and listen to his stories of New York. I miss him.

Rachel interrupts my pity party by sliding a plate of hot waffles in front of me. "You going to be at this party Byron's throwing?" she asks.

"What party?"

That's when she tells me about the party for Star Falls

residents at the Colorado Club. I glance out the window and see Byron heading into the vet. I can't help but smile. Good for him. Byron's stopped running. Slowly but surely, he's finding his way back home. It must be a nice feeling to belong to a place like this.

"Oh," I say. "I'm not really a resident anymore, I guess."

"Haven't you learned anything?" Rachel says, nodding in Byron's direction. "Once you're a resident of Star Falls, we're not so quick to let you go." She smiles at me. "I'm not sure whether I'll go. I don't want my boss to think I'm up there scouting for work. I did tell my niece in the next town she should think about applying. I hear the money's good, right?"

"Yeah," I say. "It's decent money, and the shuttle makes it easy to get into town."

"I told her about the bus. She's going to apply today. I hope she gets it. Byron's alright. He's probably a good guy to work for."

"He's a really good guy," I say. *The best I've ever known.*

AS I'M DIGGING into my waffles, my phone buzzes and Marion's face appears on my screen. My heart lifts. It's so good to see her.

I accept the call. "Hey, how's it going?"

"I found a locker at the library where I can leave all the stuff about colleges, so I don't have to risk someone finding it back home."

"That's great," I say. "Did you see your old guidance counselor?"

"Yeah," she says, sounding a little giddy. "I did. She says

she's happy to help me outside school hours. Can you believe it?"

"What else did she say?" I ask, thrilled that Marion has actually followed up on what we talked about. I can hear the excitement in her voice. "Does she think a scholarship is possible?"

"I have to apply. But she gave me things I can start doing to help with my application. It's going to take a lot of work. I don't know how I'm going to be able to do it without getting found out."

I see her issue. Mom will be in her business. She knows what hours she works, which friends she hangs out with. "Could you say you picked up a few extra shifts at the salon?"

"She might talk to my boss, or wonder why I'm not bringing home more money."

She's right. Mom has a way of finding out everything. Looking back, it was like living in a prison. I don't know why I stayed as long as I did. But I'm free now. I just want the same for Marion.

"What if you said you were doing some volunteering? You could say you were helping out at the library," I suggest. "They say the easiest way to lie is to stay as close to the truth as possible."

"You know what she'll say," Marion replies.

"Charity begins at home," we both chant.

I sigh. "Can you say you're hanging out with one of your friends?" She'll be worried they'll end up giving something away. "Or make up a friend. Someone new in town. There must be a way."

"I could pretend I got a second job."

"But she'd want some of your paycheck," I say.

"I could say I was saving up for something. Something for her. Maybe she'd give me a pass."

I blow out a breath. "I don't think she'll buy it. She'd want to know what, and then she'd be working out how much it would cost. You'd end up having to buy her the damn thing out of what little money you have left at the end of the week."

"Yeah, you're right," Marion says. "But I have to complete the applications and the essays. There's a lot of admin stuff I wasn't really prepared for."

"I know," I say. There's no way I'm letting my mom's need to control Marion stop her getting to college. "Maybe say that some of your friends are going to Applegate Lake for an overnight camping trip in the summer, and you want to go but you need to buy supplies. A tent and stuff. So you get the second job to—wait! I got it." I interrupt myself. "Ask if you can give her less of your paycheck at the end of every week, just until the summer. Tell her about the trip and how you can't afford it unless she lets you keep more of your salary."

"She might just kill me."

"When she goes crazy, suggest you can get another job. But say you want to keep the money from the extra hours because you can't fit many more in."

There's silence on the other end of the phone before Marion says, "She'll think she's so generous for not taking a cut, and she'll be relieved she doesn't have to give up any of my paycheck."

"Exactly," I say. "We're beating her at her own game. Manipulating her to get what we want."

"It could work. It's worth a shot." She squeals. "I knew you'd have a solution. You always figure everything out."

Her words take me by surprise. I've never seen myself as

a problem solver. If you listened to my mom, you'd think I was the root of most of the world's problems. "Thanks, Marion."

"I mean it. I miss you so much. Mom... she's worse since the whole wedding thing. She's constantly complaining." Then she bursts out laughing. "And the other day she suggested Lydia date Frank."

Her words are like a slap to my face. "You're kidding. Lydia and Frank?"

"Don't worry. I don't think Frank has any interest in Lydia. But that's her latest scheme."

We're all just pawns in Mom's game of chess to secure her own future. I don't know how I put up with it for as long as I did. I hope Lydia and Kitty find their way out. Or their way to me, like Marion has.

"How does Lydia feel about that?"

"She's going along with it. What choice does she have? I think the first thing Mom wants to do is get her a job at the garage."

Going along with it? My heart starts to ache at the thought of Lydia dating a man over twenty years older than her, just to keep Mom happy.

Lydia has a choice, just like I did. I only hope she realizes it before her wedding day.

THIRTY-ONE

Rosey

I stash the newly laundered napkins in the perfectly designed cubby and step back, pleased with myself. I've spent the last week learning the details of working in Blossom, because I've been moved from Autumn. It's a promotion. Kind of. I'll do half my shifts here and help out during special events, which comes with bonus pay. It's nice to be doing things on different days. I'll get to work with different people, meet different guests. I'm aware that I might not be here forever, but for now, I'm... happy.

I figure it will take some time to work out what I want to do with my life. Maybe I'll stay on as a waitress at the Colorado Club. But talking to Marion about her college applications has made me ask questions of myself I've never asked before. I don't know what I would have done after high school if I'd had the chance to choose. Would I have wanted to go to college? I knew it was never an option, so I never even fantasized about it.

Maybe I'll go to veterinary school. Or become an

English teacher. I've never thought about the possibilities because the future wasn't ever my decision. My mom said I would be a good receptionist because I was pretty. So that's what I did. Even when I stood in front of the mirror on the day I was supposed to get married, I don't think I understood all the choices I'd have in front of me if I left Oregon. I never thought of what was possible. Just what was *impossible*: marrying Frank.

As if my thoughts summon him, I see a figure in the doorway that looks exactly like Frank from the back. But it can't be.

Since my shift just ended, I head in that direction. When I get just a few yards away, the figure in the doorway turns—and I come face-to-face with my ex-fiancé.

"Frank?" It's a stupid question. It's obviously him. He looks more tired than I remember. A little older. His suit is a little rumpled and his tie a little crooked.

"Rosey!" His eyes are full of relief, but all I feel is heavy. Is he here to bring me back? Can he force me? Is my mom behind all this?

I glance around to see if anyone's spotted him. I'm sure non-employees shouldn't be wandering around this place. He probably shouldn't even be on Colorado Club land. I don't know how he managed to end up here, but he's going to get us both into a ton of trouble.

"What are you doing here?" My jaw is tight and my fists are clenched. I'm ready to fight for my freedom. I don't want to go back with him.

"I got the ring," he says, as if that answers my question.

I hurry past him. "Come with me." When we get to reception, I keep my head down and hurry out of the front entrance. We've been told we're not allowed to use this entrance once the Club has opened. But right now, it's my quickest route to get Frank the hell out of here. Not to mention, I need some air.

I lead him around to the side of the main building, toward the pathway that leads to staff housing. There are strictly no visitors allowed. The security risks have been drilled into us. Thankfully, the shuttle bus that takes staff to and from town pulls up in front of the staff block as we arrive.

"Come on," I say to Frank. "Let's get on this bus and head into town."

We let passengers get off. I get a few odd looks, but I just smile like everything is peachy, and try not to let it show that I'm in the middle of a mild panic attack because my ex-fiancé has turned up on my doorstep after I jilted him at the altar.

I usher Frank onto the bus and take a seat toward the back so the driver can't hear us.

"What are you doing here?" I ask. "How did you even get up here?"

"On this bus. I think they thought I'd come for an interview." He chuckles. "It's a nice place. Maybe I *should* get a job here."

I roll my eyes. Frank has his own successful business back in Oregon. He's not about to come and work at the Colorado Club. I just want a straight answer from him.

"I'm glad you got the ring," I say, trying to get him back on topic. "And I'm really sorry about everything that happened. I should have—" I don't want to hurt his feelings, so I don't tell him I should never have accepted his proposal. "I should have spoken to you rather than just running off."

His face darkens. "Yeah. It was a shock. I thought we were happy."

I sigh. I never gave him any reason to doubt me. "I'm very sorry. You're a really great guy."

He pulls in a breath. "Yeah, your mom said she thought you'd realize you'd made a mistake. She said you'd be too prideful to come back." He searches my face, waiting for me to confirm what my mom has said—what he's clearly hoping is true.

I glance at the bus driver. I really don't want to be having this conversation here. Or anywhere, ever. But I owe it to Frank. "I'm sorry, Frank. I regret hurting you. I really do. You've been nothing but kind to me. But I don't regret my decision."

He looks bewildered. Like he expected to waltz into the Colorado Club, sweep me off my feet, and take me home to Oregon. Like he thought I'd just been waiting for him to come and rescue me. Nothing could be further from the truth.

I try and block out the view from the bus. I don't want Frank to exist in Colorado in my mind—not even the memory of him against the backdrop of pine trees. This place is freedom to me, and I don't want anything changing that. "I'm sorry if that's why you came here," I say. "I sent back the ring because I should have never accepted it in the first place. I'm sorry if you interpreted that as me reaching out to you."

He presses his lips together, like he's trying to hold back from saying something. I'm not sure I want to hear it. It feels like a dark cloud has passed over the brilliant blue sky. A sense of dread gathers in my stomach.

"Did my mom say it was a good idea to come and visit?" I hold my breath, waiting for his response.

"When I told her you sent back the ring, she said it was your way of apologizing."

I don't think I've ever hated my mother more than I do in this moment. Looking back, it's easy to see how she manipulated and controlled me and my sisters. I just feel like a fool for not seeing it. For not breaking free sooner. It only occurs to me now that she didn't restrict her appalling behavior to her daughters. She'll do anything to get what she wants. Frank didn't deserve to be rejected by me a first time, let alone a second.

"I'm sorry she said that to you," I say. "The fact is, my mom wanted us to get married because you're rich. She saw you as a meal ticket."

He nods, like I'm not telling him anything new.

We sit in silence for a few minutes. Guilt for accepting his proposal, for not confessing to him what he was to our family, circles my chest and squeezes.

The bus pulls into the stop in town and we get off in silence.

"Let's go to the coffee shop."

Frank looks up and down Main Street. "It's small," he says.

I glance up at the mountains, jutting into the perfectly still blue sky, and wonder what he's talking about. Star Falls is huge. A place I can spread my wings. A place I can be me. This place is bigger than the entire state of Oregon.

The coffee shop—Twilight Latte—is on the corner opposite the diner. I pass it every time I come into town, but I've never gone in. Which is why it comes as a surprise that the *Twilight* in Twilight Latte is a reference to the movie phenomenon, not the time of day. There's no room for doubt when we push through the door. For a start, music I recognize from the movies is playing in the background. The barista is sporting fangs, and there's a life-size cutout of Robert Pattinson by the cash register. It distracts me from the fact I'm about to have coffee with Frank.

"This place is weird," he says from beside me.

"It's my first time in here." It *is* weird. But I can't help being kinda charmed by it. Nothing but respect for sticking to a theme.

We order our drinks—I insist on paying—and head to one of the smaller tables near the window. Pine trees have been painted around the edges, not to reflect our beautiful surroundings, but to mimic the backdrop of Forks, Washington—the setting of *Twilight*. This town is wild. And I love it.

I tamp down my smile and turn to Frank. "I don't want you to think I didn't want to marry you because I don't like you."

He lets out a rueful huff as if to say, *Then why didn't you marry me?*

"I thought that maybe we could move?" he suggests. "To a bigger house. Maybe one of your sisters could come stay with us." The hope in his expression kills me.

I upended this man's future and bruised his heart. He didn't deserve that. And even if he wasn't my choice, I should have had the strength to walk away before he got hurt. Why wasn't I stronger? Why didn't I stand up to my mother? I still haven't. I'm still running from her.

"You're a really good man, Frank."

He rolls his eyes. "So you keep saying. But what can I do? Just tell me. I'm not a man who's good at the... romantic stuff. But tell me what you want and it's yours."

I shake my head. "There's nothing you can do."

"Are you sure?" he says, his tone urgent.

Images of Byron fill my mind. Him grinning on the porch holding his hot chocolate. Him sitting across from me

THIRTY-TWO

Byron

I watch Rosey climb into the shuttle bus with a man I've never seen before. I know I have no right to feel jealous, but that doesn't stop it. Who is that guy? He's older than her, and not a local, but they clearly know each other.

"They're ready for you now," Gary calls. "Everyone's having coffee in the ballroom."

"The ballroom?" I ask. My head is fuzzy from the number of beers I drank at Grizzly's last night, but I'm pretty sure I said I wanted this meeting in the Peak Room. I've invited some of the people I've known the longest in Star Falls for a meeting. I have a proposal for them, and I want to hear their concerns. I owe them that.

"No," he says. "Not the ballroom. The room adjacent to the ballroom. The one with the views."

The Peak Room. I pull in a breath and head down. We've definitely picked up some more applications from the people of Star Falls since I stopped avoiding town. I don't know why I stayed away for so long. These people don't hate me or pity me. They just *know* me.

I open the door to find the Peak Room full of around twenty people, coffee cups in their hands, chattering away. No one pays me the slightest bit of attention. I can't help but smile. There's not a room in the Colorado Club I've walked into and been ignored—not when those rooms are full of people here at my employ. But I like this feeling. It sums up Star Falls. Not one person is more important than anyone else.

I grab a cup of coffee and see Walt coming toward me.

"Hey, man, this place is gorgeous. The views are incredible."

"You should know. You've lived here your whole life."

He chuckles. "But I don't know if it's the windows or the lighting in here or what, but it looks more magical than usual."

"Same place, different perspective," I say.

"Right," he says. "So what're we all doing here? I know we're not here for the coffee because, between you and me, Twilight Lattes does a better job."

I clutch my chest. "You're killing me."

"You know you're only going to get the truth from me," he says.

"I'm counting on it." I slap him on the back and clear my throat. "Thank you for coming, everyone," I say, raising my voice to get everyone's attention.

People turn toward me, and I gesture for everyone to take a seat. My assistant has set out chairs in a circle. I don't want to stand at the front of an audience. I'm not of the boss of the people in this room. Some of them have known me since I was born. I can only hope to be their equal.

We take our chairs.

"Beautiful place," Jim says. "You've done yourself proud, Byron."

"Thanks, Jim," I mutter. A man like Jim telling me he's proud of me shouldn't hit as deep as it does. But it's as close as it gets to hearing it from a father.

"That one of Juney's paintings?" he asks, nodding toward one of her canvasses. I hadn't realized Rosalind decided to put one in here, but it looks good.

"It is."

He nods, and a smile curls one side of his mouth. He pats me on the back before taking a seat.

"Thanks for giving up your time today. I know you're all busy. I hope not too busy to come to the party we're hosting on Monday night." People murmur amongst themselves.

Donna's hand shoots straight up. "What's the dress code for this party?" she asks. "Is it fancy?"

Shit. I should have known that was a question people would have asked. There's no doubt that in the eyes of the people of Star Falls, the Colorado Club is fancy. Hell, I hope in most people's eyes it's fancy. *Relaxed* fancy, but given the amount I've invested in this place... "The dress code for Monday is, if it's good enough for Grizzly's, it's good enough for here."

Cheers go up, and smiles light up the circle of familiar faces. I'm glad I cleared it up. I'd hate to think people might have stayed away because they didn't think they could wear their jeans.

"I wanted to bring you all up here today because I know a few of you have been concerned with the way the Club has fenced off the boundary to the property."

Mumbles around the circle tell me Jim's not the only one with concerns. "I understand that this is land you've all considered *yours* for your entire lives."

Nods and rumbles of agreement ripple through the circle.

"As you all know, I grew up on this land. Not this far up the mountain—down at the foot. I bought back the land because I understand the beauty here. I want to preserve it. So you should know that other than the trees we've already cleared for skiing, there are no plans for more buildings or any other changes to the landscape. I want the Colorado Club to be a place where people can experience the beauty of a place we've been lucky enough to grow up with. I don't want to change that."

"If they're rich," Eva shouts out.

I glance around at the people gathered. Do they all feel like that?

"It's a good point," I say. "Anyone who's a member of the Colorado Club has to be wealthy. That wealth will ensure we can take care of this land for many, many years to come."

The air almost prickles with indignation.

"But the other thing the Colorado Club does is bring opportunity to Star Falls. I left town for a lot of reasons, but leaving allowed me to spread my wings. I didn't have to follow my father's footsteps, or travel to earn a living. The Colorado Club gives the next generation of Star Falls a way of taking opportunities without having to leave a town they love. They can stay here and still plow their own path. I'm hopeful the Club will breathe new life into the town, give people more reasons to stay. I don't want to spoil anything— not the environment, and not our town."

Silence spreads across the room like a blanket.

"What about the fencing?" Jim asks.

I nod, wanting to address the issue head-on. "I have a dilemma here, because as I've said, you have to be wealthy to be a member of the Club. The membership list will be small. This isn't a huge resort where there will be thousands of people passing through. The Colorado Club will be a second home for a lot of its members—a place they can escape to. Members want peace. They want unspoiled beauty. They don't want to be one of a thousand people on a mountain. We have a good number of celebrities signed up already, and they want to guarantee their privacy. Sometimes their wealth will attract attention they don't want, which means security is of paramount importance."

"The mountain should be for everyone," a guy I don't recognize says from next to Jim.

I nod, wanting people to feel free to express themselves. But I haven't finished yet.

"Ultimately, I don't want to cut the people of Star Falls off from Club land. But access has to be limited. To that end, I want to open up much of the land one weekend a month to residents of Star Falls. You'll have to show proof of residence, but you will be free to roam during that weekend."

"So all that stuff about security and anonymity was just a bullshit excuse?" the same guy says.

"No," I say. "During that weekend, members will know they might come across residents of Star Falls. They will be offered additional security, and we'll have an increased staff presence generally outside of the main building."

People start talking to each other.

"And that's not all." An image of Rosey's smile comes into my head. I have to blink to push it away. She'd love this next bit. I wish she were here. I can almost feel the way her hand would smooth over my chest, the press of her lips against my cheek. I clear my throat and try to push her away. It's getting more difficult, not less, to forget her.

"As you know, my family owned the orchard at the bottom of the mountain. At the moment, the border of the Colorado Club on the southeast is the border of my family's farm. I'm going to change that. Most of the apple trees are still producing fruit, and I think it's kind of a shame that those apples—which are delicious—are going to waste. I'm going to move the border of the Club so the land my family's orchard stood on is excluded. And then the orchard will be run as a working farm again, the profits of which will be donated to Star Falls. It will create additional jobs, and you never know—Star Falls might get its own brand of cider."

I glance around to see people's reactions. My gaze settles on Bryan Tessay, arms folded, same scowl on his face he's worn for the last thirty years. He used to be my father's right-hand man until he lost his job after my father's death.

"We'll need your help," I say to everyone, but looking at Bryan.

He nods. I know Bryan well enough to know that's him giving me his stamp of approval.

I take a few minutes to steady my breathing and swallow past the lump in my throat. "I'm happy to take questions or chat about any other concerns."

"Are you just saying this so you get more applications for all these jobs you have?" Sue Johnson says. "Someone told me you just want to recruit waitresses and bar staff."

There's no such thing as a secret in Star Falls. If anyone knows every skeleton in every closet, it's Sue. "Recruitment was a real issue for us a few weeks ago. Luckily, we've seen an increase in the number of applicants. From people in Star Falls, but also, from surrounding towns. I think word has spread, and I have you to thank for that. At the moment, recruitment isn't a problem. I want to maintain a great relationship between the town of Star Falls and the Colorado

Club. I want us to coexist and work together to ensure the survival of... of our town." New York will always be in my blood, but Star Falls is who I am. I don't know how I've denied it for as long as I have.

"Yeah, well. We want that too," Sue says. "I like your idea about the orchard."

The air in the room shifts. Around our circle, shoulders drop and jaws unclench. Even I sit back in my seat.

"I presume access to the land doesn't include the slopes?" Nancy asks. She's grinning, like she knows the answer I'm going to give, but she has to ask anyway.

I chuckle. "I'd be very happy to receive a membership application from you," I say. "If you meet the criteria, I'll personally approve it and we'll welcome you to the slopes."

She shrugs. "It was worth a try."

I answer a couple of questions about job security, and whether or not members will use the shuttle bus. After that the meeting breaks up. Jim and Sue are the last to leave.

"You know, it's not like I'm going to be lining up every first Saturday of the month to cross into Colorado Club land and walk Jenkins," Jim says. "But it sure is nice to know that I can." He slaps me on the back. "You did good, son. Keep it up."

I try to swallow past the lump in my throat. The people of Star Falls don't care that my father was a drunk who gambled away my family's farm. They just care about me—because I'm one of their own.

THIRTY-THREE

Rosey

As the Uber pulls into the trailer park, the urge to run is far greater than it ever was when I was stuck here. I know for certain there's nothing my mom can do to make me stay, but that doesn't stop the panic rising in my chest. I can't catch a breath and my palms are slick with sweat—sensations I only realize were familiar now that I've been away from this place. I lived my whole life here in a state of anxiety. Now that I know what it feels like to live in Star Falls without those feelings, I can't fathom how I coped all these years.

The car pulls to a stop and I want to ask the driver to keep the engine running. A conversation with my mom is inevitable, but I'd do anything to avoid it. I just want to dash into the trailer, grab my stuff, and come right back out again.

"You getting out?" the driver asks, pulling me from my panic.

I grab the door handle.

I'll be back in Colorado in just over twenty-four hours. I checked into my motel on the outskirts of town straight from the airport. Tomorrow morning, I'm meeting Frank to sign paperwork. After that, I can leave and not look back.

There's a small deck on the front of the trailer, but the single chair Mom likes to sit in to see what's going on in the park is unoccupied. I glance up at the darkening sky. It's about to pour with rain. She'll be inside. Part of me hopes she's out, though it's unlikely. She rarely leaves the trailer. I have a niggling feeling that although I don't want to see her, I need to face her. Maybe because I need her to see that I've broken free of her lies and manipulation.

I'd like to see Lydia and Kitty, but I don't know if they want to see me. The burden of Mom's demands will be heavier for them since I've left. They'll probably resent me, and I don't blame them. Still, I want to show them life can be different to how they imagine it's always going to be. They can break free, just like I have.

I walk up to the deck, knock three times, and open the door. The familiar orange scent of Mom's favorite air freshener sends me right back to my childhood. I scan the living room and there she is, watching the TV as always.

She knows I'm there—there's no missing me—but she doesn't greet me. She doesn't even turn to look at me.

"It's you," she says, emotionless, not taking her eyes from the screen.

"I came to collect some things." I manage to keep my voice steady.

"And where the hell have you been? Embarrassing the family like you did by running off on your wedding day."

Embarrassing the family? She means embarrassing *her*. She doesn't care about what happened to Frank or what drove me to run out on my wedding. She cares about herself and only herself.

"You don't need to know where I've been," I say. I know

it will rile her that I'm being so rude, but I can't help myself. In Star Falls, I've tried to forget about her, block her out of my thoughts. But there's no escaping her now. She's here, and she's a monster.

The door to the bedroom I used to share with my three sisters opens and Lydia comes out, followed by Kitty and, finally, Marion. My heart lifts in my chest but sinks lower than it was before when I see the fear on their faces. They look so young. So vulnerable. They glance at Mom, unsure whether they're allowed to speak to me. If they do, there's no doubt they'll suffer the consequences.

"It's so good to see you," I say, looking at my sisters. I try to keep it together, but I want to bundle them out of here and take them back to Colorado with me. I don't want them to waste any more years doing what Mom demands of them. It's more obvious than ever that despite the lack of bars, we lived in a prison. They're still living in it.

Love surges in my chest for these young women who still have so much living ahead of them. I want to hug them. But doing so might create more difficulties for them when I leave. Mom will punish them. A huge wave of guilt for leaving them all here crashes over me. I should have been looking out for them. I should have been protecting them.

"They don't want to see you," Mom barks.

I glance back at my sisters to find their expressions say something very different.

"I haven't changed my number," I say. "I'd love to hear from you."

"They have you blocked," Mom spits. "We all do. You left this family the moment you ran out on us."

I try to keep my expression blank, but inside it's hard to hear what she's saying. I know how she is, but *who* she is remains the same: this is my mother. There's a tiny part of me that hoped she'd see me today and remember she loves me.

I face my sisters. I don't want to engage with Mom. There's no point. She'll twist my words, try to make *me* the monster.

"I didn't run out on you. I just knew I couldn't marry a man I didn't love to keep Mom happy." My voice is calm but small. It feels so grating to be speaking against her like this, in front of her. We'd all complain to each other about her, but we always went along with what she said in the end. We didn't feel we had any choice. But for the life of me, I don't understand why I stayed as long as I did when I became an adult. I didn't have to give her my paycheck. Why didn't I just keep it and find my own place?

Because she was my mother and I thought it was her job to do what was best for me. I thought it was my job to do what she told me.

I was wrong on both counts.

"I miss you," I say, looking at all my sisters.

Marion's eyes are glassy. I don't want her to cry. I don't want any of them to face the consequences of missing me too.

Unless.

Unless.

Unless I could encourage them to break free as well. They've all finished high school. None of them have to be here. I can't scoop them up and bundle them into the back of a cab, but maybe I can give them hope.

I glance back to Mom, whose gaze is stuck on the TV. She's so mad, she can't even look at me.

I look at my sisters, trying to convey, without words,

how much I love them. I have to tread a tightrope. I want to show them how good it feels to be independent, but at the same time I don't want to make their lives more difficult when I leave.

"You don't have to stay here," I say to them, not looking at my mother.

"Exactly what I was about to say to you," my mother hisses, suddenly coming back to life, as if she knows what I'm saying threatens her. Like she thinks there might be a chance my sisters will listen to me and break free from her. "Why are you here anyway? I've burned all your things. There's nothing left for you here. Just get out."

Even though I've always known my mom can be cruel and nasty and hurtful, I don't think it's until this moment that I realize she doesn't love me. Not like a mother should. She doesn't love my sisters either. If she did, she wouldn't lash out like this. She's not concerned about how I'm feeling, where I've been, how I've been surviving. All she cares about is herself. Aren't all mothers supposed to love their children? Mom doesn't love any of us.

Of course she doesn't love me. She can't. It's not in her.

The last thread of attachment I have to this woman withers and dies. A deep sense of sadness settles over me. It's grief for the mother I should have had.

"You deserve a happy life," I say to my sisters, pushing down the feelings of betrayal I feel straining to get to the surface. "You don't exist to serve this woman, even though she's your mom."

"I thought I told you to get out." She switches off the TV and turns to face me.

"I will not," I say, meeting her eye to eye for the first time since I arrived. "I own this trailer. For now. I can stay as long as I like."

I've never spoken to my mother like this. Never stood up to her, stood against her.

She narrows her eyes like she's just waiting for the right time to strike back, then she snaps her head around to my sisters. "Get back to your room. You don't need to see this."

Marion scuttles off back into the bedroom. It hurts, but I can't blame her. She's sweeping up hair at a salon. She's the only one who might not be able to afford her own place, even without giving up most of her paycheck to Mom.

"Mom," Kitty cries. "Don't be mean to her. She's our sister."

"She's no daughter of mine," she spits. "She always was a troublemaker. She's a little bitch. She's probably been sleeping in a bus shelter since she left here. She's got a snowball's chance in hell of surviving. And that's what she deserves. Hell!"

I laugh. I can't help it. Years of pent-up frustration just spills out of me and it comes out as laughter. I don't know why, but she seems so pathetic, spouting off the most awful things about her daughter. A daughter who's devoted her life to her.

It's so clear to me. The lack of love and care is every-where. It's not that she's selfish and mean and cruel. She doesn't love us. Doesn't care if we live or die. A part of me dies at the realization, but the rest of me is free—truly free.

"Do you see it?" I ask Kitty and Lydia. "You only exist to serve her. If you escape, she doesn't want to know you. Because you no longer serve a purpose."

"That's right," Mom interrupts. "That's why they're here. With me. You can get out."

"Is that what you want?" I ask my sisters, ignoring Mom. "To be stuck serving a woman who'd disown you as soon as you do something she doesn't like—like try and create a life for yourself?"

Panic and fear fill Lydia's and Kitty's faces, but they don't flee to the bedroom. Part of them wants to hear this.

"There's a way out. And I can help you," I say. I'm sure I can get them jobs at the Colorado Club. What's left of my savings could get them cheap flights out to Colorado. It would be tight, but I could do it. "It's frightening. I get it. But when you're ready—when you see what she's really like and you decide you don't want to put up with it anymore—I'll be waiting."

"That's it, get out of this house." Mom stands and moves toward me. I don't need to know what happens if I say no. I've said what I came to say.

"I'm sorry," I mouth to Lydia and Kitty. I need to leave. I haven't gotten my things or even the papers to the trailer that I came for, but I'll have to figure out another way. There's no way I can force my way into the bedroom and start going through things. Even if I technically still own this trailer, my mother will find a way to punish me or my sisters. I hadn't planned for things to go like this, but I know I've done the right thing. I've given my sisters an alternative to the life they have. Hopefully, I've planted a seed, given them something to think about, convinced them that life beyond this trailer and Mom is possible.

Mom steps toward me, and I back away. She grins, like my acquiescence fuels her power—like she's only happy when I'm weak. Except I'm not. Not anymore. Because I've found a place where I'm free of her.

I bolt out the door, sick to my stomach with the scent of orange and the hatred in my mother's eyes.

I get to the bottom of the steps and am about to head to

the exit to call a cab when something catches my eye. I turn my head to see Marion at the window. She's waving furiously at me. When she sees I've spotted her, she points her fingers down.

I can hear my mother shouting inside the trailer. Marion drops the curtain and disappears.

I glance down where she was pointing and see something on the ground, outside the bedroom window. It looks like she's dropped a bag of something—two bags of—

I race over and realize Marion has stuffed my belongings in trash bags and dropped them out the window. Mom didn't burn all my stuff. I don't know if she thinks she did or if she was bluffing, but Marion saved this for me.

As quick as I can, I gather up the spilled items. I don't stop to examine anything, but it feels like I'm stuffing an entire lifetime of memories into two shopping bags. School pins, greeting cards, the odd certificate. A high school diploma. I pick up the bags and scramble to the exit of the park before I call an Uber. I don't want there to be a chance Mom figures out I have everything I need from that trailer. There's nothing more I want from her.

In the car back to the motel, I pull out a dream catcher I made for Marion when she was born. I hold it to my chest. When Mom was pregnant with Marion, I couldn't wait to have a baby sister. I was desperate for someone of my own. Someone to love. Kitty and Lydia had been born when I was too little to understand what was going on around me. When Marion was born, I used to wake up and feed her in the night. I liked when it was just the two of us in the dark. I'd tell her stories of princesses and knights in shining armor, dragons slayed and fairy-tale castles. I sang to her. I rocked her. I loved her. I was the mother to her I never had.

I have the chance to care for Marion and all my sisters again—to be what they deserve, instead of what they were born into. I can't hand-feed them freedom, but at least today I got to tell them how it tastes. When they decide to venture past the walls Mom has put up around them—both literally and figuratively—I'll be there, waiting on the other side.

THIRTY-FOUR

Rosey

On the shuttle bus back to the Colorado Club, I can't stop looking at my phone. I'm desperate for one of my sisters to call or text me. I just want to know they're okay, that Mom calmed down after I left. There's still a glimmer of hope in me that she'll learn from her mistakes, or be slightly kinder to them if she worries they'll follow in my footsteps.

I step off the shuttle bus outside the Club and slam right into someone, dropping my bag and my phone at the same time. "I'm sorry," I say, gathering up my things.

Whoever I bumped into crouches down and picks up my phone. As soon as I see his hand, I know who it is.

Byron.

We stand, and I tip my head back to look at him. I feel myself unfurl and relax under his gaze.

"Everything okay?" he asks, concern in his voice.

I don't know how to answer that. Everything's okay and nothing's okay and now he's here and he seems... different.

"I just got back from Oregon."

He raises his eyebrows in surprise. "How was that?"

I sigh and realize how much I miss him. I miss porch swings and hot chocolate. I miss talking and kissing and feeling safe.

Byron never tried to control me. Despite being my boss, he had no agenda other than being with me. Maybe I'm confused. My emotions are running so high at the moment, Byron's familiarity seems like a safe harbor. But is that all he is?

"It was a lot," I say.

He takes my bag from me. "Did you see your mom?"

I nod. "Yeah." I let out a breath. "And my sisters. I feel so guilty for leaving."

"And Frank?" he asks.

"Him too. I mailed him back the ring, but I had to sign some papers to transfer the trailer back to him."

His Adam's apple bobs as he swallows. "How was that?"

"Frank's a good man. It was fine. I hope he finds someone."

"That person still isn't you?" he asks.

"That person was never me."

Our gazes lock. I want to tell him how much I miss him, that he came to mean more to me in a few short weeks than Frank ever did.

"I heard about the party tomorrow night," I say. I want to tell him I'm proud of him, but something stops me. "It's a great idea."

"If anyone shows," he says. He nods in the direction of the staff housing block and we begin to walk.

"Of course they'll show. This town loves you. They want to support you."

Hope brightens his face. I want to press my palm to his

cheek and tell him everything is going to be okay. I've never felt so certain that things are going to work out.

"Are you working tomorrow?" he asks.

"Yeah," I reply. "I've been moved into Blossom and events." We reach the door to my building and stop to face each other.

He nods. "Good. Are you happy?"

My heart clenches. Does he mean with my job? Or does he mean without him?

"Could we find some time to talk?" I ask without thinking. I just don't want this to be the last conversation we have. I'm not quite sure what I want to say. But I know there are things that *need* to be said.

"Now?" he says, glancing around.

I shake my head. Seeing him has stirred something in me. I need to figure out what before we talk. "No. Maybe... after the party? We could meet in town."

He nods, but he's uncertain. "We can do that."

"Breakfast on Tuesday?" I suggest. I don't start work until midday. "Eight?"

He searches my eyes but remains quiet. Voices from behind us interrupt and he hands me my bag. "Eight at the diner."

He goes to leave and I catch his arm, a familiar buzz passing between us. We lock eyes. The chemistry we had is still there. But now it's something more.

"Thank you for the card," I say. It was kind and thoughtful and asked nothing of me. It just said he was thinking of me. "It's one of the nicest things anyone has ever done for me."

"Oh, Rosey," he says, his tone full of sadness.

My stomach lilts at the way he says my name. "Don't

feel sorry for me. I'm so lucky, Byron." Lucky to know him. Lucky he's standing right in front of me.

People are coming toward us. We need to end this conversation. We both know it. But I don't think I'm strong enough.

"Until Tuesday, Rosey Williams," he says.

A smile curls around my lips at the way he says my full name.

His smile matches mine, and I have to look away. It's too much. Whenever he's near, I always want more.

He turns and heads back down the path we just came from. I open the door and I turn to watch him down the path. He's just about to step out of sight when he turns back and sees me watching him. I can't help but laugh at getting caught.

The smile I see spread across his face tells me he knows exactly what I'm thinking.

THIRTY-FIVE

Byron

I know Hazel is talking at me, I just can't hear what she's saying, My mind is too full. I check my watch again. Six twenty. The first shuttle bus with guests for the town party should be on its way by now, ready to arrive for six thirty. But there's another bus that will leave from behind the library around now. I have no idea if there'll be anyone on either bus.

I shouldn't care. If no one turns up, I'll save money on booze and I can head back to the cabin for an early night. The thing is, I do care.

Kathleen messages me, asking me where I am. I reply I'm in the ballroom and instantly she appears.

"Byron, hey, I have some good news for you."

Is she about to reveal she's got the ability to teleport?

"Your chalet is ahead of schedule," she says. "And before you complain that I've prioritized it over some of the member chalets, I haven't. They're all ahead of schedule. We had a shipment of the marble we're using in the bathrooms come in early. So you'll be able to move in before the grand opening."

Her eyes search my face, waiting for my thrilled reaction. I haven't told her about my change of plans yet. She'll either be delighted or pissed beyond measure.

"Thank you, Kathleen," she deadpans, "you're amazing. I'm going to give you a bonus for finishing my chalet early."

"Sarcasm doesn't suit you."

She shrugs. "But it fits like a glove. What are you about to tell me? I know it's something I'm not going to like."

I glance at the door, willing people to arrive. "I've just bought some land," I confess.

"You want to build more chalets?" she asks.

"I'm not quite sure what I want to build," I reply. "There are two cabins on the land at the moment."

"Is it guest accommodations?" she asks.

I pause. When I made Beth and Mike the offer for the two cabins, I didn't think much past getting the land. "No," I say. "The land is just on the outskirts of town."

She draws back. "Really? Well, what are we building?"

"A home," I say. "For me." As soon as I say it, I realize that's exactly why I bought the land. I didn't want to be up here on the mountain, onsite at the Colorado Club and always the boss. I want to be home. In Star Falls. I glance at the door, wondering if anyone is ever going to arrive.

She sighs. "So you're never going to live in this chalet I just killed myself getting ready on time?"

"I'll need a place while you build my new place," I say. "And I'll keep it to host my friends and their families." There's no way I'm letting the New York crew pay for membership.

Kathleen sighs. "If that's what you want."

The chatter of voices wafts in from the corridor and my insides clench. God, I hope more than two people show up.

Jim is the first to step inside, Sue at his side—followed by about thirty other people. Waitresses offer trays of beer and champagne. There's also a full bar.

Where did all these people come from? They couldn't have all fit into one shuttle bus.

"Hey, Byron," Jim says, approaching me. He hands me a beer, and I take it.

"You came on the shuttle?" I ask.

"Most of us. I left a line of people behind me too," he says. "And a few people drove."

My shoulders drop from where they had risen to my ears. "That's good. People are here."

"Of course they're here." Jim pats me on the back. "Everyone wants to see what you've been doing up here and drink free booze."

I don't care why they're here. I'm just happy they came. The people of this town have given me a lot. I'm glad I can give them something in return. Even if it's a night of free booze.

"You're a son of this town," Jim says. "We want to support you. Show you we'll be there for you." He pauses. "You just gotta let us."

I look at the small crowd laughing and chatting, the twinkling lights of Star Falls sparkling in the windows behind them. These are the people I belong with. This is why I bought Beth and Mike's land. I belong in the valley, not up here on a mountain.

Sue envelops me in a hug. "I'm so proud of you," she says. "So very proud."

Her words touch something deep inside me. I shouldn't

need someone to feel proud of me. I'm a man. I've made a fortune from nothing. But it feels good.

"Thanks," I choke out.

"Now, what's happening with you and that nice lady in the wedding dress?" she says.

"Dear god, none of us have seen her in the wedding dress since that first night she spent in Star Falls," Jim replies. "It's not like she's wandering the streets dressed as a bride." He rolls his eyes. "She doesn't want her past following her around like that."

It's my turn to pat Jim on the back. He's so protective. It looks like Rosey's earned her place in Star Falls, too.

Sue rolls her eyes like she's used to Jim complaining about her. There's obviously been another shuttle bus drop-off, because more Star Falls locals start to file into the ballroom.

Juney spots me right away.

"Byron!" Her eyes light up when she sees me. "I'm so excited to be here. I can't believe—" She puts her hand over her mouth and shakes her head. Her eyes fill with tears. I get another back slap from Jim. "I just can't believe you bought so many."

"You're a talented artist. We have something of yours in every chalet," I say. I'd almost had to force my designer to visit Juney's studio, but as soon as she got there, she was spending my money faster than the water falling over the rocks that gave Star Falls its name.

"You don't know what it means to me," she says. "You've bought more from me than I've sold in my entire career combined."

"That only tells me the rest of the world is missing out on your talent," I reply. "I should put you in touch with my friend Fisher. He knows a lot of agents back in New York.

He might be able to introduce you to someone who could give you a bit more recognition."

Juney's eyes go wide. "That would be great. I met Fisher, didn't I? At Grizzly's a couple of weeks back."

"I hear he's been quite the inspiration," Sue says.

I glance between her and Juney, not clear what she's saying.

"I don't know what you mean," Juney says, a blush creeping up her neck.

"From what I heard, you've been painting a lot of naked torsos since the storm."

She rolls her eyes. "I paint everything."

"Well, Fisher's coming over for the opening. Maybe I can reintroduce you two then," I say. I might also be playing matchmaker.

"Perfect," Sue says, before Jim lovingly guides his wife toward the bar.

"He's single. But a committed New Yorker," I say.

"Just ignore Sue," she says. "She doesn't know what she's talking about. I'm not painting your friend."

I might not have spent a lot of time with Juney in the last fifteen years, but I know a liar when I see one.

"What about you, Byron? Has Sue married you off yet?" she asks.

It's then that I see Rosey across the room. She's carrying in a tray of beers. She looks beautiful, her hair swept back off her face, her eyes sparkling as she offers people drinks and familiar greetings.

"Not yet," I say.

"Well, I think you need a nice woman with a big heart. Like the woman you came to Grizzly's with."

I shoot her a look that says, *You're not being subtle.*

Juney shrugs. "I don't know a lot about a lot of things, but I can spot chemistry a mile away."

There's no doubt in my mind that Rosey and I have chemistry. But that's not enough. She works for me. She's fresh out of a big bag of shit in Oregon. She's not looking for a relationship. Especially with a man who's her boss.

My mind starts to reel through possibilities. Maybe next year when things have settled for her. Maybe she could get a job in town rather than at the Colorado Club. But I can't suggest that. This job comes with a roof over her head. And she's good at what she does—she's already been promoted.

I miss her. I want our nights back on the porch. But as much power as I have, I can't get everything my own way.

"Well, thanks for the tip," I say to Juney. "I'll bear it in mind."

"Make sure you do, or the women of Star Falls will have to take matters into their own hands."

"What does that mean?" I ask.

"Fuck around and find out, Byron."

"That sounds like a threat."

"It's meant as a promise."

I chuckle. I might have changed her life by buying up her artwork. I might be a billionaire New Yorker. But around here, I'm still going to be the guy Juney went to high school with, the running back on the football team, the boy who ran away to New York—and a son of Star Falls. For the first time in a long time, I'm okay with that. That's my legacy. Not my father's.

Rosey turns and catches my eye, then heads toward me with the tray of drinks. Juney swoops one up. "Thanks," she says and heads off, leaving me and Rosey alone in a sea of people.

"Great turnout," she says. "You must be delighted. Want a beer to celebrate?"

It takes my brain a minute to register what she's saying. I just can't stop staring at her. The way her kindness seems to radiate from her, the way her skin gleams and her eyes dance in delight at seeing me.

"Yeah." I swipe a second beer from her tray. "You look lovely," I say, because I can't *not* say it. Something about Rosey pulls the truth, the most authentic me, out of myself.

"Thank you," she mumbles and her cheeks pink. "Are we still on for breakfast tomorrow?" She glances around as if she's checking that no one's heard about our illicit plans. No one seems to have taken any notice of us. Although there's no doubt most of Star Falls will have registered the conversation. I'll get more shit from Juney and Sue next time I see them. All part of the charm of Star Falls.

"I wouldn't miss it," I say. I'm not sure why she wants to meet. Maybe it's just a friendly catch-up. I don't care. However I get to spend time with Rosey, I'll take it.

She bites back a smile and the sparkle in her eyes is back. I'd like to think part of it's about the thought of our breakfast tomorrow.

THIRTY-SIX

Rosey

It's hours since the party for the people of Star Falls finished. Even longer since I saw Byron. I don't know if he left early because he got called away on some urgent business, or maybe he was meeting a date. There are a hundred scenarios vying for space in my head, which means I can't sleep.

I check the time on the clock by my bed. It's ten minutes before midnight. There are only eight hours until I'm going to be sitting across from Byron at the diner, but it feels like it's going to take three months for those eight hours to pass.

I don't know if I can wait.

I sit up in bed. I *can't* wait.

There's a shuttle down to Star Falls that leaves the Club in ten minutes. If I run, I could catch it. I could be down at the cabins in twenty minutes.

I push the covers off and start pulling on some socks. There isn't enough time to change completely. I'll just put my coat over my pajamas. I grab a hat, a scarf, my phone, and keys, and I head out.

I exit the staff accommodations and I can see up ahead the bus pull up to the designated spot. No one's waiting. I hope it doesn't leave early because no one's there. It won't be expecting passengers. There are no late shifts at the moment outside the party, and we all got off hours ago.

I don't even know if Byron's in the cabin, but it's worth a shot. I can't wait another minute to tell him how I feel. I run to the bus, but it pulls out before I get to it. I race behind it, trying to catch up. The driver must see me in the mirror, because the bus jerks to a halt and the doors hiss as they open.

"Hey," I say. "Thanks for stopping."

"I thought this journey would be a waste of time," he says. "You going into town?"

"I just want to stop by Beth and Mike's cabins," I say.

"Sure thing," he says. "Although they won't be Beth and Mike's cabins for much longer."

"How come? What's happened?"

"I heard they sold them to the guy who owns this place. Byron Miller, is it?"

The mention of his name sends sparks of electricity dancing over my skin. "He bought them?" I don't know what it means, if it means anything. Maybe it was just a good investment. But it feels like it means something. Something important.

The lights in the cabin are on when the bus pulls up.

"Do you want me to wait?" the driver asks.

"I'll be fine. I can Uber back if there's no one home."

"Right you are." He gives me a quick salute and the doors hiss closed. The bus pulls off, leaving me standing in front of Byron's cabin. But the lights are on in the cabin where I stayed, not Byron's. Maybe someone else is renting? I climb up Byron's porch, ready to knock on the door of the darkened cabin, but I pause. I can't hear any signs of life at all.

What am I doing here?

If I wake him up, he's going to wonder what the hell I'm doing. We're due to meet in a little over seven hours. And I'm in my pajamas. It's not my best look.

I pull out my phone and double-click the get-me-out-of-here also known as Uber app. Just then, there's a noise over at my old cabin.

Byron stands in the doorway wearing plaid pajama bottoms and a white t-shirt stretched over his muscled torso.

We lock eyes from across the cabins. "Rosey?"

"I just couldn't wait until eight," I say, as if that explains everything. "I have all these things I want to say. And I'm sorry I woke you but—"

"You didn't wake me," he interrupts. "And I want to hear all the things you want to say."

"You weren't asleep?"

He lifts his hand to scratch the back of his head. The hem of his t-shirt lifts, exposing his stomach. I want to talk about important stuff, but his body? It has the ability to distract me from a nuclear war. "Way too much on my mind," he says, breaking my focus on his abs. "I'm making ragu. Want some?" A sexy smile curves around his lips.

I definitely want some ragu. Especially if "ragu" is a euphemism for something else entirely.

I scramble down the steps to get to him and he meets me halfway.

"You moved?" I say, glancing back at his old cabin. But I don't wait for a response before I say, "I went to Oregon and I figured all this stuff out and I want to tell you about it.

Because it involves you. You and me. And I realize... so much now."

He gives me a small smile, scoops up my hand. It feels so good to be touching him, to feel his hand in mine. It feels safe and secure. He's protective without being controlling. I see the difference now. We head into the cabin as if all the time since I've moved out has been erased.

"Come inside and tell me everything."

He heads to the burner and turns off the heat.

His skin against mine feels so right. Warm and safe and solid. I've never experienced Byron as controlling or selfish. He's always let me do what I want to do. I've met his friends and seen how they love him—as much or more than this town does. I've been expecting him to be like the people around me in Oregon, but I'm not in Oregon anymore. I'm right here in Star Falls, Colorado.

My life changed forever the day I was supposed to marry Frank. Because I met Byron.

"You want some hot chocolate?" he asks.

I just want you, I want to say. I manage to hold back. "Sure." That should give me room to breathe, time to organize my thoughts. I glance around and see Athena curled up on the floor by the fire. She opens one eye, sees me, but goes back to sleep. Cats.

I take a seat on the couch and he sets about heating milk in the pan and taking mugs from the cupboard. He's calm and considered, like me turning up in the middle of the night telling him I've been to Oregon happens every last Tuesday of the month.

"How come you couldn't sleep?" I ask.

"Tell me about Oregon first. That's why you're here."

He's right. I'm stalling. I just don't know how to start. "I saw Mom and my sisters."

He turns, catching my eye. "You okay?"

"Yes. I mean, no." I sigh. "Kinda. It was tough to leave my sisters. But they're all adults. They have their own journeys to take with my mom. I can't force them to break free."

He sighs and turns back to the stove.

"I can only decide what *I* want. What *I* do. And..." And what? I decide I want Byron? What if he doesn't feel the same way? He has his reasons for not wanting anything serious.

He drops marshmallows into the two mugs and brings them both over to the couch. I take the cup from him and our eyes lock. I want to kiss him. I want him to hold me. I want to skip everything before the *really* good part. But I owe us both more.

"That sounds... logical," he responds.

"And I want to stop running."

His eyes widen slightly. "So you're staying in Star Falls?"

I can't read him. Is he happy? Disappointed?

"I don't mean running away from Oregon. I mean running away from... everything. When I left Mom and Frank, I wanted my freedom. I thought geography would solve that problem, but of course, it's never that simple. I thought if I could keep myself separate, stay on an island, I'd be okay. I'd be free. But the opposite happened. Being on an island is isolating. It's lonely."

Sadness shadows his face and he reaches for my hand. I realize that he cares. Really cares. About Star Falls and the Colorado Club. And maybe about me.

I glance up into his eyes. "Freedom doesn't mean being on an island. It's making decisions that feel good for me. Decisions that are right for my hopes and dreams for the future. I thought I had to shut down any vulnerability, stay on my island, so I didn't fall back into the pattern of doing things for other people—so I didn't end up marrying a man I didn't love, or having a life I don't want to please someone who doesn't care about me. But I figured out that being vulnerable wasn't the problem. The problem was—is—my mom." I slide my mug onto the table beside the couch before I spill it. "I came to Star Falls thinking I had a choice: be alone or be controlled. But being with you... it's shown me a new possibility."

"Me?" he asks, his expression confused.

"You're kind, Byron. And caring. And you seem to want me to want things for myself. You sent me that card. Why? It wasn't going to do anything for you. You took in Athena. You let me move into staff housing. You didn't insist I delay my move-in date. You didn't even suggest it. And I know we haven't known each other very long, and they might seem like little things to you. But to me, they're everything. You let me be me. You like me for me."

"I told you, Rosey—I don't want you to be anyone but you."

I pull in a breath. Being this close to him is comforting, reassuring. And I miss it. I need to pull the trigger now. I need to ask for what I want. It feels so jarring to be so selfish, and there's a real possibility that we don't want the same things. But I'm so clear that Byron is who I want. I'm not sure I'll ever have this clarity again. So if I don't start here, asking him for what I want, I never will.

"Like I said, I know we haven't known each other very long, and I know you have the Colorado Club and it's stressful and all-consuming. I know you're not based in Star Falls forever, and I'm just some girl who got on an airplane for the first time less than a month ago, and you probably normally date sophisticated New Yorkers who were born in

Paris and vacation in Sorrento—" I groan. Why would Byron pick me? Any woman would be a fool not to want him. He could take his pick.

I tell myself it doesn't matter—the important thing is I tell him I want him, not that he wants me back. The power is all in the asking.

"What I'm saying is that I know it might not be mutual, but I don't want to give this up." I glance at his chest, unable to look him in the eye. "I really like you. Like, really *more* than like you. I don't want to only see you for a second or two in the hallways of the Club or once in a while at Grizzly's. I want to curl up with you at night. I want to hang out at the diner with you on a Sunday. I want you all the time." My voice has dropped to a mumble. But I got it all out.

I clasp my fingers together, my eyes on my hands, waiting for the letdown. Waiting for him to tell me I'm a nice girl and everything but—

He reaches under my face and lifts my chin.

"I think you're incredible," he says. "Everything you've been through and you're here, one hundred percent yourself, making yourself vulnerable." He shuts his eyes in a long blink, like he's having to steel himself. "I think you're the strongest person I know. And the most beautiful. The kindest and... and sexiest. And I've really, really missed you."

I don't think I'll ever be able to look away from him. I don't want this moment to end. I don't want him to get to the *but*.

"It's tricky," he says. "Me being the owner. You working at the Club. I think we can figure it out."

My eyes widen. I didn't hear a *but* there.

"And you're right, my plan isn't to stay in Star Falls

year-round," he says. "We can figure that out too. Nothing stays the same. We'll have to navigate the changes together."

No *buts*. Where are the *buts*? I need him to jump to the goddamn *buts*, because otherwise I might just die of hope.

His mouth curls up at the corners and his eyes sparkle at me. "I think I knew the moment you walked into Grizzly's that you were it for me," he says. "Worth knew. He saw it in me. But I needed you to pick me for me, to know for sure that you weren't going along with things." He pauses and narrows his eyes. "I didn't realize that until tonight, but you turning up here, telling me you want me—it's all I needed. We can figure the rest out."

I sit up straight and take his head in my hands. I'm not sure if I'm dreaming, but if I am, I hope I stay asleep. I press a kiss to his lips, and we crash against each other like lovers who've been separated months rather than days.

I just know I never want to be without him again. Not days, not hours, not a goddamn moment.

He pulls away, and for a fleeting second, doubt creeps back in. Until he says, "I know this is soon, but I need you to know..." He holds my face, our gazes locked, lips swollen from our kiss. "I love you, Rosey Williams. I think I did from the moment we met."

All doubt disappears, melting into my past where it belongs. All I can focus on now is my future. With Byron. "I love you too," I say.

THIRTY-SEVEN

Byron

Nothing has ever quite felt so right as saying *I love you* to Rosey and hearing it back. It's like when the last piece of the jigsaw puzzle fits into place and you can finally see what the picture is. Everything I've done in my life has led up to this moment. I feel so fucking lucky to have found her. I've made peace with so much in my past by being here. A big part of that has been seeing Star Falls through Rosey's eyes. She's shown me the town through fresh eyes and she's helped me see how the town sees me.

Meeting Rosey and starting a life with her is only possible because I've managed to close a chapter on my past, which means I can finally open a new one.

"I didn't know if you'd laugh at me," she says, her breaths coming short and sharp as I pull her pajamas over her head. I can't get her naked quick enough.

"I'd never laugh at you," I say, tugging at her pants.

"But turning up in the middle of the night. You might have thought I was crazy."

I pull my t-shirt over my head. "*I* was going crazy, thinking about you."

She sighs, relief rolling off her, and presses her hands to my chest. "I've missed you so much."

Naked, we stand facing each other and pause. This moment feels big. We're stepping over a line and nothing is going to be the same ever again. But it also feels entirely right.

"I love you," I say.

"I love *you*," she replies. "And we're going to figure it out so we can date. Maybe I can get a job at Twilight Lattes or—"

She stops as I pull her toward me. "We're going to be together," I say. "Forever. And we'll figure it all out. You don't need to work if you don't want—"

"I want to work," she says quickly. "I don't want to be with you so I don't have to work." She looks horrified that I might think such a thing.

"I know," I say. "I just want you to be happy. With me. I want to give you everything."

Her eyebrows pull together like she hasn't got a clue what I'm talking about. "I'm always happy with you." She says it like no other possibility exists. Like she could only ever be happy with me. Something within me that's been churning for years finally settles. She creates a peace in me I never knew I was missing.

I smooth my hands down her back and cup her ass. "I want you," I huff out.

A small smile curves around her mouth. Then she leads me into the bedroom. I was happy to fuck her bent over the couch, but she's a woman who knows what she wants and isn't afraid to tell me—to show me. And that's what I love best about her. She's found her voice with me. I hope that means I'm as good for her as she is for me.

She sits back on the bed, pulling me over her. I glance down at her, feeling a sense of satisfaction that she's mine. Finally. And forever. I've never been so sure about anything or anyone as I am about Rosey.

She slides her legs up either side of me. I'm so hard, I might explode as soon as my dick hits her wetness.

"Let me taste you," I say.

She lets out a small sigh in response, threading her fingers through my hair. The sound is like her fist around my dick, it feels so good. I work my way down her body, trailing my tongue over her hot, smooth skin—tasting and sucking, breathing her in. She's mine now. *Every part of her* is mine. I chant as I work my way down, "Mine, mine, mine."

"Yes," she cries out. "I'm all yours." She's not giving herself to me because she has to, but because she wants to. I know I'm a lucky man. I'll spend my life being everything she needs me to be.

I graze her puckered nipples with my teeth, savoring her moans, wanting to shout out loud that I have this woman. Forever.

I work my way down her body with my hands, my mouth. All the focus is supposed to be on her, but every time she moves, blood rushes to my cock. Her hips undulate under my hands as I try and hold her still. The idea of her being so turned on that she can't keep still fills me with a power even making millions of dollars can't come close to matching. Giving this woman pleasure is all I need to feel good.

I drag my hands down her thighs and push them open. I groan at the sight. She's so wet, she's glistening, like her pussy is flirting with me, inviting me in. I dive in, sliding my tongue through her folds. She's slippery, like just the thought of me tasting her sends her body into overdrive. She's hot and drenched. I want it all.

I eat her up like I'm starved, like I can't get enough—I'm greedy. We have forever, but I want to be all over her now, now, now. Her muscles tighten underneath me far too quickly. I want to feast for hours. She comes on my tongue, chanting my name.

I've been successful a long time in this world, but now, with Rosey under me, I feel invincible. The money and the power fade into the background. All that matters is her. Being here, in this tiny cabin on the edge of the prettiest town in the world with her, is the most important place I could ever be.

She sinks into the mattress and I crawl up the bed so I'm next to her. She reaches for me immediately, like she's trying to get closer. Her hands snake down my body and she grips my cock.

"Rosey," I say on a sigh.

"I'm shaking, I want you so much. I just came and all I can think about is how much I want more. I want you endlessly and forever." She looks at me, panic in her expression.

"You have me," I say, smoothing my hand up her side.

She nods, reassuring herself. "Yeah."

She kneels beside me and takes me deep in her throat, right to the back, rocking back and forward, getting deeper and deeper with each movement. I think I might have died right then, it feels so fucking blissful. I fist my hands and let out a guttural groan. "Fuck, Rosey." But I want more too. Just like she does.

As she releases me, I reach for her and encourage her to

shift so she's over me, her pussy over my face, my dick in her mouth.

Fuck, now *this* is something I'm never going to recover from. The taste of her on my tongue and her swallowing my cock. I reach around her, pulling her ass down, so I can get deeper. She whimpers at the flick of my tongue and the sound vibrates around my shaft. Jesus fucking Christ, how did I ever think I could give her up? It's pleasure times infinity and I swear to god, if I'm still alive in the morning, I'm going to wake up a different man.

A changed man.

She's mine, but I'm hers.

We're all tongues and fingers and mouths. Giving, taking, pushing, pulling. It's desperate and needy and erotic, and I've never felt so close to anyone as I do to Rosey right now. Our bodies fit, and so do our minds and souls.

Her moans are needy around my cock, the reverberations pushing pleasure from her into me. I pull her over my mouth and I reach deeper with my tongue and fingers—everywhere. I feel the start of her climax crawl up her body, and it unleashes something in me and we come, desperate, panting, together.

But it's still not enough. I need to be inside her.

I grab a condom from my table, roll it on to my hard cock, flip Rosey to her back and plow into her without warning. It's urgent. Desperate. Maybe I'm claiming her. Maybe I've just missed this. Maybe it will always be like this between us.

"Yes," she cries out as I slam into her. It's hard and fast and merciless.

"You like that?" I know she does, but I want to hear it.

She nods, effusive, like she's worried I might stop if she's not clear. "I like asking you for what I want, but I like you taking what you want too," she pants out. "Because I want what you want."

I tense my jaw and I push against her tight walls. "I know," I say. "I want what you want too."

We're perfectly in balance.

Sweat sheens my body and I brace up on my arms. I want to watch her. Watch what I do to her. See how defenseless she is when she's like this. How defenseless she allows herself to be because she feels safe. She *is* safe with me. I'm here to protect her. To love her. To fuck her.

I press her thighs wider, desperate to get deeper, wanting to mark her, to fill her. I want to fuck myself into her. I want to come inside her, to have her full of me.

I've never had this feeling before—like an underlying knowledge that we're at the start of a journey that will last longer than either of us. We're just at the start of us, and whatever we'll become.

"I love you," she whispers, like she can hear every thought.

I slam into her again and she screams. I hold her still, keeping her in place so I can drive deeper and deeper.

Her head tips back and the convulsions of her climax shimmer over her body, but I keep fucking, keep pushing into her, until I erupt, my orgasm rolling through me like a tornado.

I collapse on top of her and she wraps her limbs around me like she's worried I might leave.

There's no chance of that. I'll never go anywhere without her. I've never been surer of anything in my life.

I push myself up and realize she's shaking underneath me.

"You okay?" I ask her.

Her breaths are still coming short and fast, but she nods.

"It's just a lot. It's intense. I love you so much and you make me feel so much, even when you're not fucking me. And when you are..." Her eyelids flutter open and closed. "It's perfect."

I growl and pull her into my arms. "You're perfect."

"We're perfect," she says, and I press a kiss to the top of her head.

Star Falls. The Colorado Club. It all led here. And *this* is perfect.

THIRTY-EIGHT

Byron

My assistant tried to convince me to wear a suit tonight, but I just can't. Not even without a tie. The Colorado Club isn't New York, and I have no desire to turn it into New York. This is a place to escape to—even on opening weekend. I've traded the plaid shirt I wore the night I was in Grizzly's and a runaway bride walked in and sat down beside me, because I've worn it every day since Rosey came back to me. I figure it's lucky because the Colorado Club is open on time. Instead, I've gone for the cable-knit sweater that Rosey says is her favorite of mine.

"You look handsome," Rosey says as she comes out of the bedroom of my chalet. This is our home for now, until we can get a place built on the site of the cabins. As long as we're together, I don't think it matters where we live. "You excited?"

"Yeah," I say. "It's going to be a long weekend."

"Did you win the argument with your party planner

about not having fireworks?" she asks. I roll my eyes and she laughs. "They're used to New York, Byron."

"I guess. It was such a stupid idea. Setting off fireworks in the woods? Sending every living thing in the forest into a tailspin and starting a fire?"

"They clearly haven't seen the Star Falls sky at night. They don't realize the Colorado Club doesn't need anything else."

I nod, grinning at her. Rosey's appreciation for my hometown has let me see it through new eyes. She's changed everything for me.

"Where's Athena?" she asks.

"She left about five minutes ago. She can tell when we're heading out. Doesn't want to risk being shut in."

Rosey laughs and I feel the sound deep in my bones. It's a sound I hope I hear until the day I die.

"You ready?" I ask.

She's changed into her waitressing uniform and is looking around the kitchen counters.

"I just need to find—"

"I got it." I hold up her water bottle.

Her face breaks out into a grin. "You made me my water bottle?"

"I unscrewed the lid and turned on the faucet, if that's what you mean."

She pulls at my waistband. "You thought about me. You knew I needed my water bottle and you got it for me. It's kind. And I love you."

She lifts up on her toes and presses a kiss to my lips. I glance at my watch. If we had a little more time before people were scheduled to arrive...

She swipes me on my ass. "Don't even think about it. I'm due on shift in seven minutes. And seven minutes with you just won't do." She steps into her shoes, pulls on her coat, and takes her water bottle from me. "Besides, you have a party to get to."

We have some ground rules at work. We don't speak when we're on site unless we're in the chalet. We don't ignore each other, but we don't chat, or say, "Honey, can you pick up some milk?" There's no evidence of our personal relationship at work. But people know. I've told Hart. Rosey's told the people she works with. It's not a secret. But I've also told them Rosey doesn't expect any special treatment.

The chalet is on the far edge of the resort, so we take the golf cart to the staff entrance. As usual, there's no kiss good-bye, but as she gets off, she turns to me and says, "Have the night of your life. You deserve it." She flashes me a smile and heads off to her shift.

I know she means it. She's rooting for me every step of the way.

Members and potential members have been arriving all morning. I've been on site all day, shaking hands and smiling. There's nothing more for me to do.

Cocktails are being served in the lounge in ten minutes. I head there so I'm the first to arrive. But as I take the steps down from the lobby, I see a group of people have beaten me here. Five guys I'd do anything for are sitting around one of the low tables by the window.

"Byron!" a woman's voice says from behind me.

I turn. It's Efa, Jules by her side.

"This place is so—it's incredible. I don't have the words. I want to move here."

They pull me into a group hug and it feels like family. A pang of regret hits me in the belly. I wish Mary could be here. I haven't been close to my sister since we were kids—

since I left Star Falls and we started living separate lives. But having spent some time here and reclaimed this town, I think about her more often. I sent her an invitation to this weekend, but she couldn't make it. Maybe she will another time.

Fisher's the first of the group to hug me. Instead of cracking a joke—which is usually how Fisher greets me—he just whispers how proud of me he is. It hits me like a mallet, and I have to blink back tears.

"We wanted to ensure we were the first to your party," Bennett says. "Nothing like standing in an empty room wondering if anyone's going to show."

I chuckle. Doesn't matter how much money we have, we're all human.

"And by the way," he adds. "There's no fucking way this place qualifies as a hotel under the terms of our bet. You're going to make a killing in this place, but you're fucking disqualified from our arrangement."

"And that's why Bennett always wins," Jack says. "Because he decides the rules."

"Exactly," says Bennett. "There's a lesson in there for you."

"You've left Manhattan twice in a month," I say, greeting Jack. "Proud of you for expanding your horizons."

I expect him to say something about how he'll have to stay on Lennox Hill for the next three years to make up for it, but instead, he says simply, "Wouldn't have done it for anyone else."

God, I'm a lucky bastard. All my friends—the family I chose—are here, celebrating with me.

"Where's Rosey?" Worth asks.

"She's working," I say. "It's all hands on deck." We talked about her attending as my date, but she didn't want to create any awkwardness among her colleagues. Tonight is work. For both of us.

"Have you talked about what happens when you come back to New York?"

I pull in a breath. "Yeah," I say. We've done a lot of talking over the last week. All we know is wherever we'll be, we'll be together. Rosey knows she doesn't want to be a waitress her entire life, but she doesn't know what she wants to do yet. Neither of us is in a rush to get to the next part of our lives, so long as we're together.

"I thought when all this is done tonight, we could go into town," I say. "Drink some beer and shoot some pool at Grizzly's." I've arranged for the place to be open late and the bar's free from ten. I'm hoping the people of Star Falls will help me continue the celebration of the Colorado Club's opening.

"Grizzly's wings?" Fisher says, his eyes popping out of his head. "Hell yeah. That's music to my ears."

"These wings better be good," Leo says. "That's all we heard about on the way over."

"Yeah, the wings are the best you'll find," I say. "But they're not the best part of Star Falls." The people are. I'm hoping Fisher feels the same—about one of the people of Star Falls in particular. I know for a fact Juniper French will be at Grizzly's tonight.

I push my hands into my pockets, my fingers brushing the velvet ring box I stuffed there before leaving the chalet. There's only one thing that could make tonight any better—when Rosey says she'll be my wife.

EPILOGUE

A month later – New York City

Rosey

I face the floor-to-ceiling bedroom window. It's like I'm looking at a picture or something. I still can't believe what I'm seeing—the Chrysler Building, the Empire State Building, the East River. The entire city is laid out in front of me like I'm in an art gallery. I can't even drag my eyes away to watch my fiancé as he comes into the bedroom—and that's saying something, because there's not much that can keep me from ogling him.

"It's like you have an enormous picture of New York in your apartment."

"Our apartment," he corrects me. He stands beside me and circles his arms around my waist. "You look beautiful."

"It's your apartment," I say. "I just arrived twelve hours ago."

"You're right," he says. "We'll move."

I laugh. Byron's so keen on giving me anything and everything I want, it's comical. If I didn't love him so much, I might be tempted to take advantage and have him cart-wheel down Broadway naked. It's funny, but it's also like being wrapped in cotton balls and cashmere. I've never felt so safe. I just hope I make him feel the same way. That's what I'm aiming for—to show him the love he shows me. We both know we feel it, but I've learned from a lifetime without it that love is a *doing* word. I don't want a day to go by when Byron isn't sure that I love him.

"We don't have to move," I say.

"I want you to feel like this is *our* home."

I pause. I don't want to upset him. It's not that I don't think I'll be happy when we're in New York. But it's so vast, so busy. I'm not sure I'll ever feel entirely at home here. "Star Falls feels like our home."

He buries his head into my neck and kisses me, tightening his grip on my waist. I know how this one ends. I put my hand on his, about to encourage him to release me, when the buzzer to the apartment sounds.

"Are you ready?" I ask.

"I should be asking you that question, but nothing's going to prepare you for this."

I'm excited about seeing all Byron's friends in New York. I've met most of them already, but it will be interesting seeing them outside of Colorado.

As we head out of the bedroom, Worth and Sophia are coming toward us.

"Brunch!" Sophia yells as she opens her arms and sweeps me into a big hug. "So good to see you. I'm so excited you're here."

I can't help but grin at her infectious enthusiasm. "I'm excited too."

"This is your first time in New York?" she asks. She looks incredible. Her hair is swept up in a high pony and she's wearing all black. She's so stylish. For the first time since I sat at the bar at Grizzly's, I feel self-conscious about what I'm wearing.

I glance down at my denim skirt and white blouse. I must look like a country hick. "Can you tell?"

Sophia fixes me with a stare. "Don't you dare do that. There's a place for everyone in New York. You don't have to look a certain way or dress a certain way or be a certain way." She winces. "Well, maybe you do to fit in certain circles, but no one who matters cares about any of that. We care about *who* you are and how much you love Byron. Not about what you're wearing—which is very cute, by the way."

Anxiety gathers in my throat. "I do love him."

"Good," she says, taking my left hand. "That ring is completely beautiful. He did such a good job."

I wiggle my finger, the round diamond solitaire sparkling in the sunlight. "He did."

Byron puts his hand on my waist. "Everything okay?"

I nod a little too enthusiastically.

"New York can be intimidating," Sophia says in explanation. "The key thing is not to let yourself get sucked in by the assholes who spend their time trying to out-dress, out-talk, out-lifestyle everyone."

"Hmmm," Worth says. "You're right. There are a lot of people in New York who compete with each other about..."

"Stuff that doesn't matter," Byron says. "The six of us were always focused on business. We didn't notice any of the other noise."

Worth nods. "Are we all the same?" he asks, just as Fisher walks through the door, with Jack following behind.

"Jack notices," Byron says.

"What?" Jack asks.

"You notice stuff the rest of us don't—like the shoes people are wearing and whether their last name is a family that came over on the Mayflower. That kind of shit."

Jack is intimidating. He seems a little less friendly than Byron's other friends. Byron speaks fondly of him, but I don't seem to have warmed to him the way I have his other friends.

He takes a deep breath. "Yeah, I notice. It's ingrained in me. Generations of Aldens have been judging everyone they come across. I swear, if I was to die tomorrow, my mother's first thought would be whether her hair stylist could come out on a Monday, and whether Ferragamo has a new black pump." He shrugs. "I know it's ridiculous. But just because I notice it, doesn't mean I value it. It's just information."

"Well, I'm sure my ancestors didn't come over on the Mayflower," I say.

Jack shrugs and kisses me on the cheek. "But thankfully they found their way here. Because you make my very good friend here very happy." He pats Byron on the shoulder, and I smile.

"Does he not make you want to play matchmaker?" Sophia whispers beside me. "We need to find him a woman who's going to rock his world."

"Me first," Fisher says, coming in between us and making us jump.

"You want someone to rock your world?" Sophia asks. "You meet literal rock stars every goddamn day. You shouldn't need us to set you up."

He shrugs. "I don't want to go out with a singer."

"You've been out with a hundred singers," Sophia says.

"And where did it get me?" he asks.

"Laid?" Sophia says.

"There's that." He sighs. "But I wonder if there's something else out there. Someone else. Someone who'll care more about me than publicity and a good time."

Byron joins our group and pats Fisher on the shoulder while Worth and Fisher continue to chat. "What are we talking about?" he asks.

"Finding Fisher a woman," Sophia says.

"Yeah, you'll have to go back to Colorado for that," Byron says.

I narrow my eyes and look up at him wondering what he must mean.

"I happen to know someone who's interested. Didn't know who the fuck you were. She just liked your vibe."

The corner of Fisher's mouth twitches. "I'm taking Vivian Cross out there to record soon. I'm just there to babysit really—make sure everything goes smoothly so she can write songs and be incredible. I'll have plenty of free time."

I can't wait to hear who Byron's talking about. He never mentioned anything to me about someone he knows liking Fisher.

"Star Falls is the place to go if you want to fall in love," Byron says dramatically, and all his friends groan. I can't stop laughing. He's such a goofball.

"Where do you go to fall in love?" a short, dark-haired woman I've never met before says as she enters the room. She's with another woman who's blonde.

Sophia immediately scoops them both up into a hug.

"Rosey, meet my sisters, Poppy and Avril," Worth says.

"Your soon-to-be-in-love sisters, because we're going to Star Falls," Avril corrects him before she pulls me into a hug. "It's so good to meet you."

"I feel like I might be entering my lumberjack era," Poppy says. "Do you have lumberjacks in Star Falls?" she asks.

Worth just rolls his eyes but doesn't say anything.

"I'm not sure about the lumberjack options in Star Falls. But if you get the chance to go, you absolutely should. It's a really magical place." I glance over at Byron, who's looking at me with a familiar expression that says he can't believe he gets to marry me. It never gets old.

"We're all going to go," Byron says. "You know I own a private members resort there."

"You do?" Avril asks. "I had no idea. You know, you should call it the Colorado Club. It has a nice ring to it."

"Good idea," he replies, as he nudges Avril. "But seriously, it's an open invitation. Any of you can come anytime. And maybe we should all go for the holidays this year."

"By then, Fisher and Jack will be engaged," Sophia says.

"Or even married," Fisher says. "I'm an impatient man."

"Don't forget about us," Poppy says. "Avril and I are lumberjack shopping, remember? My man will cut down our Christmas tree."

Byron finds his way to me and wraps his arms around me, like everything he needs in life is right here.

The buzzer sounds again. "That will be Bennett, Efa, Leo, and Jules. They texted me to say they're all in the same car."

"Everyone will visit us in Star Falls. You have no worries on that score."

He nods. "Everyone," he says. "And it won't be today, but I spoke to Mary. She says she's going to meet us in Colorado later in the year."

I squeeze Byron tighter. "That's amazing." His expression tells me how much it means to him that he's going to reconnect with his sister. Hopefully now he's come to terms with so much of his past, his future can involve his sister. All our sisters, hopefully. Maybe that's the answer. Maybe I'll gently encourage my sisters out to Colorado, and they can heal from their pasts too.

After all, Star Falls is a magical place.

14 months later - Star Falls

Rosey

I see Marion's name flash on my screen and send up a silent prayer. Please god let her have good news today. I want her to have it, more than I want it for myself.

I break into a grin and accept the call.

Marion doesn't speak, she just squeals. "I got into Columbia," she eventually says.

Marion applied to Oregon State as well as a local community college. When I suggested an Ivy League college, she laughed. But over time, she came to see she's way more than Mom would have her believe. She applied but never expected to get in.

"Holy shit," I reply. I'd like to say I knew she would, but honestly, I'm shocked. We're just two kids from a trailer park. We don't get to go to the Ivy League. "That's amazing! I'm so proud of you."

"*I'm* so proud of me," she says. "But I couldn't have done it without you."

I can't think of anything nicer she could have said to me. All I've done is encourage her, buoy her up when she felt like giving up. And of course, I've kept her secret.

I'm in touch with Kitty, too. At first we just shared

memes via text. Now we speak pretty regularly. I've asked her to come and live with us. But she's still under Mom's spell. Still doesn't want to upset her and probably scared to leave Lydia but scared to tell her and have her tell on her or not choose to come with her. I can't push too hard. I have to be patient and let them find their own way to me. Of course, Mom doesn't know. I'm hoping when they all find out about Marion, things will shift.

"Have you told Mom?" I ask her. Mom and my sisters had to move to another when Frank sold their trailer. Apparently it's the exact same size, and on the adjacent lot. Life changes, but everything has stayed the same for them.

"You're my first call," she replies. "What am I going to say to her?"

"You have to have a plan before you tell her. She might throw you out on the spot." I don't say it, but she needs to be ready to never see Mom again after she tells her the news. "You could leave it until the semester is about to start."

Silence echoes at the end of the phone.

"I'm impatient. I've been just trying to get to this day and now... now I want the rest of my life to start. I don't want to be stuck in this trailer anymore."

My heart lifts in my chest like it's had a dose of helium. I'm so thankful that she wants more from her life. I've been preparing for this moment. When we bought the New York house, Byron insisted on getting a place large enough that all my sisters could move in, if that's what they wanted. I hadn't told Marion before because I want it all to be her decision.

"Come to New York early, or go to Colorado." She can keep a close eye on Athena if she goes to Colorado. She knows most things about our life, how Byron and I travel between the two states. "I'm sure the Colorado Club is recruiting this time of year. I can put you in touch with the manager there."

"You love Star Falls, right?"

Of course I love Star Falls. It's the place I found my freedom. And my husband. Who, as ever, has great timing. He appears in the doorway.

"It's the best place in the world," I say through a massive grin, as Byron stands bare-chested, fresh from the shower, looking at me like I'm ice cream. "Wanna tell Byron your news?"

Marion agrees, and I put her on speaker.

"I got into Columbia," she squeals. "Full academic scholarship."

Byron's gaze flits from me to the cell and back again. "Whoa, that's amazing. So you'll stay with us." It's not a question. Byron has the room allocated already.

Every day I fall a little more in love with him, but today, the way he says that to my sister like it's a foregone conclusion—I don't know if it's possible for me to love him more than I already do. He's such a good man. He understands what we've all been put through and he wants to make it right. He's offered to helicopter all my sisters out of the trailer park on some kind of pseudo-CIA mission, but I've told him kidnapping them is not the answer. They need to leave on their own terms. Hopefully, Marion is just the first of three to find her way back to me.

"You think there might be a job at the Colorado Club for her between now and September?" I ask.

Byron looks at me as if I've lost my mind. "Just tell me when she's arriving and I'll make it happen." Towel or no towel, glistening skin or not, he's never looked so hot.

"Marion, I'll talk to you later," I say, and hang up the phone. We don't have to decide when Marion's going to move out and where she's going to go right this moment. My husband's standing in front of me half naked, saying things that make him a total god. I have things to do. To him.

"Did I ever tell you how much I want to have your baby?" I ask.

One corner of Byron's mouth turns up in a shy smile. "You do?"

In answer, I unbutton my blouse and pull his towel from his waist.

Love Deep is the next book in the series.

For Louise Bay news and releases, including bonus content, sign up to my newsletter at www.louisebay.com/newsletter

Read on for a sneak peak of Mr. Mayfair.

MR. MAYFAIR

Beck

"Kevin Bacon is full of shit," I said as I thwacked the small, black rubber ball with my racket.

Dexter lurched away as the ball ricocheted toward his bollocks. "What did he ever do to you?"

"The six degrees of separation thing—it's bullshit."

"What?" Dexter asked, panting. I was kicking his arse, and I knew that had to hurt his delicate ego. No doubt he'd chalk up his losing to that skiing injury he still complained about. As far as I was concerned anyone who skied deserved every injury they got—hurtling downhill with metal flippers on your feet could end only one way.

"You know, the idea that everyone on the planet is just six people removed. So, a friend of a friend of—"

"You can't blame that on Kevin Bacon. It's not like he invented it," Dexter said before serving.

"Okay then, if you're going to be pedantic, Frigyes Karinthy is full of shit."

"I can't tell if you're swearing at me or speaking Ukrainian."

"Hungarian," I replied, wiping my forehead with my sleeve. I measured exercise not on calories burned or time spent in the gym but on the amount I sweated. Someone needed to develop a machine to measure perspiration—I'd pay good money for it. As far as I was concerned it was effort that always earned the best results. "He developed the bullshit theory. I looked it up on Wikipedia."

"Fuck," he spat as the ball hit the plaster below the red line, giving me the victory I'd expected since we got onto the court. Dexter only lost at squash when he had business trouble, so I wasn't going to crow about my win.

"Yeah, I get it. What's the problem?"

I bent and scooped up the out-of-play ball as it trickled toward me. "The theory is flawed. I have dredged every single one of my contacts and I can't get an introduction to Henry Dawnay."

"You're still trying to get a meeting with that old billionaire?" Dexter grinned, as if my failure in business was going to make up for his shitty performance on the squash court. "You might have to give it up."

"Henry Dawnay is not just some old billionaire. He's *the* old billionaire standing between me and nine-point-four million quid. And I'm not about to give up on that kind of money. I've plowed every contact I have and come up empty. I thought one of you lot would have some kind of connection to him. What's the point in having rich, successful friends if they're no use to me?"

"Us lot? You mean your five closest friends who'd walk through fire for you?"

He knew I was joking as sure as I knew United were going to win the league. The fact that the guys I'd forged bonds with as a teenager were rich and successful was simply circumstance. Their jobs weren't important. They were the best men I knew outside my own dad. And I'd walk through fire for them just as I knew they would for me. But that didn't mean I couldn't complain about the fact that none of them had been able to score me a meeting with Henry Dawnay, even if it did make me sound like the moody git Dexter always accused me of being.

I rolled my eyes and nodded toward the changing rooms. I needed a shower and then I needed a plan. "I don't need anyone to walk through fire for me. I need someone to introduce me to the man who owns the property standing between me and ten million quid."

"You said nine point four."

"Have I told you how annoying you are?"

"A couple of times," Dexter said, pushing through the door to the changing room. "Look, if you can't get an intro from someone you know, why don't you track him down, bump into him, and introduce yourself."

I fixed him with a thanks-for-the-advice-mum look. "I did. Last month in the lobby of the Dorchester. He shook my hand and swooped right out without stopping to get my name."

Dexter winced, and he was right to. It'd been embarrassing. I'd felt like a nine-year-old boy meeting Cristiano Ronaldo.

I opened my locker door and pulled out my phone to check my messages. Two more missed calls from Danielle. *Shit.* Another thing I had to deal with. "I've managed to get access to his calendar so—"

"How the hell have you managed that?"

"Don't ask. You need plausible deniability so you don't end up in prison." From what I understood, I'd broken several British laws and a couple of international ones by getting that information. I hoped it was worth it.

"Well, I hope you and Joshua end up in jail."

I ignored his assumption that another member of our brothers-in-arms, Joshua, was involved. It was an obvious assumption—Joshua liked to hack into government agencies to unwind. The rest of us played squash. "I'm well connected—some would say powerful in real estate circles. I've got money and resources. For Christ's sake, I know the brand of loo paper this guy uses. But apparently, it's not enough to get a meeting." Things would be very different if my birth certificate had carried my biological father's name.

"You need to calm down and figure it the fuck out."

"Great advice," I mumbled as I scrolled through my emails. One was from Joshua with Henry's itinerary and schedule for the next couple of months. I slumped onto the bench and opened the attachment, hoping to find he'd finally arranged a lunch or a meeting with someone I knew.

But no. Nothing. Although there was an entire week blocked out. Perhaps he was going on holiday?

"This is the guy who you want to buy the building in Mayfair from, right?"

"Yeah, I own every other piece of property in the row except that one—the most run-down of the lot of them, and he's done nothing with it. It's standing empty and prime for redevelopment. It's prime for *me* redeveloping it." It was a building I'd been obsessed with since I could remember.

"Look, worst case, you just work around it."

I shook my head. "I don't work around things. I take a wrecking ball to them." I'd crunched the numbers. I wouldn't make a profit if I didn't have Henry's building. And I didn't take losses. And anyway, it wasn't just the money.

It was the building my mother lived in when she found out she was pregnant with me.

It was the building my mother was evicted from as soon as her boyfriend, the owner of the building and my biological father, found out she was pregnant.

When he died, it had been inherited by a distant cousin, and since my mother told me the story when I was a teenager, I'd been laser-focused on buying that building. Maybe I thought if I owned it—owned what I should have inherited—wrongs would be righted.

Then I could tear it down and start again.

I'd rewrite history.

I studied the document Joshua had sent. Why had Henry blocked out an entire week? The man didn't take holidays. I looked closer. The only reference in the entire week was M&K. I typed it into the search engine on my phone. What could M&K stand for? As I scrolled through the results, I couldn't see how a furniture shop in Wigan or an American DJ could be relevant. Henry wasn't just old money, he was titled—an earl or something, although he didn't seem to use it. I was pretty sure he wasn't shopping in Wigan or entertaining DJs.

I switched screens, and just as I was about to call Joshua to try to get more information, another email flashed up with an attachment. When I opened it, the dates of the M&K week were the first thing I saw. It was a glossy, electronic wedding invitation. Apparently Joshua had been just as curious as I had. A wedding that lasted an entire week? Did these people and their guests not have jobs? M stood for Matthew and K for Karen. The bride and groom. I plugged their names into Google. They were no one I knew. But there was no surprise there. They looked like the type to have met on a croquet field—Matthew was all sports jackets and straw boaters. I didn't know how old-Etonians and people with inherited wealth looked different from most normal human beings, but they did. It must be the floppy hair or the air of entitlement they wore.

A society wedding would be a perfect place to approach Henry. He'd be relaxed and in a good mood as he spent time with his people.

But his people weren't my people.

My money was as new as the dawn and that left me on the outside of the wedding party, peering inside, at the end of unreturned phone calls and unable to meet with Henry Dawnay.

"Speaking of wrecking balls, how's Danielle? Managed to destroy that relationship yet?" Dexter asked, pulling me out of my Henry obsession.

I glanced up from my phone. "What? She's fine." I wasn't sure she was exactly fine. I'd pissed her off. Again. The last conversation we had over dinner, she'd started to talk about taking things to a deeper level. But I liked the shallows—dinner a couple of times a week followed by a sleepover. I didn't have time for anything else. The rest of the time I was working—figuring out the next deal, scoping out new opportunities, firefighting issues on current sites. It didn't leave time for much else in my life other than for my five closest friends. As much as it might make me a dick, women were important in the generic sense. But a particular woman wasn't. So the last few months it had been Danielle. Before that it had been Juliet and by the end of the summer, it was likely to be someone else. But I should return Danielle's calls. I'd been busy and this Henry thing was getting to me.

"When's the last time you took her to dinner? Or even had a conversation with her outside the bedroom?"

"Jesus, are you my therapist now?" Guilt prickled beneath my skin, and I kept my eyes on my phone. I'd cancelled dinner this Saturday. Again. She'd been pissed off, so I'd given her some space. But it was Thursday. *Shit.* I should have called her back by now. If I confessed to Dexter, he'd tell me I was a dick. But it wasn't like I planned it that way. I was just wrapped up in everything else I had going on, and somehow Danielle had fallen off the bottom of my call sheet. I switched screens and dialed my messages to check her tone of voice and see if I was still in the dog box.

I deleted the three "Call me back" voicemails. The fourth escalated into "Where are you?" The fifth another "Call me back." She sounded calmer, more relaxed. Perfect. Just as I'd hoped. But the sixth voicemail was one I hadn't been expecting. Or maybe it was. I listened as she dumped me—her tone resigned, her words cutting.

"You okay?" Dexter asked, studying my expression.

I ended the call. "Yeah. I'm a selfish, piece-of-shit workaholic. And Danielle Fisher's ex-boyfriend."

For the second time this morning, I got a well-deserved wince from Dexter.

I shrugged—as if it couldn't be helped. As if it wasn't entirely my fault. "I should have called her back sooner."

Dexter nodded as he fixed a towel around his waist. "Yeah, you should have. But at the same time, if she was the right woman for you, you wouldn't forget to ring her. Or avoid her calls. You'd want to speak to her."

"And what the fuck do you know about dating the right woman?"

"I know," he said.

"But it's not Stacey," I said, referring to the woman he was currently sharing a bed with.

"Stacey's not . . . Just because I fucked up with the right woman doesn't mean you have to. Learn from my mistakes."

I rolled my eyes and went back to the email from Joshua. "I'll be sure to mention to Stacey she's in an interim role next time I see her."

"Don't be a dick."

"You first," I replied. I was being a dick. Danielle had sounded kinda resigned, like I'd lived down to her expectations, which stung. It was the tone my form teacher had used when I'd told her I had no intention of going to university. My grades had been good, but I wasn't interested in more studying. I didn't belong in that world. I wanted to be out in the world earning money. I doubt she'd use that tone with me if I ran into her now. She'd thought I was being lazy except it was the exact opposite. University was good for people like Henry and whoever this Matthew and Karen were—I had better things to do. I needed to earn my fortune.

But no matter how rich I got, I still didn't mix in the circles that Henry Dawnay did.

Well, that needed to change. I had to figure out a way to score an invite to the society wedding of the year.

Beck

I traced my finger down the guest list for a second time. I must have missed something. Some*one*.

"I checked it three times, sir," my assistant, Roy, said from the other side of my desk. "I even searched against contacts of your contacts."

By the time I was out of the shower and back at my desk, Joshua had sent me the guest list from the wedding Henry was attending, and I'd been determined to find my way in. The groom's father was well known in the City—a partner in one of the oldest investment banks in London. I knew the type—hated it when clubs in London were forced to let women in, longed for the days when no one expected you back in the office after lunch. I should be grateful—they were the men who left meat on the bone that I came along and gobbled off. The bride's father was a landowner, so he didn't do a lot except drive about in a Land Rover dressed in tweed. If I just knew someone who would be going. Then I could get them to speak to Henry at the wedding and talk me up, explain how I was good for my word and easy to trust—maybe even mention how I had a business proposition for him. I'd have to be careful who it was. Dexter and I goaded each other, but if he was going to that wedding, Henry would think I was his fairy godmother by the time Dexter was done—any of the six of us would do the same for each other. We were brothers in all but name. But anyone else? I wasn't sure I'd trust someone outside our circle with something so important. It would be better if I was a guest at the wedding myself. Then Henry would be a captive audience and I was sure I could convince him to sign on the dotted line.

"And you're sure that I don't know *anyone*?" I might not have been to the right schools or grown up in the right circles, but I'd been successful for years. I was earning more money than most of London put together, and I dealt with lawyers and people in business all day, every day. But I didn't know a single person who would be at this three-hundred-fifty guest wedding.

"As sure as I can be. I've cross-referenced against your contacts and your LinkedIn page. And I checked the last five years' Christmas card lists to see if I'd missed anyone."

It wasn't so surprising. We might all be British and

living in the same city, but I still existed on a different planet to these people.

"I don't suppose there are any single women on the list?" There must be someone going without a boyfriend. I was single. So I'd track them down, seduce them, and be available as a plus one for weddings and bar mitzvahs. No, that was a shitty plan. I needed to be sure I was getting into this wedding—I wasn't going to leave it to chance. I wanted some kind of guarantee or contract or something.

"The ones invited with an un-named plus one are at the bottom of the list," Roy said. I turned the page to find one male name and three female names.

"Do you have their ages?" Or photographs.

"No, sir. I can find that out for you though."

I needed to know exactly who these three people were.

Candice Gould

Suzie Dougherty

Stella London

Three single women—it had to be my way in. As invitees to M&K's wedding, they had something I needed more than oxygen. I might not be able to guarantee a plus one by seducing them, but everyone wanted *something*. And I had considerable means at my disposal. I just needed to figure out what they wanted and then do a swap—a plus one for a pony or a week on a yacht or whatever it was people who didn't work wanted in life. I just needed to track them down and make them an offer they wouldn't want to refuse.

One of these women was the key to the Dawnay building.

Stella

Another day, another dollar, so the phrase goes. But for me another day meant another twelve hours at my crappy office with the crappiest boss who ever lived. Placing people I didn't know into jobs they didn't want was the worst. It might have only been two months into the role, but I'd never get used to being a recruitment consultant.

My mobile buzzed on my desk beside me and I glanced over my shoulder toward my boss's empty office. She hated people taking personal calls. If breathing took time out of the day, she'd ban that too.

It was Florence. She never called me at work. Taking my life in my hands, I swiped to accept the call. "Hey," I whispered.

"Are you in front of your computer?" she asked.

"Of course I am. I'm chained to it, what—"

"I'm five minutes away. Whatever you do, don't check your emails. Get your coat and meet me downstairs."

Florence must be crazy. I was constantly checking my emails. "I'm staring at my inbox, Florence."

"I mean your personal emails. Promise me. Log off and meet me downstairs or I'm going to march into your office and haul you out."

"It's only just gone six. I can't just leave. What's the problem?" It sounded serious. "Are you and Gordy okay?" She and Gordy were the perfect couple. If there was trouble in paradise, then anything was possible.

"I've just turned into Monmouth Street. Have you got your jacket on?"

Oh God. She didn't say that they were okay. Florence needed me. And she trumped the wrath of my boss. "I'm coming," I said, wedging the phone between my shoulder and my chin as I logged out.

I pulled my jacket off the back of my chair and headed to the exit, ignoring my boss's assistant's pointed look at the clock as she saw me leave.

I saw Florence as soon as I stepped out of the lift. She was facing me from the other side of the glass doors of the office, her shoulders slumped, her forehead furrowed, and her face as pale as a corpse. It was clear something catastrophic had happened.

I was going to kill Gordy.

"I'm so sorry, Florence," I said, and I opened my arms and pulled her into a hug.

She held me so tight, I struggled to breathe. She must be devastated. We all thought Gordy was one of the good guys.

"I wanted you to hear this from me," Florence said as she pulled away and snuck her arm around my shoulder.

"Of course. I'm here for you," I replied as I grabbed her hand. "I'll help you bury the body if you want me to."

She frowned as if she was surprised by my offer, but how could she be? There wasn't anything I wouldn't do for Florence. For either of my two best friends.

We crossed the street and found an outside table at the bar opposite my office on Monmouth Street. One of the few positives about my job was that it was based in the West End and surrounded by bars and restaurants. "We're going to need wine," I said.

We were going to need a shovel. If she didn't kill Gordy, I would.

We ordered a bottle of wine and took a seat. "So you saw?" Florence said. "You seem very calm."

"Saw what?" I asked. "Oh," I said, pulling out my

phone. "You said there was something in my personal email."

"You didn't see?" Florence asked.

"What?"

She pulled my phone from my grasp and grabbed my hands. "What body are you helping me bury?" she asked.

"Gordy's, of course. Tell me what he's done."

She shook her head. "It's not Gordy. It's Matt."

My stomach dropped straight through the seat of my chair and I froze. If Florence had raced over here from where she worked in the City at six on a Wednesday, it couldn't be good news. Had he been in an accident? Had his dad died?

"He's getting married," she said, squeezing my hands.

I pulled away from her as I tried to understand what she was saying. "Of course he's not getting married. We've only been apart two months." I didn't like to say we'd split up because it wasn't an accurate description of what was happening. We were just apart right now. It was just a temporary thing. He was just freaked out that all our friends were getting married and people kept asking us when we were next. He was just doing that guy thing where, just before they pop the question, they have a man meltdown. Just look at Prince William and Kate Middleton. They had a three-month break before William proposed.

"I'm so sorry, Stella."

Florence looked up at me, her eyes filled with tears, and my heart began to gallop. She was serious. "What do you mean? Who to? How do you know?"

"The invitation was delivered to Gordy's office. And then there was the email follow-up with the schedule. Never mind."

I tried to swallow but my throat was too tight. I reached

for the glass of wine that Florence was hastily pouring. "I don't get it. There must be some mistake." How could Matt be getting married? He hadn't proposed to me, and we'd been going out for seven years. We'd been living together for six. It wasn't possible. Florence must have it wrong.

Florence shook her head. "It gets worse. I really don't know how to say this, but he's marrying Karen."

I shivered as my body turned cold.

I couldn't speak.

I couldn't breathe.

I couldn't think.

Florence slid a white card in front of me.

I traced the embossed writing with my fingertip as my stomach churned slowly and relentlessly, like it was mixing concrete. It was the invitation I would have picked out for my own wedding—thick white card, a thin gold surround, and an elegant black font. Simple. Classic. Refined.

Apparently stealing the love of my life wasn't enough. My best friend had to have my taste in wedding invitations, too.

"Karen and Matt?" I searched Florence's face, looking for answers. "*My* Matt? *My* Karen?"

Florence tilted her head to the side. "For some reason, they've invited you. I had no idea they were even a thing. Neither did Gordy."

They sent me an invitation? I suppose I was the common denominator between them. "How long have they . . .?" Was this the real reason Matt left me? His excuses when he left seemed so lacking, looking back—

I'm not sure we were meant to be together forever.

We don't want the same things in life.

I'd assumed he was just getting jittery as we approached the time for weddings and babies.

Apparently, I was wrong.

"Karen swears it's since you two split up but . . ."

"You spoke to her?" Now that I thought about it, I hadn't had an actual conversation with Karen or an in-person catch-up for . . . Well, I couldn't remember how long. We messaged each other. All the time. Most days. But I hadn't seen her or spoken to her in weeks.

"Called her as soon as Gordy called me when he got the invite. It was delivered to his office. Which was weird. It wasn't like I wasn't going to find out."

I was only taking in half of the words that Florence was speaking. "What did she say?"

"Just that . . ." Florence paused and drew breath. "She and Matt had realized they had feelings for each other and it was serious, and she didn't really say anything more. As soon as I mentioned you, she made up some excuse about another call and rang off."

So my boyfriend was getting married. Ex-boyfriend. Potaytoes Potahtoes. The man I'd shared a bed with for seven years up until two months ago was getting married. On any other day, that would have been the worst thing that could have possibly happened. But to my best friend?

Why?

"Is she pregnant?"

Florence sat back in her chair. "You think that's why?"

Why was any of this happening?

Why was Matt getting married to someone else when he was supposed to be marrying me?

Why was my best friend getting married and hadn't told me?

Why were they marrying each other?

"I'm not sure any explanation would really be an answer," I said. "But if they'd shagged and she'd got knocked up that might be some kind of logical reason for a quick wedding." It was certainly easier to understand than my best friend catching feelings for my boyfriend because that led to questions—how long had they had feelings for each other? Had Matt always wanted Karen when he was with me? Had they been having an affair? For a few months? Years? Since the beginning of our relationship?

"I don't understand why she didn't tell me," I said. "It wasn't like I wouldn't find out. She was going to let me find out by opening my invitation."

"I don't have an answer to that, other than she's a total bitch."

That would have to do. For now. "I guess that's why she invited me. To announce the news. Because she was too much of a traitorous coward to tell me to my face that she'd stolen my boyfriend."

"Do you think they were having an affair while you two were still living together?"

"That's at the top of my list of questions I have for them both." Had I seen any signs? Since we'd moved to London, Matt had worked late a lot. But we'd come down from Manchester because he was offered his dream job. Of course he was going to put body and soul into it.

When had he had time for an affair?

We were at the stage where I bought Matt's underpants and he reminded me that I'd not called my brother for three weeks.

We were a team.

We were in love.

We were going to spend the rest of our lives together.

Or so I'd thought.

I should be crying, but for some reason the tears hadn't

arrived. Perhaps I didn't believe it was true. Perhaps the fizzle of anger I was beginning to feel had dried them out.

Karen had been a part of my life since the day we'd both started school. I always felt slightly unkempt next to her. Even then. At five, her knee-high white socks never fell down, wrinkling at the ankles like mine did. At thirteen she never suffered with acne and wrestled with cover-up, and in our twenties, I'd never seen her with a single clump of mascara or eyeliner that was smudged.

Karen had known Matt since before we were a couple. She'd come up to visit me in Manchester, during our first term at university, twirling in, making the boys drool and swapping make-up tips with the girls in my block. She'd been struggling to fit in at Exeter, which made no sense to me. All my friends loved her.

When Matt pulled me onto the dance floor during the summer ball, told me I brought out the best in him, and he liked my boobs, I was thrilled Karen had already met him so she could help me overanalyze every part of our relationship.

Seven years later, Karen knew Matt almost as well as I did.

"Maybe you should go to the wedding and when they do that bit about impediments, you can stand up and ask that question," Florence suggested. "But obviously, you can't go."

"Of course, I can't go," I replied. Despite the invitation, I was almost certainly the last person Karen wanted at her wedding. It wasn't as if seeing my ex-boyfriend—the man I'd thought I was going to spend the rest of my life with—marrying my ex-best friend was top of my list of things to do this summer.

"Are you going to go?" I loved Florence like a sister, and

if Karen was capable of sleeping with my boyfriend, what could she do to Florence?

"Of course not," she replied.

"But Gordy will want to go. And he won't want to go without you. If more time had passed and I was married or at least dating someone, I'd definitely go." If nothing else, I'd love to see Karen's face when she got my RSVP.

"There was a schedule that came with the invitation," Florence said.

I frowned. I'd been so focused on the white card that looked so much like the one I would have chosen, I'd forgotten about the email.

"It's like a week-long thing up in Scotland."

I slumped back in my chair, grateful that my jacket covered the mole-hill sized goosebumps that popped up all over my arms. "His uncle's castle?" I asked.

Florence nodded and the dull churning in my stomach kicked up a gear like an idling car put into drive.

"That's where he always said he wanted to get married." We'd visited last summer and hiked, ridden horses, slept under the stars. It had been amazing. Magical even.

"He's a ginormous wanker," Florence said.

Matt Gordon was having the life he and I had always planned—with someone else.

Read Mr. Mayfair to find out more.

BOOKS BY LOUISE BAY

All Louise Bay Books are available for free in Kindle Unlimited or on Amazon to buy.

Each book is a stand alone

The Colorado Club Billionaires

Love Fast

Love Deep

Love More

The New York City Billionaires

The Boss + The Maid = Chemistry

The Play + The Pact = I Do

The Hero + Vegas = No Regrets

The Doctors Series

Dr. Off Limits

Dr. Perfect

Dr. CEO

Dr. Fake Fiancé

Dr. Single Dad

The Mister Series

Mr. Mayfair

Mr. Knightsbridge

Mr. Smithfield

Mr. Park Lane

Mr. Bloomsbury

Mr. Notting Hill

The Player Series

International Player

Private Player

The Gentleman Series

The Ruthless Gentleman

The Wrong Gentleman

The Royals Series

King of Wall Street

Park Avenue Prince

Duke of Manhattan

The British Knight

The Earl of London

The Nights Series

Indigo Nights

Promised Nights

Parisian Nights

Standalones

An American in London

14 Days of Christmas

Hollywood Scandal

Love Unexpected

Hopeful

The Empire State Series

Sign up to the Louise Bay mailing list at www.louisebay.com

What kind of books do you like?

Fake relationship (marriage of convenience)

Duke of Manhattan

Mr. Mayfair

Mr. Notting Hill

Dr. Fake Fiancé

Dr. Single Dad

The Play + The Pact = I Do

An American in London

Enemies to Lovers

King of Wall Street

The British Knight

The Earl of London

Hollywood Scandal

Parisian Nights

14 Days of Christmas

Mr. Bloomsbury

The Play + The Pact = I Do

Small Town

Love Fast

Love Deep

Love More

14 Days of Christmas

Hollywood Scandal

Friends to lovers

Mr. Mayfair

Promised Nights

International Player

Office Romance / Workplace romance

Mr. Knightsbridge

King of Wall Street

The British Knight

The Ruthless Gentleman

Mr. Bloomsbury

Dr. Off Limits

The Boss + The Maid = Chemistry

The Play + The Pact = I Do

Second Chance

International Player

Hopeful

Best Friend's Brother

Promised Nights

Vacation/Holiday Romance

The Empire State Series

Indigo Nights

The Ruthless Gentleman

The Wrong Gentleman

Love Unexpected

14 Days of Christmas

The Hero + Vegas = No Regrets

An American in London

Holiday/Christmas Romance

14 Days of Christmas

British Hero

Promised Nights (British heroine)

Indigo Nights (American heroine)

Hopeful (British heroine)

Duke of Manhattan (American heroine)

The British Knight (American heroine)

The Earl of London (British heroine)

The Wrong Gentleman (American heroine)

The Ruthless Gentleman (American heroine)

International Player (British heroine)

Mr. Mayfair (British heroine)

Mr. Knightsbridge (American heroine)

Mr. Smithfield (American heroine)

Private Player (British heroine)

Mr. Bloomsbury (American heroine)

14 Days of Christmas (British heroine)

Mr. Notting Hill (British heroine)

Dr. Off Limits

Dr. Perfect

Dr. Fake Fiancé (American heroine)

Dr. Single Dad

The Play + The Pact = I Do (American heroine)

An American in London (American heroine)

Sign up to the Louise Bay mailing list on my website
www.louisebay.com

Made in the USA
Columbia, SC
30 May 2025